ABNORMAL
LIVES

STREBOR ON THE Streetz

ABNORMAL LIVES

A NOVEL

RAE

SBI

STREBOR BOOKS

NEW YORK LONDON TORONTO SYDNEY

SBI

Strebor Books
P.O. Box 6505
Largo, MD 20792
http://www.streborbooks.com

This book is a work of fiction. Names, characters, places and incidents are products of the author's imagination or are used fictitiously. Any resemblance to actual events or locales or persons, living or dead, is entirely coincidental.

ISBN 978-1-59309-382-2
ISBN 978-1-4516-4067-0 (e-book)
LCCN 2011928055

First Strebor Books trade paperback edition November 2011

Cover design: www.mariondesigns.com
Cover photograph: © Keith Saunders/Keith Saunders Photos

10 9 8 7 6 5 4 3 2 1

Manufactured in the United States of America

For information regarding special discounts for bulk purchases, please contact Simon & Schuster Special Sales at 1-866-506-1949 or business@simonandschuster.com

The Simon & Schuster Speakers Bureau can bring authors to your live event. For more information or to book an event, contact the Simon & Schuster Speakers Bureau at 1-866-248-3049 or visit our website at www.simonspeakers.com.

ACKNOWLEDGMENTS

First, thanks to Yahweh, the most high and the Blessed Mother, for giving me the strength to stay steadfast throughout this life. Thanks to Gloria Irene Johnson for always being there through all my screw-ups and never forsaken me. Now that's love. Thanks to Kevin Johnson, without you there would be no me. Thanks to Camrian Johnson for encouraging me to follow a dream I had before he was born. Camrian, I love you, sweetie. Thanks to Tiffany Smith for her encouragement also. Thanks to Maurice Johnson for all the times he has made me laugh and the times he's backed me up no matter what. Thanks to Marquerite Smith-McBride for just being her. Thanks to all my family who have been there for me at one time or another and have helped me raise my child.

Hey Casey, I have a lot of family but I don't consider a lot of them my friends. Your friendship has been a blessing to me since I was old enough to notice your presence. We've been friends since diapers and still will be when we hit that age when we'll be wearing them again. Thanks to Casey Norville, I swear we should have been sisters. Arketta Claxton, thanks for your friendship. You are such a wonderful person. Thanks to Michael (who is like God) for always being there for me 24/7, for your advice, for sharing your knowledge even when it's not what I want to hear, and for your love and protection. I love you, Michael. Thanks to Velvet Conly for encouraging me to follow my dream by embracing my beliefs and having faith everything would turn out right. I wish you all and your families the best.

It's a lot of chicks I was down with in the past and have lost contact with. I don't know whether you've thought about me and I'm sure you don't know whether I've thought about you or maybe you just don't give a shit, but shout outs to all of you for old time's sake.

A big thanks to the Virginia Food Bank and Lamb's Basket and RCAP and other such organizations for being there to help out the community.

Thanks to William Linka at Richmond Criminal Law.

Thanks to those that instilled in me the passion to write: James Baldwin, Iceberg Slim, Toni Morrison, and Donald Goines.

With the greatest amount of love, appreciation and respect, I thank you all.

AUTHOR'S NOTE

The story you are about to cerebrally consume is sizzling hot. Read carefully.

Get a cold glass of water before proceeding. Seriously, this one's a scorcher.

Read at your own risk.

Caution: This isn't the type of fiction you buy from the drugstore, so hold on to your seat.

If you're looking for one of those love stories—girl meets boy, they fall in love, boy showers girl with expensive gifts and at the end, they live happily ever after—you are in for a big surprise.

If you want happy endings, read one of those Christian inspirational novels.

If you are looking for a novel just about hot sex that you can get off on, this isn't it. I suggest you check your Yellow Pages for an adult store in your area. They have videos that might solve that problem for you.

This novel is about friendship, disappointments, lost love, revenge gone bad, and how tragedy can make someone turn their back on God. It's not just about hot sex.

Parental Advisory: Don't leave your children unattended while they are in reach of this novel.

Scream it down the block: Fuck fairytales, romance novels and all other forms of fuckery that screws with your perception of life and toys with your psyche.

Aw, did I offend anyone? If so, it wasn't intentional. Let me clear that up now because if asked about it later, I'll just laugh.

Now that we have covered all of the above, just dive in and read. I dare you.

ENJOY.

Rae

It was ten o'clock on a Friday night. Simone sat inside of the fitness center, entertaining her client, Mason. Mason was the director of the center and usually planned their meetings there after-hours. Simone sat on the edge of the hot tub wearing a pink G-string and Mason stood inside the encircling pool with Simone's thighs resting on his shoulders.

"My wife saw the present you gave me a few weeks back," Mason announced proudly, as he walked his fingers up Simone's thighs.

Simone sighed. *It's not like it's the first time and it won't be the last*, she thought. "Well, what did she think of it?" Simone tried not to disclose how humored she was by her remark.

"Let's just say she didn't like it as much as I did."

The present Mason referred to was the hickey Simone had placed on the shaft of his penis. That was her trademark. Men from all over the Tri-City area contacted her to see could and would the pretty, petite, wavy-haired, fair-skinned doll baby pucker up her plump pink lips to perform the act that all of their friends and colleagues bragged about.

Once she proved that she could and would, if they were willing to pay her fee for the priceless experience, they became loyal customers that contacted her on a regular basis to have the "O"-shaped bruise on their genitals that they held with the same regards that bikers and gangsters held their tattoos, retouched before it faded away. It had only been three weeks since she had last provided Mason with her services and there he was, standing in front of her waiting to be retouched, among other things.

Simone liked dealing with Mason. She understood what to expect from him. He never showed up drunk or flying off of the handle as a result of hallucinogens. That was behavior she'd tolerated from the petty, low-class criminals she'd started out servicing. They would beat, belittle, and refuse to pay women in her profession after they'd romped around with them on old, pissy mattresses. Simone had paid her dues to earn the status she now held in her profession and refused to deal with that nonsense. That was one of the reasons why most of her clients were upper middle-class whites; the few that were black held the same social status. The other reason for that was they were willing to pay more money. Money that the lower-class troublemakers couldn't afford to let leave their pockets.

Mason also referred a lot of his friends to Simone, which was good for business. Simone also liked the fact that Mason wasn't long-winded. She could get it down as fast as she could get it up and when it was over, it was over. Mason didn't try to stall to keep her around while he tried to have another erection. Her terms of service were, once her client ejaculated while she performed the service he'd requested, her job was done. Some of her clients had her perform one act, some paid for two or three, but after they ejaculated as the result of each service, or lost their erection, whichever came first, she was off the clock. Mason stuck to those terms. Being that Mason wasn't what she considered to be endowed, after she finished with him, she would still be in adequate condition to service another client before calling it a night.

What Simone didn't like about Mason was how he never seemed to be able to put an end to his idle chitchat. Her time was more valuable to her than her services were to him. The more time she had, the more money she had the opportunity to make. She didn't want to be rude. After all, he was a longtime customer. So she sat there in a rut while he rambled on about the weather.

It was times like those that made her wish Stefan had come along. He had a way of nipping things in the bud. Although Mason was a huge fan of anal sex, he wasn't one of her bisexual clients. She often heard him bash gays that attended the fitness center. He would go out his way to express how sickened he was by them.

Simone thought Mason might have been nervous. They had been together numerous times but, for some reason, he always seemed scared to touch her.

Simone's legs shivered as a result of Mason's jitteriness. She looked down at him and sighed.

"What's wrong?" Mason asked.

"Nothing." Simone removed her legs from Mason's shoulders. "Come up here with me."

Mason lifted himself up on the wall of the hot tub and sat beside Simone. Simone stood up, grabbed Mason's hands, and pulled him closer to her. She knelt down in front of him and blushed at the sight of semen seeping from his partially erect organ. "You mean to tell me you've been in the pool hiding this from me all this time."

"I wasn't sure if you were ready for it."

"Oh, is that right?" Simone drooled on his shaft and gently stroked it with her hand.

Mason stood up and began to slide his dick back and forth in her mouth. "That's right; get it nice and wet."

That's a first, Simone thought. Usually, Mason would lay there lifeless, not uttering a single word while she did all of the work.

Simone slid her hands up Mason's thighs and onto his hips. She thrust him forward, taking him entirely in her mouth. She could feel Mason's dick pulsate as she secured it in her mouth and gathered saliva to create a massaging motion.

Mason pressed his lips together and looked up at the ceiling. He hoped Simone wouldn't notice the ugly faces he was making while she pleased him.

Simone slid her index finger inside Mason's rectum. His knees became weak and he plopped down on the wall of the hot tub. Simone followed his motion, never releasing her grip. Mason tugged on Simone's weave and moaned at the top of his lungs as he reached his climax. He squirmed, unable to tolerate the overwhelming sensation he was being subjected to.

Simone stroked his organ with her hand to quicken his release. She almost laughed when Mason stood on the tip of his toes like a ballerina and cried out with pleasure.

"Whoo," Mason cried out in between a series of pants. He looked back up at the ceiling and ran his fingers through Simone's hair. "You've got my head spinning. If you can do all that with your mouth, I can't wait to see what the pussy is like."

Simone was puzzled. For as long as she had serviced Mason, he had never asked for pussy. Ass was his thing. Mason loved the way she slid her hips down on his dick until he fully occupied her anus and rode him like a jockey. *He* would *want it tonight when I'm on my period; just my luck*, Simone thought.

She sucked on Mason's lip as she reached between her legs and freed her tampon into the hot tub. She straddled Mason and pushed herself down on his tool. It wouldn't be long before he reached his climax. Simone could hear Mason's breaths quicken as she pressed herself down on his dick harder and harder, lingering for a few seconds so he could feel the softness of her walls. In less than two minutes, Mason clutched Simone in his arms and called on the Lord.

Stefan lay in the bed with his man, Eugene. He threw his arm over Eugene's chest and kissed him.

"Could you move over?" Eugene asked.

Stefan was fed up with Eugene's attitude. Eugene had changed since he'd landed a job. When Eugene first came home from prison, things were wonderful. They would make love all night and sleep late into the day. Eugene would beg Stefan to let him take the condom off so he could feel his flesh. But now he didn't even want Stefan to hold him. It was blatantly apparent that their relationship was only a ploy to help Eugene get on his feet. Now that Eugene had found a job and saved some money, he didn't need Stefan anymore and he was ready to free himself from their relationship.

Stefan wondered if Eugene modeled the clothes he bought for him for some female when he wasn't around. Stefan was sure Eugene was having sex with a woman in the apartment he paid the rent for. The thought of Eugene trying to impress some random chick with the things he had purchased for him made Stefan sick to his stomach.

Eugene liked females. Stefan saw the way he looked at them. Not only did he admire their beauty, he wanted to be entangled in it, he wanted a piece for himself. He'd noticed Eugene checking out the curves on his cousin, Simone, when he'd introduced them. He never brought them around one another again. He could not trust Eugene and he realized that Simone was weak.

Stefan attempted to kiss Eugene again.

Eugene pulled the covers over his head. "Come on with that. I'm tired," he grumbled.

Life is too short for shit like this, Stefan thought. If Eugene was willing to throw away the security that Stefan provided him with over a female, then he could go right ahead. He was sure Eugene would run into some shabby whore that would fool him into believing that she was a lady. She'd be a little girl who had no clue where she was going; only what she wanted from him. She'd convince him that she was high-class when she was extremely high-maintenance. Eugene would exhaust his little savings trying to keep up with her and, when his money was gone, she would be also.

Stefan got out of bed and put on his clothes.

"Where you going?" Eugene asked.

"Home."

"You're not gonna fix me nothing to eat before you leave?"

"No."

"Come on with that; a nigga's hungry."

"You've got two hands; fix it yourself," Stefan said as he opened the bedroom door and made his way down the stairs.

"Don't forget the rent is due next week!" Eugene yelled.

"And don't forget you've got a job now and you can pay it," Stefan said as he slammed the front door.

[2]

Simone sat at the kitchen table, sketching a new design for the line of fashion apparel she'd dreamed of launching since she was nine. When she wasn't servicing clients or running the streets, she was sketching lavish designs while she daydreamed about flipping through magazines and running across a few of her pieces in the fashion section. That was what she wanted more than anything. Simone and Stefan had a compilation of over twenty-five hundred designs, some of which they took the liberty of bringing to life themselves, courtesy of their grandmother's sewing machine.

Simone was trying to get inspiration for an outfit she'd promised to design for her friend, Paris, to wear the one night of the year when their hood hangout was transformed into an upscale nightclub for the drag queen beauty pageant. Simone could picture Paris slinking across the stage and taking the audience's breath away as she stood in the crowd cheering him on. That's what she would do whenever she sketched. Whether it was a beautiful woman she spotted somewhere as her day played out or an actress she saw on TV that inspired her to create a design, she'd imagine them strutting down the runway in her garment until her creation was flawless.

This time Simone drew a blank. She didn't know what to design for Paris. It wasn't that she had a shortage of ideas. It was that she didn't think her designs were exotic enough for Paris.

Simone heard Stefan unlocking the front door. She looked up at the clock that hung on the wall across from the kitchen table. It was ten o'clock in the morning.

Stefan strutted in the kitchen and slapped a sandwich bag full of cocaine on the table beside Simone. "Girl, I swear, ain't a hoe on Harrison Street that's more tired than me."

Simone looked down at the sandwich bag of cocaine. "Now what would Grandma say about you slapping that shit on her table like that if she was here?"

"The same thing she'd say if she saw this pretty-ass eyeshadow." Stefan rubbed his index fingers across his eyes. "Boy, where you get that from? Let me hold some of that."

Simone laughed. "You're a mess."

"Naw, you're a fool if you think Grandma ain't sit 'round with them things she called friends and get her nose wet."

"Damn, I ain't seen you since this time yesterday. Where the hell you been?"

"Chillin' with Paris and Crystal."

"What y'all do?"

"Nothing; same old shit," Stefan said. "Oh, we made reservations to go to Southern Decadence in September. I heard it's gonna be off the meter this year."

"Sounds fun. Who else is going besides y'all?"

"Nobody; just the three of us."

"You mean to tell me y'all not taking y'all men," Simone said. "And what about y'all friend, Jewel? Y'all not taking him neither?"

"Jewel ain't want to go and as far as our men are concerned, you know what they say, don't take sand to the beach."

Simone laughed and continued sketching her design.

Stefan paused and focused on the movement of Simone's hand. "I see you're still adding to those sketches."

Simone nodded. "Yeah, I am."

"Can't nobody say you don't keep hope alive."

"What's that supposed to mean?"

"It means, any sane person would've swept that shit under the rug and grown up by now," Stefan said.

"I was told if you want something, you should work hard to get it. Besides, Paris thinks I'm talented. Why else would he ask me to make an outfit for him to wear to the pageant?"

Stefan removed a glass from the cabinet and filled it with cold water from the refrigerator. "Well, I was told dreams and thrills don't pay the bills and it's not about talent the majority of the time; it's about who you know, and you don't know anybody." Stefan gulped down his water and placed his glass in the sink. "You really need to find something better to do with your time, like a part-time job or something."

"Been there, done that."

Stefan smirked. "Oh yeah, that's right; you did have a job. Why did you say they fired you?"

Simone sighed. "'Cause they said I had a hard time comprehending instructions and I couldn't multitask."

"I bet." Stefan tapped his finger on Simone's sketch-pad. "That's 'cause you were too busy thinking about this shit."

Simone rolled her eyes. "It doesn't matter since I don't work there no more, do I?"

"It does matter. It's something you need to handle before you start working again."

"Me? Work again?" Simone chuckled. "Yeah right; I need a job like I need an STD."

"You better stock up on business suits and penicillin 'cause if any of them places we applied at last week calls and offers you a job, you're taking it."

Simone stopped sketching and looked up at Stefan. "The hell if I am."

"The hell if you ain't."

Simone sucked her teeth. "Go ahead with that. The only reason I applied was 'cause you kept nagging me about it. I ain't doing a damn thing."

Stefan took a seat in the chair across from Simone and began to fumble with the bag of cocaine. "I don't know if you ever thought about this but we can't be running 'round town turning tricks for the rest of our lives."

"Says who?"

"Your body; that shit doesn't appreciate, it depreciates. So you better get your money's worth now 'cause when your ass starts dragging the ground, your clients gonna be looking to upgrade." Stefan sprinkled the cocaine in a line on the table. "We need to start saving a lot more money than we have been, too."

"I've been saving my money. What about you?"

"I'll tell you what; you blew damn near half of it in the last couple of months buying your car."

Simone put her hands on her hips. "And I've been pulling like two sessions every other day to make up for it, so what the fuck? What about that shit you're sniffing? You blow a lot of money on that, don't you?"

Stefan slapped his hands against the table. "Pump the brakes. First of all, don't compare the two. That car outside cost a hell of a lot more than this shit right here," Stefan said, holding up the bag of cocaine. "Secondly, don't act like you don't be sniffing this shit with me."

"And don't act like my car doesn't take you back and forth where you need to go."

Stefan paused for a moment and gathered himself. "I'm simply saying you need to cut out your little Internet shopping sprees. They're unnecessary."

"Shopping sprees?" Simone asked. "What are you talking about?"

"You'll find out the next time I find one of them bags stuck in the door and slap the return label on it and send it back where it came from."

Simone huffed. "Why you always trying to regulate my shit?"

"'Cause obviously you can't."

Simone hated getting into those discussions with Stefan. She was the only one of his cousins who'd stuck by him when everyone else figured out that he was gay. She was the one who'd stood by him and endured his shame along with him when the kids in the neighborhood mocked him. When Stefan's mother dropped him off at their grandmother's house to stay, it was her that had kept him company.

Stefan's father ran out on him and his mother; he blamed Stefan's mother for the homosexual tendencies that Stefan had displayed and refused to have any part in rearing a homosexual. Stefan's mother had promised Stefan that he would only have to stay at his grandmother's house for two weeks. She told him that she needed some time to get herself together. A week later, his mother committed suicide. Stefan was heartbroken. When he stayed up all night crying, asking why his mother didn't take him with her, it was Simone who'd sat up with him and comforted him. She'd never blamed him for his mother's suicide. She'd never rubbed his shortcomings in his face, but every time he got a chance, he rubbed her face in hers.

"Look, Simone, we're not gonna be able to live in this house and run up all these bills in Grandma's name forever. It's been eight years. Sooner or later, these people are gonna realize she's dead."

Simone nodded her head in agreement; what Stefan said was true. They couldn't run up bills in their grandmother's name forever. Sooner or later, her mother would get locked up and make it into rehab and that's when the house would gain her interest. She would discover that their grandmother had never gotten a chance to revise her will and that the house belonged to her.

Simone didn't plan on living out the rest of her days there. Although she cherished the good memories that had taken place within those walls, there were a lot of bad ones that she wanted to leave behind.

The house reminded Simone of the day, after her fourth birthday, when her mother had had a revelation. Her mother had stormed through her grandmother's door, dragging Simone behind her and had tossed Simone in her grandmother's lap. Her mother delivered a speech about how she didn't need Simone's nappy headed ass holding her down, how she could do so much more with her life if she didn't have Simone following behind her begging for shit, and how if she'd never given birth to Simone, she would've still been with Simone's father. It's odd for a child to take delight in their mother's misery but eight years later, when Simone's mother showed up at the door with more tracks in her arms than Stefan had rollers, sobbing and hollering about how her boy-friend was trying to kill her, it had brought Simone much joy. She was glad to see her mother eat her words. Her mother had blamed her for her misfortune with men and once she'd cut ties with her, her misfortune had become worse. Her mother had run the streets in search of a baller who'd take care of her. She'd wanted a man she could have the liberty of bragging about and showing off to her friends but she'd been pimped instead. There she was, running into Simone's grandmother's arms for help; the same place she'd left Simone.

There was also all the ridicule that Simone and Stefan had endured from their neighbors and peers. None of the children in the neighborhood had wanted to inter-act with them and the parents of those who did had forbidden them from doing so.

When Simone and Stefan were in fourth grade, a neighborhood kid named Anthony had befriended them on the school bus. The three of them had joked and laughed the entire ride home. When they'd gotten off the bus, Anthony had walked in the middle of the two and accompanied them across the street. When Anthony's mother spotted him with Simone and Stefan, she'd run off of the porch to get him. Anthony's mother had snatched him from be-tween Simone and Stefan and slapped him across his head. She'd yanked up Anthony's jeans that hung low on his hips.

"You'll pull your pants up when that punk and his cousin run you down and take your bummy yummy,"

Anthony's mother had said as she'd dragged him up the street.

That's when the problems with the kids in the neighborhood had started. Every day, when Simone and Stefan had gotten off of the school bus, all the boys would race past them. "Last one home is a dummy 'cause Simone and Stefan gonna take his bummy yummy!" they'd shouted as they ran across the street. Simone and Stefan had listened to them blurt out the same stale insult all school year.

The kids they rode the bus with would bring eggs from home and save their milk cartons from lunch so they could toss them at the back of their heads during the bus ride home. Simone and Stefan got off of the bus every day covered with milk and egg yolk. They would fight back their tears until they reached the living room of their home where their grandmother sat waiting for them. Their grandmother would fly off of the handle when she saw them. Once they told her what happened and she realized they didn't do anything to defend themselves, she had a fit.

"Next time y'all bring y'all asses up in here looking like y'all came from a bake shop, I'm gonna put my foot in both y'all asses," their grandmother threatened.

In spite of their grandmother's threat, Simone and Stefan came home the exact same way their grandmother warned them not to at least three times a week and she never followed through with her threat.

On the last day of school that year everything went

well. The kids on the bus were as rowdy as usual but were too excited about summer break to engage in their usual pastime of egg and milk tossing. Simone and Stefan were refreshed when the bus let them off at their stop, knowing they wouldn't step foot on another school bus for damn near three months.

When they got home, their grandmother gave them money so they could go to the store and buy some goodies to snack on that evening while they sat in front the television, out of the way of her card game. They raced around the corner to the store and came back with two bags filled with goodies. Simone carried the bags while Stefan ate a Popsicle. They passed Anthony and his father as they walked up the block home.

"Hey, Anthony," Stefan said, as he waved.

"What's up?" Anthony asked.

Anthony's father yanked Anthony by his collar. "Who the fuck is that?"

"This boy I know from school," Anthony said.

Simone and Stefan walked slowly toward their house as they listened to Anthony's father scold him.

"What the fuck you speak to him for?" Anthony's father asked.

Anthony's lips quivered as he tried to explain. "He spoke to—"

Anthony's father placed his hands on Anthony's chest and shoved him. "Oh, so you a fucking faggot?"

Anthony shook his head.

"Well, you better go over there and straighten that shit," Anthony's father demanded.

Simone and Stefan heard Anthony and his father's footsteps behind them and picked up their pace.

"Stefan!" Anthony called out as Simone and Stefan made it in front of their house.

Simone and Stefan turned around to face Anthony.

Anthony stood there with his face twisted up and his father stood behind him with his arms folded, egging him on. "Don't be walking past me, speaking like you know me and shit." Anthony turned around to his father for approval and once his father nodded his head, Anthony continued, "You lucky I don't whip your ass for that shit."

Simone and Stefan stood there like totem poles, hoping that Anthony had appeased his father and the four of them could go their separate ways. They heard a screen door slam and turned around and saw their grandmother standing on the porch.

"Little Mama, grab that Popsicle," their grandmother said as she walked off of the porch into the yard. She looked at Anthony. "You so fucking bad, beat his ass and make him unlucky."

"Whip that nigga's ass!" Anthony's father shouted as he pushed Anthony toward Stefan.

Simone grabbed Stefan's Popsicle and Anthony swung his arms wildly, landing a punch on Stefan's shoulder. Stefan rushed Anthony, tackling him onto the sidewalk, and spate punches to his face. Simone stood there in amazement, watching Stefan do what neither one of them had had the guts to do up until then. Anthony's father became infuriated at the sight of Anthony struggling to get from underneath Stefan. He drew his leg back to kick Stefan but froze when he heard a gun cock. Simone and Stefan's grandmother gazed down at Anthony's father and pulled her Glock 18 out of the pocket on the side of her robe.

"That's right, muthafucka. Don't fuck with my kids; fuck with me," their grandmother said.

Anthony's father gritted his teeth. Simone felt sorry for poor Anthony and pulled Stefan off of him.

Anthony's mother came running down the street with tears in her eyes. She grabbed Anthony and held him at her side.

Simone and Stefan's grandmother smiled. "Now who was gonna get their ass beat?" she teased.

Anthony's father fussed as he walked up the street. "I can't believe he let a faggot beat him. My son's a fucking wimp."

Anthony's mother waited until she was a few steps away from Simone and Stefan to voice her frustration. "I hate y'all muthafuckas. I wish y'all move y'all trifling asses from 'round here."

"Oh shut the fuck up!" Simone yelled, throwing Stefan's Popsicle at Anthony's mother's head.

Since that day, Simone and Stefan hadn't taken shit from anyone. They went outside freely. They didn't worry about what anyone was going to say or do to them. When the neighborhood kids stared at them, they stared back to let them know that they weren't afraid anymore.

Then there was the time Simone's mother, Tessa, had gotten out of rehab and decided to stay with them while their grandmother was in the hospital having her leg amputated. The entire time their grandmother was in the hospital, Tessa never went to see her. She invited one of her junkie boyfriends to lie up in their grandmother's room with her so she could fuck and sniff dope all day. When Tessa's man got tired of fucking her and she ran out of dope, she would run around the house trying to regulate shit. They put up with it for a short time. The way Tessa would yell down the stairs and tell them to shut the fuck up when they were laughing at a scene from their favorite sitcom. How she reprimanded them when they ordered pizza instead of cooking dinner, wanting to know what she and her man were supposed to eat. Tessa's stay came to an end the day Simone decided to visit her grandmother at the hospital and Stefan stayed at home in the bed sick. When Simone returned home, she overheard her mother cursing at Stefan for calling the police on her boyfriend while she was out trying to score. Stefan had accused her boyfriend of trying to rape him.

As soon as Simone stuck her key in the door, she heard her mother shouting, "I don't let anybody fuck with my man! You fitting to join your mama behind that shit!"

"It's whatever!" Stefan shouted back.

Naw, it's however she wants it, Simone thought. All Stefan had to do was spark it and she would follow up and slap the hell out of her mother. As soon as Simone walked through the door, Stefan and Tessa went to blows. Simone ran over and shoved her foot in her mother's behind and watched her and Stefan tumble to the floor.

Stefan flipped Tessa off of him and punished her ass, punching her again and again. Simone stood over top of them, screaming for Stefan to whip her mother's ass and kicking her mother every time she threw a decent punch.

"Stefan, let me go. I don't want to fight no more," Tessa pleaded.

"Let go of my hair then, bitch!" Stefan shouted.

Tessa let go of Stefan's hair and he released her from the floor.

"Now, bitch, get your shit and get the fuck out, 'fore I stump a hole in your ass," Stefan said.

Tessa ran up the stairs and came back down carrying a tote bag. She rushed to the door like she had received a bomb threat and was fleeing the house to save her life. Simone walked over to lock the door behind her.

"And, bitch, you ain't worth shit!" Tessa screamed at Simone. "Anytime you—"

"Whatever. Just get the fuck out." Simone kicked her mother in her back and watched her stumble off of the stoop and fall in a bush on the lawn. Simone slammed the door and she and Stefan burst into laughter.

It was three years later when their grandmother rode the ambulance to the hospital and never returned; having to say goodbye to the woman who'd raised them since they were four and five years old was the saddest incident of them all. They were both eager to leave those memories behind them and start over.

⬧

Stefan sat on the sofa watching TV. Simone was slouched down in the chair across from him with her eyes closed. She didn't know about Stefan but after a few sniffs of cocaine and half a blunt of hydro she couldn't give a fuck less what was on TV. She lay back and imagined that the cool air blowing from the air conditioner was the cool wind blowing in her face as she rode down 95-South in her pastel pink 2010 convertible Saab 9-3 with one hand on the steering wheel and the other out of the window, laying against the car door. Her daydream was interrupted by the chirp of the buttons on the cordless phone. She opened her eyes and saw Stefan making a phone call.

"Who you calling?"

"The voicemail."

"Let me know if any messages are on there for me."

Simone sat up and looked at Stefan, waiting for him to indicate that she had a message. A huge smile formed on Stefan's face.

"Who was that?" Simone asked.

"I got a job interview." Stefan stuck his tongue out at Simone before he listened to the next message. "Girl." Stefan jumped over onto the arm of Simone's chair and held the phone to her ear. "Listen."

Simone listened for a few seconds and then rolled her eyes. It was the bank downtown where both of them had filled out a job application, calling to schedule an interview. Simone collapsed across Stefan's lap. "I don't wanna work."

"So? You're gonna get off your ass and go." Stefan nudged Simone off of him. "It'll be a good opportunity to meet new clients and, above all, we need to plan for our future. As much as you love your little dream of having this established fashion line, it might be just that; a dream. And remember what I said about depreciation; sooner or later that little trap of yours is gonna wear itself out."

"Yeah, and sooner or later you're gonna have to replace that 'For Sale' sign over your ass with one that says 'Condemned'."

They both giggled.

"Don't act like you don't be giving up yours."

"I do, but unlike you, I have other options."

Stefan stuck up his middle finger as he headed up the stairs. "Finish up your daydreaming while I'm up here in the shower, 'cause when I get out we're going to the mall to find something to wear to our interviews."

"Yeah, that's what I'm going to do, daydream about flying down 95-South with the top dropped on my ride. Maybe it'll keep me from dreading over this job shit."

"Do what you must; just make sure your ass doesn't get off on that Powhite Parkway exit," Stefan said. "I'd hate to see your ass dash around that curve and lunge into that damn clock. Ain't no telling when the hell somebody will come and pull your ass out of there."

Simone grabbed one of the decorative pillows off of the sofa and tossed it at Stefan.

Why I got to get a job 'cause he wants to get his life together? Simone thought. Working wasn't her thing. The longest she'd ever kept a job was three weeks and now Stefan was talking about jobs like their future depended on it. As far as she was concerned, a job wasn't in her future unless it involved the fashion designs she was so eager to bring to life. If not she would be an old-ass hooker turning tricks for fifty dollars a pop until she came down with some crippling disability that allowed her to collect Social Security benefits.

[3]

Simone and Stefan walked through Regency Square Mall buying everything from their interview outfits to sexy undergarments.

"Damn, Stefan, we should've stayed at home and bought a few outfits online or something, instead of buying this shit."

Stefan replied, "My interview is at eleven o'clock tomorrow and I could've sworn yours was only thirty minutes after mine."

"What's your point?"

Stefan sucked his teeth. "My point is, we wouldn't have gotten our order in enough time to have something to wear to our interviews."

Simone nodded. "True, but you keep talking this shit about saving money and I just spent a grip on some mediocre shit when I could've shopped online and snagged something I really wanted."

"Do the math," Stefan said. "You got a lot more shit out here than you would've spent your money on for whatever high-priced shit you wanted to buy online. Damn, why I always got to spell shit out for you?"

Simone looked at Stefan and rolled her eyes. She couldn't win with him. He jumped at every opportunity to make her feel stupid. She was so disgusted with him that her face became flushed. She wanted to run outside, hop in her car, and leave his ass strained. At that moment everything about him rubbed her the wrong way. She hated how he walked around with his nose stuck in the air, rolling his hazel eyes at whomever he thought to be inferior to him. She hated the way he switched his high-yellow ass around in his form-fitting clothes, swinging his long auburn dreads, trying to show off his girlish figure. The entire time he had a dick hidden away between his legs but he had the nerve to criticize her.

"What's your problem?" Stefan asked, resting his elbow on Simone's shoulder.

Simone didn't answer. She shook her head and looked away.

"It's a shame, how some people walk around with their hearts on their sleeves."

"Well, it's hard not to when there's someone taking cheap shots at you every second of the day."

They both paused and Simone turned around to face Stefan with her fist rested on her hip.

"Calm down, baby girl; you don't want to take it there."

"I don't need to calm down. I'll take the shit wherever you want to go with it."

"Oh, is that right?" Stefan asked. "All I want you to do is come the fuck back to reality and realize you don't want it with me. And for future references, if I was as sensitive as your ass, I wouldn't wear my heart on my sleeve. I'll put the muthafucka up so I won't get hurt."

Simone giggled at Stefan's remark and her anger fizzled.

"How'd you get to be so damn sensitive?" Stefan threw his arm over Simone's shoulder.

Simone started to feel guilty about the way she'd snapped at Stefan. *It's just that he's been so judgmental ever since Grandma died*, she told herself. She felt like Stefan was acting out her grandmother's role, disciplining and correcting her. She was grown. She could live her own life. She didn't need him telling her what to do or how to think. She didn't spend every second they were together telling him how provoking it was for him to prance around town in his tiny sundresses and that he was inviting trouble by doing so. She stuck by him and if trouble came their way, they would deal with it however they needed to in order to prevail. She wanted Stefan to show her the same respect.

Stefan stopped in front of the Guess store and peered through the window.

"What we stopping here for?" Simone asked.

"The pool opened up last weekend and I'm buying a swimsuit so I can take a dip."

Although both of them had received a lifetime membership to the most popular fitness center in the Tri-City area, a Christmas gift from Mason, Stefan still wanted to go around the way to the pool. Not even around their way but over on the north side of town to the pool at Battery Park. Simone hated going there. Every time they went, someone felt the need to run their mouth; someone who felt the need to try them. The guys always had something degrading to say and all the little bitches that wanted to be down with them would entertain their comments and join them in shooting insults. Most of the time, the shit didn't end well. Every summer, they found themselves having to set someone straight by giving them an ass-whipping that took them and the viewers clean into the next summer to get over. But as soon as they got over it, they were ready to try their hand again. Simone felt like the shit was getting old, real old, but Stefan insisted on going there and meeting up with his friends, Paris, Crystal, and Jewel, better known as Paul, Charlie, and Jamie, and about ten others who hung out there on a regular basis.

Stefan pulled a black signature bikini off of the rack and held it up. "Simone, you like this?"

"No, I don't really go for signature stuff." Simone pulled a floral print halter bikini off of the rack. "What about this one?"

"Naw." Stefan pulled a turquoise tropical print bikini off of the rack beside it. "Oh, I like this one. I'm going to try it on."

Simone held on to the pink bikini and scanned the racks for one she liked better. Wherever they went, Stefan made sure he looked his best. Even when he was dressed in his boy clothes, he made sure he presented himself in a way that was appealing to him and those he wanted to impress.

Simone recalled the first time Stefan had gone out on the town dressed in drag. She was thirteen and Stefan was fourteen years old. They stayed up late the night before, making Stefan's dress. The next night when they ventured out, Stefan stole all of the compliments. Men walked past him doing double-takes. Simone listened as the men spit their pickup lines to Stefan:

"Damn, ma, you thrown together!"

"What you doing there with all that?" and all types of stupid shit, but Simone hadn't received one compliment or advance. She'd seen a middle-aged man leaning against his car gawking at her. She'd anticipated him making a pass at her and looked forward to the chance to curse him out and send him on his way. Before the man could make a pass at her, Stefan had strolled in front of her, grabbing his attention.

"Um, you a tall drink of water if I ever seen one," the man had said.

It was at that moment when Simone decided that she wasn't going to be Stefan's coaster. *There is no way he should be pulling more men than me*, she told herself. *After all, I have two things he doesn't have.* She promised herself to use both to her advantage whenever possible. She made an effort to look as good, or better, than Stefan when they stepped out, even if it meant showing off what he didn't have to show.

Stefan came to the dressing room door, striking a pose

in his bikini. "You like?" Stefan asked, turning around to show Simone the back of his bikini.

"Ain't nobody fucking with you."

Stefan blushed. "Who you telling?"

Simone held up the cover-up that went with Stefan's bikini. "Look what I found."

"I don't want that shit," Stefan said. "That's for them chicks with a bunch of dimples in their asses, like you."

"You're crazy; my ass is tight."

Stefan shook his head. "Naw, your ass is fat. That's what you get for sitting in front of the TV eating pizza when you're supposed to be at the gym with me."

"Fuck you, Stefan."

"See, I always knew you were a hater." Stefan turned his back toward Simone. "You wish you had an ass like this. This ass right here is tough." Stefan slapped himself on the ass.

"Please," Simone said. "My ass is so tough I could carry five niggas from here to California on one of my cheeks."

"My ass is so tough I could pick up five nickels, three nails, and a crochet needle off a scalding hot sidewalk in Miami in the middle of July with my bare cheeks," Stefan said.

Simone laughed. She threw both of her hands in the air to surrender. "I'm scared of you."

"And you should be." Stefan winked his eye and closed the door to the dressing room.

After leaving Guess, they went to the tattoo parlor so Stefan could get one. Stefan talked about it the entire ride there. He wanted an outline of a bone on the small of his back with red cursive letters inside that read: "red bone." Simone was hesitant about getting one. She had a low tolerance for pain but, after seeing the finished results of Stefan's, she decided that she had to have one. She got two strawberries that overlapped each other on the small of her back. The one on the right had a chunk bitten from it where drops of juices trickled down to the top of her hip. She was a little sore but felt extra special rocking the two strawberries on her back. She would wear backless shirts and low riders all summer. It was also an added plus when it came to enticing her clients and finding new ones.

〔 4 〕

Paris sat at the bar, sipping his fourth mojito. He was trying to numb his envy. Every time he went out with his boyfriend, Michael, he had to deal with his flirting. It didn't matter where they went; it could be a bar, club, or park and Michael would find someone or something to flirt with, be it a man, woman, or dog. This time it was Paris's friend, Jewel, who was at the bar when they arrived, drinking his sorrows away and trying to find someone drunk enough, or low enough, to spend the night with him.

Jewel dressed in drag like Paris did but was uglier posing as a woman than he was dressed as a man. He had eyes the size of grapes, a wide nose and itty-bitty nostrils, thin lips, and a box chin. When he added his blonde weave and drew the mole on the top of his lip, he looked like he belonged on the island of misfit toys, but you couldn't tell him that. Jewel would go around telling people that he was the shit. He said it so much that he had brainwashed some poor folks into believing that he was a hot commodity.

Paris scanned the bar for someone who would give him the attention that he deserved. He put too much into himself; waxing, putting on makeup, buying breast and butt pads, sitting for eight hours for his micro-braids. He refused to be ignored. If Michael preferred to look in Jewel's rough face instead of admiring his smooth chocolate skin, his big brown eyes that he went out of his way to glue lashes on, his pearly white smile, and the deep dimple on his left cheek, then fuck him. Paris could find someone else who would.

Paris walked over to a handsome, light brown-skinned guy. He was definitely Paris's type. He was tall, muscular, and the exact opposite of Michael whose dark, short, frail body could be masked by a barstool. Paris realized that Michael would be jealous. Michael had a serious color complex. He was threatened by the lighter-skinned people he had to compete with in the dating game and had an unyielding partiality for the ones who were his potential love interests. Paris never understood what the big hype was about color. He felt black people practiced supremacy amongst each other. Some light-skinned people thought being fair made them better than other members of their own race. They thought that they were special when they really needed special education. Any person with good sense would understand that if any-thing made one person better than another, it was their morals and values. Then there were some dark-skinned people who stereotyped light-skinned people as being whores, gold diggers, or snobbish based upon light-skinned people that they'd had negative experiences with, or something they'd heard or seen on television. Paris guessed the brown-skinned people in between thought that they had serious ego and inferiority issues and needed to see a shrink. Paris planned to use Michael's complex to his advantage.

Paris walked over to the muscular, light-skinned man and tapped him on his shoulder. The man glanced up at him.

Paris held out his hand. "Hey, I'm Paris."

The man grabbed Paris's hand and kissed it. "My name's Frank, boo."

Paris smiled and looked down at Frank's firm lap. "Is that seat taken?"

"It is now." Frank grabbed Paris by the waist and sat him down in his lap.

Paris sat in Frank's lap, flirting with him and sipping on his drink for a half-hour before Michael drew his attention away from Jewel long enough to notice.

Paris was too busy looking in Frank's eyes to notice Michael approaching him. When he did notice Michael, it was too late. Michael stood in front of him, emitting smoke from his nostrils like a bull. Before Paris could utter a word, Michael threw his drink in his face. The bar became silent as everyone turned their attention to them.

Paris was fuming. *This nigga has lost his mind*, he thought. That was one of the most degrading things you could do to your mate.

Frank slid Paris off of his lap and stood up to confront Michael. "Man, what the—"

Before Frank could finish, the sound of Paris's fist slamming into Michael's chest echoed throughout the bar. Michael pushed Paris into the table and Paris dove onto Michael and sunk his teeth deep into the skin on his cheek. Security ran over to break up the fight and threw Paris and Michael out of the club.

Frank left the club to offer Paris a ride home. He saw Michael prying the Rolex watch off of Paris's wrist and heard him demand that Paris give him the bracelet and earrings that he'd purchased for him.

Frank started up his car. "Come on, Paris; I'll take you home!"

Michael cursed and yelled as Paris made his way to the car. "I don't know why I even settled for some trash like you! You ain't fit to eat shit out my ass!"

Paris got into the car and shut the door. "You're right; that's your mama's job!" Paris yelled out of the window as Frank drove off.

Michael chased the car to the end of the block and then stopped and cursed at Paris as he caught his breath.

❖

Simone and Stefan arrived at the Crowne Plaza Hotel on East Canal Street at eleven o'clock. They were thirty minutes late. Stefan yawned as he got off of the elevator and Simone thought about whether she should apologize to their client for being late. As they approached the room, they spotted Thomas peeking out of the door. The two looked at each other and grinned.

"He must be in a hurry to get his hands on us," Simone joked.

"What you expect? I'm a hot commodity," Stefan said, snapping his fingers.

Simone slowed her pace and allowed Stefan to enter the room first. She was starting to have a case of the giggles like she often did when they went on jobs together, something that happened when she became nervous. She wanted to contain herself before she walked into the room.

Thomas flung open the door and welcomed them with a hug and a kiss on the cheek. He grabbed Stefan's hand and spun him around, looking him over. "Um…um… um," Thomas said, before kissing Stefan's hand.

"I know that's right." Stefan wasn't surprised by how pleased Thomas was with his appearance.

"Would you two like something to drink?" Thomas asked, glancing at the bottle of Glenlivet on the stand beside the bed.

Simone looked over at the bottle. "Glenlivet, hell yeah. That's my baby daddy."

Stefan rolled his eyes. "Sure, I'd love to have some."

Stefan stood there, watching Thomas pour their drinks while Simone scanned the room.

"Is he a doctor?" Simone whispered in Stefan's ear, nodding her head toward the white lab coat that lay across the bed.

"Yeah," Stefan mumbled.

"Oh, and he's married, too. Look at that wedding band on the table."

Stefan kept his eyes on Thomas, trying to ignore Simone.

"I wonder how much I can get for that bad boy at the pawnshop."

Stefan stomped down on her foot.

Simone quickly slid her foot from under Stefan's shoe. "What the hell is wrong with you?"

Stefan looked at her and squinted. "We're about to make fifteen hundred dollars and you want to damage our credibility by stealing his wedding band so you can get duped out of it at the pawnshop."

Thomas handed the two of them drinks. "Is there something wrong?"

Stefan looked at Simone and then back at Thomas and smiled. "No, everything's fine."

Their session moved by quickly. Thomas put on his Garth Brooks album and they sat on the bed, sipping their drinks while Thomas rambled on about the stress of his job and the new baby his wife had given birth to two weeks earlier. Stefan got off of the bed and began easing off his dress as he swayed his hips to the rhythm of the music. Simone had seen some strange and funny things in her profession but up until that point, she had seen nothing funnier than the sight of Stefan stripping to country music.

Stefan made eye contact with Simone, signaling for her to get up and join him. She gulped down her drink and joined Stefan, sliding off her clothes and tossing her G-string to Thomas. He held onto it for a minute, inhaling the scent before licking the string and tossing it across the room. Thomas grabbed the bottle of Glenlivet and joined them.

Thomas poured the liquor on Simone's neck and she rubbed it in as it ran down her breasts. Thomas began to suck on Simone's nipples. Stefan took the bottle out of Thomas's hand, poured the liquor down Thomas's back, and rubbed it over the mass of his hips. Stefan stooped down and Simone heard the sound of him lapping between Thomas's hips. That was her cue to drop to her knees and take care of the part of Thomas that she had been assigned to. She drooled on Thomas's dick and stroked it until it was fully erect. Semen dripped from his dick and his knees began to buckle. For a moment she wondered whether his pleasure stemmed from her or Stefan. She dismissed the thought. It was none of her concern. She engulfed Thomas's dick with her mouth and Thomas reached behind himself to stroke his anus. The pitch of his moans increased. Stefan stood up and crammed his dick into Thomas's anus. Thomas placed his hands on the wall behind Simone to balance himself. Simone was stunned. She had seen Stefan take dick plenty of times but she had never once seen him dish it out. Hell, this was the same man that sat down on the toilet to take a piss. As far as she knew, Stefan didn't know he had a dick.

Thomas moaned. "Ahh, yeah...that's what I've been waiting for all night."

Simone rubbed Thomas's balls with one hand as she continued to stroke his dick with the other as she slid it in and out of her mouth. Stefan pounded Thomas so vigorously that his pelvis smacked against Simone's forehead, causing her to bump her head against the wall. She took a deep breath. *Please hurry up and be over with*, she thought.

Thomas's breathing became heavy and Simone could taste his semen. Thomas leaned forward onto the wall and squealed as he filled Simone's mouth with cum.

⟦ 5 ⟧

Stefan drove down Cary Street while Simone lay back in her seat with her feet propped up on the dashboard, laughing about the night before.

"Damn, Stefan, you can lay *pipe!*"

"Just 'cause I like to get dealt to doesn't mean I can't deal. Don't get it twisted."

"Ooh, I heard that," Simone said, slapping Stefan on his arm. "Shit, I didn't know you realized that you had a dick. When you find out? Last night? I bet Thomas's ass is all tore up."

Stefan sucked his teeth. "You just make sure yours doesn't end up that way."

Simone's cell phone rang and she fumbled around in her purse to retrieve it.

"Who is that?"

"Let's see." Simone looked down at the caller ID.

"A private caller," she said, rolling her eyes.

"Didn't you say you've been getting a lot of them calls lately?"

Simone nodded her head. "Un-huh."

"Go ahead and answer it," Stefan said. "It might be

one of your clients calling from home. Make sure you power your damn phone down afterward. You don't want that thing to start ringing during your interview."

Simone flipped open her phone.

"Hello," a woman's voice said before Simone had a chance to greet her.

"Who's this?" Simone asked.

"Who the hell you think it is?" the woman replied. "It's your mother."

Simone immediately hung up the phone.

"Who was it?" Stefan asked.

Simone sighed. "Your aunt, Tessa."

Stefan looked at Simone and grinned. "You mean it was your mommy; how sweet."

Simone raised her eyebrow at Stefan to let him know how displeased she was with his comment. The phone began to ring again. Simone looked at the phone and then back at Stefan.

"Go ahead; answer it. You can put it on speaker. It'll be fun."

Simone flipped open her cell phone and put it on speaker. She waited for her mother to say hello.

"Hello," Tessa said.

"Answer me this; how you get my number?" Simone asked.

"Trust me, it ain't hard to get when you're into the type of shit you're into."

Stefan leaned over and yelled into the phone, "Tell that bitch, fuck her!"

"Tell that punk to get on the phone and tell me his damn self."

"I don't talk to the less fortunate," Stefan said.

"Less fortunate? I ain't the one selling my ass for money," Tessa said.

Simone clapped her hands to applaud her mother. "You're right; you're such an upstanding member of the community. You make me so proud, I wanna go out and cop you a gigantic needle full of dope."

Stefan burst out into laughter, almost hitting the wall as he pulled into the parking deck.

"Fuck you; you always standing up for that fucking faggot. I'm your goddamn mama."

Simone's face turned red. *This bitch has got nerve, saying she's my mother*, Simone thought. "And I'm the nappy-headed girl you tossed in your mother's lap for her to raise."

"You know what? I ain't worried about y'all; carry it however y'all want." Tessa sighed. "And you tell that damn Stefan I know what the fuck he did."

Simone looked over at Stefan, noticing how red his face had become. "What did you do, Stefan?"

"He called the police on Tony that day at the house, accusing him of trying to rape him, but get this; now he running 'round fucking him," Tessa said.

Stefan pounded his fist on the steering wheel. "That bitch is crazy. She knows damn well I don't fuck junkies."

Simone giggled. "What are you trying to say, Stefan?"

"That he's a fucking junkie," Stefan answered.

"Hey, Tessa, you heard that, didn't you?" Simone asked.

"His punk ass is lying," Tessa said. "But I ain't worried; payback's a bitch. His foolish ass did something to spite me and he's fitting to die behind the shit and he's too dumb to even realize it."

"Who's gonna kill him, you?" Simone asked.

"I don't have to lay a hand on him and as dumb as your ass is, you're probably gonna join him. God knows what you two do together. And who is he to be calling my man a junkie when he's a fucking abomination."

Stefan took a deep breath. "Here we go with the religious shit."

"Damn right, 'cause that's what the fuck you are; running 'round craving dick at a young age," Tessa said. "That's why my sister killed herself; she was tired of dealing with your faggot ass."

"Whatever! If you were so concerned about it, why you didn't come to the funeral?" Simone asked.

"'Cause she was too busy selling her pussy so she could score," Stefan answered.

Tessa paused for a moment to think of what she could say to get underneath Stefan's skin. "Hey, Simone, did Stefan tell you that he used to peek through the keyhole of his mama and daddy's bedroom so he could watch his daddy undress?"

"Bitch, I've never done no shit like that," Stefan said. "Don't make me jump through this phone and bash you in your damn face."

Simone decided it was time to end the conversation. It had gone too far and it was obvious that her mother's accusation had pained Stefan. "Blah…blah…blah… Take your delirious ass somewhere and score; that's if you ain't done so already."

"Yeah, I'm surprised you ain't nodded off by now," Stefan said.

Simone hung up the phone, looked at Stefan, and took a deep breath.

Stefan got out of the car and shut the door. "See, I told you it would be fun," he said, before making his way into the building for his interview.

Simone sat in the car, thinking about what her mother had said. She wondered if there was any truth to the claim she'd made about Stefan sleeping with Tony. Tony wasn't even Stefan's type. He was too scrawny and unkempt. She had never seen Stefan date anybody that was missing teeth like Tony. Stefan liked his men with wide, lean, muscular frames, dark brown skin, and he was crazy over the ones that wore grills in their mouths. Besides, Stefan was dating a man named Eugene that his friend, Paris, had hooked him up with. Stefan had written to Eugene while he was in the penitentiary and when he got released, he and Stefan had instantly become an item.

The man was fine. Simone told Stefan that he was lucky that Eugene was a full-fledged homo, 'cause if he weren't, she would've cut his throat and gotten with Eugene. Between Stefan's clients and Eugene, she didn't see where Stefan had the time, or a need, to sleep with Tony. If Stefan did sleep with Tony, he had done it to be spiteful. But Stefan thought Tessa was the nastiest, scummiest bitch on the face of the earth and, for that reason, Simone didn't believe he would knowingly sleep with anyone she had been with.

Simone rubbed her hands together, feeling how dry they were, and searched her purse for the tube of lotion she usually carried with her. She took it out of her purse so often to soothe her dry hands, there was no telling where it was. After not finding any lotion in her purse, she searched the car, starting with the glove compartment and ending with the creases in between the cushions of the back seat. That's when she remembered that Stefan carried lotion in his gym bag. They'd packed their stuff in Stefan's gym bag so they could go to the pool after their interviews. Simone popped open the trunk, grabbed the gym bag, and hopped back in the car. She poked around in Stefan's bag longer than she'd anticipated before finding the lotion hidden away in a small zip compartment inside of the bag. After drenching her hands, she placed it back.

She noticed a bottle of prescription medication lying in the zip compartment. She picked it up and began reading it. She was curious. As far as she knew, Stefan didn't go to the doctor. He thought seeing the doctor was a waste of money. He'd even taken the liberty of going to the bookstore and buying a book of home remedies for them.

The year before, when Stefan had come down with the flu, he'd remained in the bed for four weeks. He'd only gotten out of bed to splash salt water on his face and to drink glasses of water that he mixed with cayenne pepper three times a day. Simone had to bring his meals up to his room and force him to eat.

After two weeks, she'd started to become worried. He'd lost at least ten pounds and his eyeballs had sunk so far back in his head that she swore they would dry up and roll out at any moment. Simone had pleaded with him to let her take him to the hospital but he'd refused. One night she'd sat in his room, watching BET while he slept. He'd lain there with his eyes slightly open and his hands resting on his chest. It was the first time since childhood that Simone had viewed Stefan as a male. He didn't have on any makeup or nail polish. His facial hair had started to sprout out. The sight of him frightened her so much that she'd knelt down beside the bed to pray for his recovery. It was one of three prayers she had ever said in her life. That's what she seemed to do in her times of severe anxiety and confusion and only then.

The day she walked into her grandmother's room after she'd just had a heart attack, Simone had cried out to God. She was so loud that Stefan had heard her and run up the stairs. He'd entered the room just as Simone had begun to perform CPR on their grandmother. Simone didn't know what she was doing. She did what she had seen on TV and it worked. By the time the ambulance arrived, their grandmother was breathing and conscious.

Simone and Stefan rode the ambulance to the hospital with their grandmother and after sitting in the waiting room for two hours, the doctor gave them the okay to go back to her room. She'd seemed full of life. She'd told them that she expected to be home the next day, to clean up so she wouldn't be coming home to a messy house, and told Stefan to have a pot of turkey necks ready for her. They went home that night and did as their grandmother requested before going to bed. Early the next morning, before the sun rose, they'd received a call from the hospital saying that their grandmother had passed away.

Simone had gone into the bathroom to shower before they made their way to the hospital while Stefan made a few calls to their relatives so they could pass the word. Simone knelt in the center of the bathroom floor, naked and dripping with suds, crying out to God. Stefan banged on the bathroom door, asking her if she was alright. The thought of their grandmother was too much for her to endure and it was all she could think about during her shower. She got out of the shower to ask God why He'd reneged on her blessing, why He'd taken her grand-mother. It was at that moment that Simone made up her mind about God. She thought God was undependable and didn't hesitate to snatch back what He had given. He was like a spoiled child who had given His toy to a friend and when He saw His friend taking pleasure in it, He snatched it back.

Despite her feelings about God, there she was with

Stefan, on her knees, asking for God's assistance again. It took a couple of weeks but Stefan did get better. She walked up on him two weeks later in the bathroom, making up his face, bearing witness to cayenne pepper and salt water.

She looked at the bottom of the bottle. It read: "Original Fill Date September 6, 2010." She sat there, struggling to pronounce the name of the medication, when she caught sight of a white man wearing sunglasses and a blue suit parked beside of her in a black BMW. He was gorgeous. He had deep, wavy, light brown hair like Matthew McConaughey and when he took his glasses off and they locked eyes, she swore he had the most seductive baby blue bedroom eyes she had ever seen.

The man lifted himself up in his seat to inspect her body. His eyes crept down the imprint of her breasts that protruded through her white satin cap-sleeve blouse, down to her dark gray mini-skirt that stopped midway of her voluptuous thighs.

"Have you ever seen a cat clean itself?" the man asked.

Why would he ask me that? Simone thought. *Something ain't right with his ass.* "I can't say that I have."

"I just wanted to give you an idea of what I want to do to you," the man said.

Stefan opened the car door, startling Simone. Simone quickly shoved his medication under her seat and looked up at him to see if he'd noticed. Stefan rolled his eyes and turned his head in the opposite direction.

Simone turned back around to her potential client and

responded to his comment. "How much are you willing to pay to put your tongue on this?"

The man laughed. "I'm sure we can come to some sort of agreement."

Simone looked him over and then smiled. "How about I give you my number and you call me so we can work something out?"

The man picked up his cell phone and prepared to enter her number. "What's your name?"

"Mona," Simone answered.

After giving him her name, she followed up with her number and they made plans to meet that night. Simone couldn't help but notice that Stefan hadn't looked in her direction since he'd gotten into the car. He seemed to want to distance himself from the situation. She thought it was because he had dressed in his boy clothes to attend the interview and felt insecure about his appearance. She didn't know why he would feel that way. Stefan carried himself in such a way that he rarely projected a masculine image. He was always pretty and feminine. His clothes didn't take away from that. His girl clothes merely enhanced those qualities like her girly clothes enhanced her feminine qualities. She figured that if a man wasn't attracted to him, it wasn't because they didn't find him good-looking; it would be because they didn't play on that side of the field. She decided to ask if Stefan could accompany them that night.

"By the way!" Simone yelled, trying to catch her new client before he drove off. "What's your name?"

"Ivan," the man answered.

"Ivan, do you mind if my cousin over here came along?"

Ivan paused to look at Stefan before he answered. "Of course not; I've got a friend that would be crazy about him."

"Okay; we'll see you then."

Ivan put his car in gear and drove off. Simone and Stefan didn't say a word to one another until Ivan was out of view.

Stefan grinned from ear to ear. "If a man that fine told me that he'd lick in my crevices like a cat, he would've been a freebie."

"Well, I don't do freebies."

"Now, if I had a man like that, I'd never leave the house."

"Whatever; that's what you say."

"Naw, that's what I mean. I wouldn't care if he was missing four teeth, strung out on crack, wouldn't do shit for me, and couldn't do shit else," Stefan said. "As long as I could lie up in the house with him lapping on me all day, I'd be one raggedy bitch. I might even go out and suck some dick so his ass could get high."

Simone shook her head. "Now you're tripping."

Stefan laughed. "You're right; I *am* tripping."

Simone got out of the car and straightened up her skirt. "Do I look okay?"

"You look fine," Stefan said. "Maybe you'll pick up some more clients on your way in."

"Maybe so," Simone said, as she winked her eye and then made her way into the building for her interview.

❧[6]❧

S imone stood in front of the mirror in the ladies dressing room of the Battery Park swimming pool, putting on sunscreen. She and Stefan were scrambling to join their crew outside.

"Can you rub some of this on my back?" Simone asked.

Stefan reached for the bottle of sunscreen and began to rub it onto Simone's back. "Let me ask you a question. Why were you snooping through my gym bag?"

"Snooping? I wasn't snooping. I was looking for some lotion."

"Then how did my prescription fall into your clutches?"

"I found it in the compartment with the lotion," Simone said. "You never mentioned not feeling well, or going to the doctor. I was wondering what it was for."

"Well, if you must know, they're hormone pills."

Simone was puzzled. "Hormone pills?"

"Yes, I finally decided that I want to have my operation," Stefan said. "I mean, who would make a prettier woman than me?"

Simone hugged Stefan. "Aw, that's why you're so hung up on saving money. I can't wait. I'm so happy for you."

They heard the sound of flip-flops coming toward them and turned around. It was Paris. He leaned against the wall, resting one foot on the other with his arms folded. He wore his long black micro-braids in a bun, showing off the beads dangling from the tie of his low-cut yellow swimsuit.

"What y'all doing in here?" Paris asked.

"What does it look like we're doing?" Stefan asked. "We're getting ready."

"Y'all should've done that before y'all got here. Ain't no telling what might happen up in here," Paris said. "Y'all will start getting dressed at home when one of y'all get y'all choke broke messing 'round up in here."

"If that's the case, I see why you get dressed at home. As worn out as your ass is, you wouldn't know someone broke in it until you damn near made it home," Stefan joked.

Paris stuck up his middle finger and made his way out of the dressing room.

When Simone and Stefan stepped out of the dressing room, Paris, Crystal, and Jewel were posted up against the wall with three others Simone had never met before. They all wore pastel-colored swimsuits. They either had on bikinis or halter-style swimsuits and everyone had a fresh manicure and pedicure with bold designs except for Simone, Stefan, and Paris, who always wore a French manicure. They thought multiple colors, candy paper, and cut-up dollar bills looked better scattered across the sidewalk than they did on their nails and swore never to wear that tacky shit. As soon as they all noticed Simone and Stefan, they walked forward, one behind the other, as if they were ready to strut down the runway in a fashion show.

Simone and Stefan slid in the middle of the group. As they entered the pool area, they received stares and smirks from all who were present, even the lifeguards. The guys began to jump out of the pool. One guy damn near knocked his girlfriend on the pavement, trying to get out of the pool before they could jump in and *taint* the water. Simone's heart began to race. The contempt in the men's eyes warned of what was about to go down. The guys walked past them on their way out and the girls that were with the guys cackled. Jewel reached his trembling hands over to play with the ties hanging from Stefan's top. He complimented Stefan on how nice he looked. Jewel was trying not to notice the stares they received as the guys walked by. A guy name Calvin paused in front of them and eyed them.

"I hate y'all faggot muthafuckas," Calvin spat, then spit on the ground near Stefan's feet.

"Hold the fuck up!" Crystal yelled.

Stefan kicked off his sandals, thrust his arm back, and delivered a blow that made Calvin's knees buckle. The brawl was on. Fists were flying so fast that Simone couldn't determine whose were whose. The girls that remained in the pool jumped out and the lifeguards left their posts to assemble around the fight. Calvin grabbed a handful of Stefan's dreads and banged Stefan's head against his knee. Stefan rammed Calvin into the wall and deluged his sides with punches. Paris and Jewel struggled to separate Stefan and Calvin. Simone decided to join them in their efforts. Simone grabbed Stefan's arm and was slung to the ground as he threw his next punch. Four of Calvin's friends, Robert, Gerald, Haywood, and Xavier, ran over to break up the fight. Robert and Gerald pulled Calvin away from Stefan, and Haywood and Xavier ran up on Paris and Crystal.

"Y'all can't be ganging up on my man like that. That shit ain't gonna ride," Haywood spat.

Paris stood his ground and bucked back at Haywood. "We ain't got to gang up on your man. My nigga handled his business."

"Your nigga?" Xavier said. "You mean your girl."

Haywood laughed and dapped Xavier up, enlivened by his comment. Paris stood in silence, thinking of a comeback.

"Y'all walking 'round here like a bunch of bitches," Haywood snapped. "Switching and shit with y'all dicks bulging out y'all bikinis. People ain't trying to see that shit."

"Ol' take-it-in-the-booty-ass niggas," Xavier said before he and his friends walked off.

Stefan picked up one of his sandals and tossed it at Xavier, hitting him on his shoulder.

"What the fuck!" Xavier turned toward Stefan.

"Yeah, nigga!" Stefan shouted. "Fuck you gonna do?"

Paris stood beside Stefan with his hands on his hips, Jewel held onto Stefan's arm, and Crystal reached inside his top and inconspicuously pulled out his razor. Simone stood beside them thinking about how she was too delicate to be scuffling with a bunch of men. She hoped they would make their way out front before anything went down so she could get her hands on one of the loose bricks that laid beside the entrance and wallop the hell out of whomever came her way.

"Nigga, y'all don't want to fuck with me. I'm an O.G. and y'all, y'all some bitches, some wannabe hoes," Xavier said, and then followed his friends out front.

Stefan jolted toward Xavier and Jewel attempted to restrain Stefan with one hand on his arm and the other tugging at his top. Stefan broke free and rushed out front behind Xavier and his crew. Everyone followed Stefan except for Jewel, who stood there holding Stefan's top in his hand.

"Bitches!" Stefan ran up behind Xavier. "I'll put some lipstick on yo' ass and make you my bitch. After I finish with you, your girl's gonna wonder who should be fucking who."

Xavier stopped in his tracks and squinted at Stefan, then began to approach him.

Simone picked up a brick and joined Paris and the rest of the bunch, who stood behind Stefan.

Robert threw his arm in front of Xavier, prompting him not to go forward. Xavier slapped Robert's arm away.

Robert squeezed Xavier's shoulder. "Man, fuck them; let's go."

"Yeah, that's what he wants to do; fuck me. That's why he's so hot and bothered," Stefan said.

Paris snapped his fingers. "You ain't never lied."

"I ain't going to stand here and let no fucking faggot disrespect me like this," Xavier said.

Robert whispered in Xavier's ear and nodded his head toward his SUV.

The crowd became anxious and started to belittle Xavier for not attacking Stefan.

Crystal started to become jumpy. He thought there was a gun in the SUV and that was why Robert was so eager to get to it. "Oh, hell naw; don't let them damn niggas make it to their jeep," Crystal said.

Xavier waved Stefan and the crew off and headed to the SUV with his friends. Crystal ran up to Calvin and tagged him. Stefan followed suit and ran up to Xavier, punched him in his groin, and then followed up by slamming his elbow against Xavier's jaw. Robert rushed toward Simone and she hurled the brick that she held behind her back into his head. Robert staggered, knelt down, and grabbed his head. Simone picked up the brick, ran toward him, and smacked him with the brick repeatedly until he hit the ground, and then began to kick him. Robert covered his face with his hands to prevent Simone's foot from slamming into his face. Simone felt something warm splash across her face. She turned around and saw Crystal pulling his razor from Calvin's bleeding face.

Somebody's going to jail today, Simone thought. *Well, ain't like we don't have the money for bail.*

Simone, Stefan, Paris, and Crystal were all in the same profession; they conducted their business in different circles so there wouldn't be any hard feelings behind one of them cutting the other's throat on a customer. If need be, Simone and Stefan would pack their belongings and leave town. Neither one of them was willing to give up their freedom, not even for a day.

Simone looked over at Stefan to see how he was holding up against Xavier and scoped the area for Paris, but was unable to locate him. She continued to kick Robert, who laid beside her feet, trying to inflict more pain each time she jammed her foot into his gut.

The sound of sirens drowned out the roots of the spectators. Simone's eyes met with flashing blue lights and she ran over to Stefan to warn him of the arrival of the police. Before Simone could reach Stefan, she was blinded in her steps. She stood there, gasping for air, until she was snatched off of her feet and handcuffed.

❖

Simone, Stefan, and the rest of the bunch sat on the sidewalk in handcuffs, flushing their eyes out with tears. They could hear Crystal yell obscenities as he slammed his feet into the door of the police car.

Crystal was dragged to the squad car after he attacked a police officer. The police officer clenched his hands around Crystal's neck in a poor attempt to pull him off of his opponent.

Two officers went around, obtaining the statements of witnesses, and two other officers on the scene searched Robert's SUV. They confiscated what appeared to be a kilo of cocaine and an ounce of marijuana from the SUV.

Stefan sucked his teeth. "Damn, I wish I could've gotten my hands on that shit."

Simone remained quiet. She sat there, mentally chastising herself for tagging along. She knew it was going to happen. It went down that way every year. They kicked off the summer scrapping with the patrons of Battery Park Pool. The incidents increased in their severity each year. It started out as bickering and unkind gestures, and then escalated to heated arguments that threatened bodily harm, and then shortly afterward turned into fist-fights.

The previous summer Stefan and Paris had gotten into a quarrel with two guys after accidentally bumping into one of them as they walked up the hill on their way leaving the park. The guy shoved Stefan and they began to tussle and rolled down the hill. Stefan spotted a forty-ounce bottle and beat it against the man's head until it broke. The man lay there unconscious, covered with blood. The guy's friend charged Stefan, threatening to kill him for what he had done to his friend. Paris picked up a remnant from the bottle and forced it into the charging man's side. Luckily, they managed to slip away before the police arrived but this time, they weren't fortunate enough to have that opportunity.

Simone looked down at the curb as she questioned her association with the bunch. It seemed like every time they went somewhere together, there was some type of drama and it wasn't always finding its way to them. It seemed like they went on a pursuit to find drama and she followed behind them like a foolish child. She didn't know what else to do. They were the closest things to home girls she had and whenever she needed them, whether it was to borrow money or go snatch some hoe's ass, they were there for her. Simone dismissed her questioning as selfishness, her not wanting to do for them what they wouldn't hesitate to do for her.

Simone looked over at Paris. She was sickened by the bluish abrasions that covered his face. "Damn, what happened to you?"

Paris frowned. "What you think happened to me? I don't know about y'all but when the cops started spraying that mace, I was like, whoo—thank the Lord."

Stefan laughed, disregarding the serious expression on Paris's face. "That nigga must've given you a run for your money."

"Humph, if I could've got my hands on my cell phone, I would've called the police my damn self," Paris said.

Simone and Stefan sat around, teasing Paris, until one of the officers came to release them. The officer explained to them that they were banned from the property and if they stepped foot on any area of it, pool or park, they would be arrested for trespassing. They nodded their heads in agreement. They were glad that they weren't riding to the city lockup with Crystal and Robert.

The officer hopped in his car and slammed the door. "Y'all better be on y'all way. I ain't leaving until y'all remove yourselves from this property."

Paris stood there with his arms folded and sucked his teeth.

"One of you over there got some kind of problem?" the officer asked as his partner came and stood beside the car.

"No, ain't no problem, officer," Stefan said.

"You should be thankful; we could've hauled y'all asses downtown along with your friend here, but based on the reports we got from some of the witnesses, we decided to cut your asses a break. So if I was you boys, I'd run my asses on home 'fore we change our minds," the officer said.

They all paused for a minute. Stefan and Paris stood there, pissed, wanting to be defiant in order to regain their pride, but the others that accompanied them didn't feel the same way. They felt like getting the fuck out of there before the man did change his mind. A couple of them slowly departed across the street, Simone followed suit and shortly afterward, Stefan and Paris did the same.

⁅[7]⁆

S imone and Stefan sat outside in the parking lot of
the Courtyard by Marriott on West Broad Street.
They hadn't said much to each other between getting dressed and arriving there. Simone was exhausted
and Stefan was still in a funk about the incident at the
pool. Stefan asked Simone to stop by the store on their
way to the hotel so he could get a pack of cigarettes.
Stefan hadn't smoked since he and Eugene had become
an item. Eugene couldn't stand the smell of cigarette
smoke and was completely turned off by it. Stefan decided
he would rather be without the cigarettes than be without Eugene, so he stopped smoking. But after the stress
of that evening, Stefan disregarded Eugene's feelings,
and calming his nerves became his top priority.

Stefan struggled to free the cigarettes from the plastic
that sealed them. He became frustrated and threw the
pack against the dashboard. He grabbed his head and
squealed before retrieving them from the floor.

Stefan began to unravel the plastic and turned to look
at the lock on the car door. "And, you'll start locking these
doors when somebody slide in here beside you and slit
your throat," he snapped at Simone.

Simone continued to clean her nails with her ice pick, not uttering a single word. Stefan was upset and whenever he was, he always found something to nag the hell out of her about. She never locked her car doors and he never had an issue with it up until then. Sometimes she would leave it outside for hours with the top down and never had a problem with anyone trying to steal it or with any of her belongings coming up missing, unless it was a pen or pack of gum that Stefan confiscated from the glove compartment. She didn't give Stefan's comment a second thought.

Simone sat in the car, trying not to doze off. If it were anyone else, she would've rescheduled but she couldn't wait to get acquainted with her sexy new client and take him up on his offer.

Stefan flicked the ashes from his cigarette out of the window. "I swear that muthafucka made me so mad, I could've plucked his fucking eyes out."

"I know," Simone said. "What do you think is going to happen to Crystal?"

"Shit, you know Paris got him. They're like you and me; they're gonna look out for each other."

"What happened to Jewel?"

Stefan cut his eyes at Simone. "What you think happened to him? He bounced."

"Well, that's your friend."

"Correction," Stefan said, snapping his fingers. "That's Paris's friend and I doubt if Paris will still fuck with him after this shit."

Simone shook her head. "Jewel is terrible."

"He's a pussy."

Simone leaned back in her seat and placed her hands behind her head, waiting for Stefan to elaborate on his comment.

"We all be walking 'round here primping, trying to be cute and shit, but when it's time to brawl, it's time to brawl." Stefan pulled his cigarette before he became roused. "It's time to put that bitch shit on hold and handle business."

Simone nodded. She understood where Stefan was coming from but, on the other hand, she wondered had he considered that Jewel didn't crave drama like he did. Yeah, Jewel liked to party, drink, and get high, along with all the other bullshit they were into, but when it came to fighting, he didn't want any part of it. And although Crystal was a bit temperamental, he seemed to stray away from trouble until he felt like it could no longer be avoided. It was only Stefan and Paris who were on a hunt for it.

◈

Simone and Stefan sat at a small table in a room on the second floor of the hotel. They looked out of the window, watching the cars that cruised up and down Broad Street as they waited for Ivan to retrieve his friend from the adjoining room.

Stefan sighed. "I hope my client's as fine as that thing you're gonna be romping with tonight."

Simone looked at Stefan and smiled. "He probably will be. You know what they say; birds of a feather..."

"Well, I hope this little birdie has a tongue he wants to put to work as badly as yours does."

Ivan swung open the door to the adjoining room and stepped to the side as his friend walked in. Stefan's eyes widened and Simone smirked as they eyed the blond, spike-haired man. Tattoos overlapped his face and thoroughly covered both arms. Strains of thread hung loosely from the arms of his tee where the sleeves had been torn off and his stomach protruded and hung over his black boot-cut jeans. He turned to Stefan and smiled, revealing his enamel-striped teeth. He then walked over and extended his hand to Stefan.

"You must be Stefan. I'm Earl."

Stefan reached out his hand and Earl kissed it. Stefan looked at Simone and rolled his eyes. He was pissed and Simone was tickled to the point of no return. Stefan's face turned three different shades of red and Simone's grin became broader with the change in his color.

Earl motioned toward the door. "I think it's time to retreat to my quarters, don't you?"

Stefan sighed and made his way to the door where Earl stood.

Earl leaned forward and licked Stefan on his lips. "Smile; we're going to have a lot of fun tonight."

They walked into the adjoining room and shut the door.

Ivan turned to Simone and smiled. "Would you like something to drink?"

"Sure, why not."

Ivan's smile made Simone wonder what sort of acts Stefan might've begun to perform on the not-so-handsome, gray-toothed man in the next room. She sat there with her hands on her stomach, giggling to herself as she imagined what Stefan was being subjected to.

Paris stood in front of the altar in the corner of his room. His naked body was still wet from his ritual bath. He allowed the warm breeze coming in from his window to dry his body as he prepared for his spell work. He held his intention clear in his mind while he anointed a purple candle with Just Judge oil. The purpose of his spell was to get the charges against Crystal thrown out at his preliminary hearing. Paris invoked Isis, lit the candle, knelt in front of his altar, and prayed Psalms 37 repeatedly.

Paris had been interested in the occult since his mother had taken him to a New Age bookstore. His mother was desperate for his father to come home. His father had left a week earlier. He had gotten his mistress pregnant. Paris overheard his father explain to his mother how he could not walk away from his mistress, how she was so young and vulnerable. Paris listened as his father asked his mother what kind of man he would be if he turned his back on his mistress after planting his seed, knowing she had no one else to look out for her. Paris watched his mother beg his father to stay as she tried to wrestle the trash bag he carried his belongings in out of his hand. His father shoved his mother away and walked out of the door. Paris hoped his father never came back. He was tired of his father's criticism about the tone of his voice and how he held his head down and swung his arms when he walked like a little wimp. But his mother spent days in the bed crying. She didn't bother to bathe, brush her teeth, or comb her hair; she just lay there groaning about how she could not live without him.

At the end of the week, his mother got out of bed and put on a pair of sweatpants and a blue tee with a college logo on the front and a big hole under the arm. His mother woke him up and told him to throw on some clothes so he could accompany her to the store. Paris was so happy his mother was out of bed, he put on the wrinkled clothes he had worn the day before and ran downstairs to ride with her to the store.

The exterior of the store had the visage of an antique shop but as soon as Paris walked through the door he was greeted by candles, incense, powders, New Age books, and washes that brought fortune and dissolved various problems. Paris scanned the store while his mother consulted with the shop owner about a spell to bring his father back.

Paris was drawn to a picture of a tall, slender woman who wore a sheath dress and held a staff in her right hand and an ankh in her left hand. The woman had dark eyes that appeared to be able to disregard flesh and look right into the soul, and a throne sat on her head. She stood out from the other deities that were displayed throughout the shop. She was beautiful but her stance was one of strength and fearlessness. Paris asked the shop owner about the woman while his mother gathered the supplies listed in the spell book the shop owner had shown her. The shop owner told Paris that the woman was the goddess Isis. She explained that Isis was the mother of all mankind and the goddess of magic. Isis loved all of her children, sinners and saints, and she heard the prayers of the wealthy as well as the oppressed. She went on to tell Paris invocations of Isis were extremely powerful, being that they not only involved her powers but the powers of her offspring, the god Horus, as well. The shop owner showed Paris a book about Isis that he could read to find out more about her. Paris asked his mother to purchase the book for him. His mother ignored him, only concerned with buying the spell book the shop owner had shown her and the supplies for her spell. Paris pleaded with his mother and told her that she wouldn't have to give him his allowance for two weeks if she bought the book for him. His mother snatched the book out of his hand and put it on the counter so it could be rung up.

Paris peeked in on his mother as she performed the

spell to bring his father back. He could feel the energy in the room increase as his mother chanted. Later that night he snuck into his mother's room and took the spell book out of her underwear drawer. He had to learn the craft. The knowledge of it would be beneficial to him in the future but he had no idea how soon he would actually use it.

Within three weeks, Paris's father was back and his mother loved his father more than ever. His mother directed all of her attention to his father and began to ignore him. His father was more critical of him than ever. Every time Paris spilled something or knocked something over, his father would call him a doofus. When he retreated to his room to read his mother's spell book, or his book about Isis, his father would poke his head into his room to tell him how strange he was for reading such nonsense and how he should be out playing with other boys his age instead of wasting his time reading about demonic shit. He would finish the conversation by telling Paris that if he caught him trying to work a root up in his house, he would beat him within two inches of his life. Paris was upset that his mother never intervened and told his father how helpful the craft could be; especially since she had it to thank for bringing him back.

A man named Larry, one of Paris's father's friends, was the only outlet that Paris had. Larry would come home with Paris's father after work so they could sit around and smoke marijuana. Although Larry spent most of his time talking to Paris's father and mother, he would find time in between to talk to Paris to see how his day had gone and help him with his homework.

Larry offered for Paris to come over his house to get help with his homework. He assured Paris that there would be fewer distractions there. Paris had taken him up on his offer and went to his house to do his homework.

Larry leaned over Paris's shoulder, explaining how to come up with the correct answers to his equations. Paris turned around to ask Larry a question and their lips touched. Larry did not turn away, nor did Paris resist. During the fourteen years he had been on earth, Larry was the only male who had ever paid him any attention and the only male that had ever shown him any type of love. Larry did not have to tell Paris not to tell anyone, or that it was their little secret; Paris already knew.

After a few months passed, Paris began to think of himself and Larry as an item. His relationship with Larry made him feel loved. That love gave him the confidence he needed to be content with himself.

One afternoon, Paris came home from school and saw Larry sitting in the living room with his arm around a light-skinned female. Paris's mother and father announced to him that Larry was getting married and the female was his fiancée, Jackie, whom he had purchased a house with. Paris looked at Larry and Larry looked away. Paris's eyes filled up with tears and he ran upstairs to his room and slammed the door. He could not believe Larry would do something like that to him. The love he had felt was fake. All the time Larry had spent showing him affection was only a scheme to gain access to his body until he found someone that he liked more. He couldn't believe Larry had the nerve to sit in his home with his arms wrapped around some woman. Paris hated her; green eyes, long, stringy brown hair, and all. And to make matters worse, she had a body out of this world. One that women dreamed of having but could only be witnessed on cartoon characters little Betty Boop and Jessica Rabbit. The kind of body he wished his head were attached to. Paris wanted Larry to pay for his deceit and he was not about to wait on karma. If he waited on karma, he might not be around to witness Larry's misfortune and he wanted to witness it as soon as possible.

Paris went in his parents' room and searched his father's pants pockets. He took twenty dollars and then slipped out of the back door and walked to the New Age store to purchase spell supplies.

Paris was nervous about casting his first spell. He had practiced performing rituals and visualization but he was not sure if that was enough. He planned to stay in his room the entire night. He shoved a towel under his door so the scent of burning wax and incense wouldn't go out into the hallway. He doubted that the little bit of smoke that seeped through the vents would alarm his parents. He would have been surprised if they could have smelled it over their cigarette and marijuana smoke. Paris opened the window so the smoke from his candles and incense could escape his room and carry his spell out into the world. He took his pre-ritual bath and gridded his space with stones. He held the image of his intention in his mind's eye while he cast the spell three times. He visualized Larry and his fiancée arguing, pushing dishes off of the table, calling each other derogatory names, and breaking their vows of happiness. In his mind's eye, he saw Larry sitting at the table resting his head in his hands, weak from hunger; his heartache prevented him from eating. His lips were chapped and his arms were thin and flabby from his weight loss. Larry would feel as inadequate as he made him feel and it would drive him to tears and to the point of madness.

Paris looked at the clock. The night had passed and it was two o'clock in the morning. He was exhausted and decided to take a nap before he disposed of the leftover materials from his spell. As he slept, the energy from his spell surged through his body and brought him a dream.

Paris sat at the table doing his homework while his mother and father watched television in the living room. There was a knock on the door and, all of a sudden, Larry floated through the door, defying the laws of the physical realm. Larry screamed for help and said some-one was trying to ruin him; someone was trying to kill him. The screams jolted Paris out of his sleep. Paris went into the bathroom and splashed water on his face, and then went back into his room to prepare the final part of his spell. The final part of his spell was sure to speed things up. He filled a small gris-gris bag with the contents said to bring quarrels and ill luck to the person whose home it entered. Among its contents were black pepper and animal feces. Paris slipped out of the house and walked four blocks down to Larry's house and slipped the gris-gris bag through the mail slot in the door. Afterward, Paris walked to the store and bought a bag of chips so if his parents had woken up while he was gone and decided to question him about his whereabouts, he would say that he had been to the store and he would have the chips to prove it.

Three weeks later, Paris sat in the kitchen doing his homework, taking in the fumes of his parents' marijuana smoke, when he heard someone pounding on the door. Paris's father opened the door. Larry fell on him, screaming for help.

"Oh God, help me!" Larry screamed. "They're after me; they trying to kill me!"

Paris's mother ran to the phone and called the police. Paris's father tried to get Larry to take a seat on the couch but Larry refused and continued to say someone was trying to kill him. When the police arrived, they called crisis intervention for Larry and he was committed to the psycho ward until he was able to function in society again.

While Larry was in the psycho ward, his home was foreclosed on. Paris was pleased. Revenge was sweet. He felt powerful, so powerful that he had taken his father's advice and decided to play with other boys in the neighborhood. He was not worried about anyone breaking his heart; he pitied the fool who did.

{ [8] }

Stefan drew his attention away from the road long enough to roll his eyes. "I swear, I could strangle your ass for that shit last night."

Simone sank down in her seat and laughed.

"You think that shit's funny, huh?"

"Shit, don't blame me," Simone said. "It ain't my fault."

"The hell if it ain't."

"The hell if it is. Why it got to be my fault?"

"'Cause of this, 'Ivan, do you mind if my cousin comes along,'" Stefan said, mimicking Simone.

"Whatever; I didn't force you to come along."

Stefan nodded his head. "I know."

"Awight then, you came 'cause you wanted that money."

"True, but goddamn, I could've done without rolling around with his weird repulsive ass."

Simone looked at Stefan and grinned. "Whatever; you loved it."

Stefan drew back his hand. "Don't make me slap your ass."

Simone laughed. "Shit, I ain't worried."

"Your ass ain't smart enough to be worried."

"Don't keep fucking with me, Stefan. You must've forgotten about the ice pick in my glove compartment. Don't think I won't use it on your ass."

Stefan sucked his teeth. "Oh yeah, don't think I won't whip your ass and toss you out your own damn car."

"Oh, you'd do me like that?"

Stefan looked over at Simone, making eye contact with her. "You ain't know?"

Simone threw her head back and laughed at the threats they made against each other.

Stefan looked over at Simone and smiled. "Girl, you're a retard; I don't know where the hell they got you from."

"Me either," Simone said. "All jokes aside, why you still holding onto that shit? You act like we out recruiting mates. We're only trying to get some paper."

"Yeah, but it helps when they look like something. He could've at least taken a bath. Goddamn."

Simone giggled. "Was he funky?"

"Funky ain't the word. And when he whipped out that pinky of his, I thought I was gonna faint."

Simone leaned on Stefan and tugged on his shirt as she laughed.

Stefan nudged Simone off of him. "Damn, girl; calm down before you make me wreck this car."

Simone sank back down in her seat. "Well, I know why Ivan loves working his tongue so much."

"Why is that?"

"'Cause he got a dick like a Ring Pop."

"You lying."

"The hell if I am," Simone said. "I had a hard time prying that joint from between his balls."

"Serves you right."

✦

Simone and Stefan sat in the parking lot of the auto detail shop, frustrated by the sight of all the cars that waited to be serviced.

Simone got out of the car and took a deep breath. "Damn, looks like we're gonna be here for awhile."

"I don't know what you're complaining for; it's your damn car," Stefan said. "And the last time we were here, you met four new clients."

"You did, too."

"Only because I met them through the guys you met," Stefan said. "These bastards up in here be hiding behind their newspapers when I walk by, too damn scared to come out the closet."

"Whatever," Simone said. "Just bring your ass in here and sit pretty. You never know; you might meet some new money."

Simone paused to admire the car parked directly in front of the door. She was taken by the way it appeared translucent as it reflected her image. She ran her fingers across the door.

"What kind of car is this?"

"It's a Bentley," Stefan answered.

"If I was driving this bad boy, couldn't nobody say shit to me."

"I bet they couldn't. They already can't tell you shit when you driving around in that slob," Stefan joked.

Simone looked at Stefan with a raised eyebrow. "It's Saab, bitch; don't make me hurt you."

"Yeah right," Stefan said. "Anyway, I can't believe you've never seen one before."

"How many people in this city do you think drive a Bentley?"

"A few; if you hoed outside the neighborhood more often, you would've seen one by now."

Simone waved Stefan off and continued into the shop, swaying her hips until she reached the line for the service desk.

Simone huffed as she listened to the guy at the front of the line loudly dispute the amount of his bill while he searched his wallet for his credit card. Simone immediately became irritated.

Simone and Stefan didn't get home until four o'clock that morning. When Simone got out of the shower, she plopped down on the sofa instead of joining Stefan in the kitchen to eat the breakfast he had cooked. She was more interested in regaining the energy she'd lost during her sexually immoral acts than she was in filling her belly. A couple of hours later she woke up to the sound of Stefan clapping his hands above her head.

"Chop chop," he said. "If you want to go to the detailing shop, you better get a move-on 'cause I plan to spend the evening with Eugene and there's a ton of shit I'd like to do before then."

Simone had put so much thought into primping herself and ignoring Stefan's complaints that she had left the peach she'd planned to snack on during the ride there on the table. The taste of the chunk she'd bitten off before she'd left still lingered in her mouth as a reminder of her hunger and forgetfulness.

The annoying man holding up the line made her stomach roar.

Simone huffed. "If people don't want to pay for shit, they need to take their asses to the gas station down the street and have them teenagers posted up out there clean their shit for twenty dollars instead of holding me the fuck up."

Simone's comment grabbed the attention of the sales associate and everyone who stood in line, except for the man in front who handed over his credit card, still expressing how displeased he was with the price.

Fuck this! Stefan's gonna stand his ass right here while I go to the snack machine, Simone thought. "Stefan, wait in line for me. I'm going to the snack machine."

"Sure, why would I mind? I played chauffeur for you this morning; I'm sure I can handle one little business transaction while you carry your fat ass to get a snack," Stefan said. "Hell, you want me to digest your food for you?"

The employees drew their attention away from their duties and the customers who sat in the waiting area peered from behind their newspapers and magazines as if they were about to witness a fight. The guy who was making his way out of the door after holding up the line paused and looked back to watch them carry on.

Stefan turned his nose up at his audience. "What the fuck y'all looking at? I mean, goddamn, can I help y'all with something?"

Simone shook her head and made her way to the vending area.

"Hurry up and make sure you bring me something back," Stefan said, as Simone walked off.

Simone stood in front of the snack machine holding two bottles of water between the fingers of her right hand while she debated on what to get for her and Stefan to snack on. She really wanted a candy bar but didn't want Stefan to ridicule her for eating it the entire time they waited to be serviced. The day had barely started and Stefan had already managed to piss her off. He had a way of dramatizing things. He could create drama from scratch; he didn't need an antagonist. He did a damn good job by himself. The attacks on her weight were getting old. Yeah, she was a little heavy in the hip area but she was far from fat and the words "fat" and "ass" that were constantly rolling off of Stefan's tongue were starting to become more annoying than a scratched CD.

Simone decided to get two bags of baked chips and

leave it at that. She reached down to retrieve her items from the vending machine and felt someone place their hands on her waist. She immediately turned around to lay eyes on the person who had the nerve to do such a thing. They were going to get cursed, that she knew for sure. But as soon as she caught sight of the perpetrator, she changed her mind. There was something about his smooth, fudge-colored skin and able body that mellowed her mood. And once he smiled and revealed how deep his gorgeous dimples were, she wanted to run her fingers over the deep, dark waves that were magnified by his Caesar haircut.

Simone removed his hands from her waist. "It's not nice to touch things that don't belong to you."

"Oh, is that right?"

Simone nodded.

"That's funny; you didn't seem to feel that way when you were outside probing my car."

Simone was baffled; she hadn't considered that the owner of the car might be looking out the window watching her while she stood outside admiring and touching his property. "Oh yeah, you're the man who was holding up the line when I came in. I hope I didn't leave any finger-prints on your car. You seemed to be having a hard time parting with your money at the service desk. I wouldn't want to put you out-of-pocket. I can't imagine how much that would inconvenience you. Or did you come in here to ask me to reimburse you?"

"No, I thought you could make it up to me another way."

"How's that?"

The man looked at Simone and smiled. "By letting me take you out to dinner."

"That does mean you're paying, right? 'Cause I ain't paying for nothing."

"Did I ask you to pay for it?"

"Naw, but—"

"Awright then. I don't know what you're used to, ma, but it ain't like that with me."

Simone sighed. "Oh, for real?"

"Yeah, for real. I got my own money. I can pay my own way."

"It sure didn't seem that way a few minutes ago."

"What? Let me ask you something. If someone charged you for something that you didn't buy, would you pay for it regardless of how much money you had?"

Simone shook her head. "Probably not."

"Then why hold that against me?"

Simone nodded. "Well, where do you get this money from?"

"Excuse me."

"This money you got that you can pay your own way with. Where'd you get it?"

"Work."

"And that would be what? Laying bricks, drug trafficking, plumbing, I mean, what?"

The man paused for a moment and frowned. Simone could tell that she had succeeded in irritating him.

He placed his arm over Simone's shoulder and began to walk her back in the direction of the service area. "I'm a boxer," the man announced proudly.

"What you mean? Like, street fights or something?"

"No, I'm a professional boxer."

"What's your name?"

"Wayne."

"Do you have a last name?"

"Jasper."

Simone sucked her teeth. "I don't believe you."

"If you don't, you don't. That's neither here nor there; all I'm asking you is to let me take you out for dinner tonight."

"I don't see anything wrong with that," Simone said. "Unless what they say about y'all is true."

"What's that?"

"You know, the stories about how y'all like to grope all the girls at the club so you can get them all hot and bothered and lure them to your hotel room and when they refuse, y'all toss y'all drinks on them and call them every degrading name you can think of."

"Whoa, hold on, ma."

"Simone."

"Excuse me?"

"My name is Simone."

"Simone. That's beautiful. You look like a Simone.

Anyway, *Simone*, you can't judge me by what you heard someone say about somebody else. Know what I mean?"

"I guess."

"And besides, I thought you didn't believe me."

Simone grinned. "Maybe I'm starting to."

"So are you up for dinner or what?"

"Sure, I don't think it will be a problem."

Wayne entered Simone's name and number into his cell phone and they continued to make their way back to the service area where they parted company. Wayne headed for the door and Simone took the seat beside Stefan where a magazine lay to reserve her spot.

"Damn, you met somebody already?" Stefan asked.

"That's right," Simone teased. "And guess what." She slapped down on Stefan's thigh. "He's a boxer and that was his car."

"Stop playing."

"I ain't playing."

Stefan sucked his teeth. "Then he's lying."

"Why he got to be lying?"

"'Cause, if he's a boxer, what the fuck he doing down here?"

"I don't know; maybe he has family down here."

Stefan rolled his eyes. "I'll be damned."

"Believe what you want; all I know is he's gonna be my baby daddy."

"Just be thankful that I ain't get to his ass first."

Simone frowned. "What?"

"You heard me."

Simone looked Stefan up and down. "Whatever."

"Please, did you see the way his pants were hanging off his ass? He's begging for some dick," Stefan said. "I swear, I think that shit is sexy as a bitch."

"Whatever; he ain't like that."

"Yeah right; he'd probably say the same thing if he heard about your after-hour activities," Stefan said. "You'd be surprised what niggas be into."

Simone aimlessly flipped through the pages of the magazine, trying to draw her attention away from Stefan to let him know she wasn't interested in taking their conversation any further and that he could stop running his mouth since she wasn't listening. She wondered why every time she had a moment of happiness, Stefan would go out his way to shoot it down. She could say numerous things about his relationship with Eugene. Like, if he's your man, why do you only see him once a week? Who's with him the other six days? Or I hope you ain't letting him run up in it without a rubber because you don't know how many men he was sleeping with while he was in the pen. But she didn't. She held her tongue and that's what Stefan needed to do sometimes; hold his tongue.

Choo-Choo; Simone's text message alert went off. It was a sound she didn't hear too often so when she did, she snatched her cell phone from her purse and quickly flipped it open.

Meet me at the Berkley Hotel in the lobby at eight o'clock.

Simone could feel her blood rushing to her face as she blushed.

"Who is that?" Stefan asked.

"Wayne."

"Who is Wayne?"

"The guy I just met."

"Oh, let me see."

Stefan leaned over to read the screen of Simone's cell phone, not giving her adequate time to turn it in his direction. Stefan was especially interested in the signature portion of the message. *The mind is a powerful thing.*

Stefan sucked his teeth. "That's some bullshit."

Simone grinned. "Watch this."

Simone hit reply and responded back to Wayne's message. *See you then. P.S. So is my pussy.*

Stefan laughed. "You ain't right."

Wayne responded right back. *Am I gonna find out?*

Stefan leaned over and read the message along with Simone. "Don't front; we both know it's as good as his."

"We're talking about me, not you," Simone said. *We'll see,* Simone replied back and then flipped her cell phone closed.

"So I guess you won't be sitting at home by yourself, eating pizza, dripping tomato sauce all over those sketches of yours, huh?" Stefan said.

Simone giggled. "You're jealous."

"Damn right," Stefan said. "I see you didn't ask him if I could come along."

[9]

The cab driver dropped Paris off in front of Michael's apartment. Michael lived on the first floor of a Victorian-style house that had been renovated into an apartment building with four units. Paris carried the paper bags that contained the dinner he'd made Michael for his birthday up on the porch. Michael had taken him to the beach for his birthday so Paris wanted to do something special for Michael in return. He hoped Michael had gotten over their fight at the bar. It was nothing out of the ordinary. They often fought and a week or two later, they were back in love again. He knew the night would be special. He had it all planned out. They would have a candlelight dinner and then he would put on his red lace teddy and put on a show, grinding to the slow jam CD he had brought along.

Paris rang the doorbell and waited for Michael to come to the door.

Paris rested his hands on his hips. *What's taking him so long?* he thought. Michael was there. He could see his car parked on the corner. *Maybe he's asleep*, Paris thought.

Paris stuck his key in the door and turned the knob. He was unable to open the door because Michael had a deadbolt lock put on it.

"Who is that?" Paris heard someone whisper on the other side of the door.

Paris banged on the door. "Michael, you better open this damn door before I kick it in."

Michael cracked the door open and peeked out at Paris.

"Hey, baby, happy birthday; I made you dinner," Paris said.

Michael glanced down at the paper bags in Paris's hands. "That was nice of you, but now isn't a good time."

"Why not? What are you doing?"

"Me," Jewel said as he walked up behind Michael and placed his hand on Michael's chest.

"Oh hell naw!" Paris shouted.

Paris tried to force his way into the house but Michael shut the door and put the deadbolt back on. Paris kicked the door, trying to get in. "Michael, if you know what's good for you, you'll let me in."

"Don't worry about it, baby; let's go back to your room and finish what we were doing," Jewel said.

Paris tried to open the windows but they were all locked. He didn't want to hurt himself by breaking the windows out with his fists. What sort of condition would he be in once he got inside if he did that? He wanted revenge but not at his own expense. Paris screamed to the top of his lungs and then went into a frenzy, slinging the dinner he had prepared all over the porch while the neighbors watched in amazement.

※

"The nigga wasn't lying!" Simone yelled out to Stefan, who was directly across the hall in the bathroom with the door wide open.

Simone was excited about all of the information that her Internet search had pulled up on Wayne. She stood there scanning her grandmother's room, noticing how the spiders had made claims to it and how dust covered the dresser and windows. It hadn't been cleaned since their grandmother had died and that wouldn't change anytime soon. She tapped her foot on the floor, eager for the printer to finish printing her people search results so she could get the hell out of there.

"What does it say?" Stefan asked.

"I'm printing it now so I can show it to you."

"Don't be using up all the damn paper."

"Ain't like you be using it," Simone said. "This paper has been in here for years."

"You just make sure it stays in there."

Simone sucked her teeth. "Whatever."

"You heard what I said."

Simone sighed. "Yeah, I heard you."

The results to Simone's people search printed out. She

rushed into the bathroom, took a seat on the counter, and began to share the results with Stefan.

Simone bounced around on the counter with excitement. "Wait 'til you hear this."

"Damn, don't keep me waiting; just tell me."

Simone organized her search results in order of importance, saving the most important for last. "Awight, here we go."

Simone was distracted by the sound of running water and then realized it was the sound of Stefan urinating and gave him a puzzled look.

"May I help you?" Stefan asked offensively.

"Shouldn't you be standing up?"

"I don't think it matters."

"Well, that's how most guys do it," Simone said. "I've never seen a nigga piss with his dick in the toilet."

"In case you haven't noticed, I'm not your average Joe," Stefan snapped. "Now get on with it or get out."

Simone sucked her teeth and continued. "Okay, let's see, this right here says Wayne was twenty-four years old and the middleweight champion in 1998 and hasn't fought in a match since he lost his title in 2002."

"So he's 37 now, in the '11.' Damn, that means he's fifteen years older than you."

Simone nodded. "Um-hmm."

"I'll tell you one thing; you sure can pick them."

"Anyway, it also says he got a divorce in 2006 and he has five kids," Simone said. "I wonder if they're all by his wife."

"Who gives a damn? I don't want to hear that shit," Stefan said. "Damn the nigga's kids. I want to know about his money."

"The background check I ran says he has three homes, one in Florida, one in Pennsylvania, and one down here. Look at the value," Simone said, handing Stefan the background check.

Stefan looked at the value of the homes. "Oh, this nigga is getting it."

"Eight hundred thousand apiece; I'd say so," Simone said. "And look at how it lists everybody's name and age that lives in the house."

"Yeah, it says somebody name Martha and Kirk live in the one down here."

"What I'm thinking is this, since they have the same last name as Wayne and it lists their ages as sixty-five and sixty-seven, those are his parents."

Stefan looked up from the paper for a minute and nodded his head in agreement.

"And this lady right here listed beside the one in Florida, that's the ex."

"Well, I'll be damned," Stefan said. "Who was it that said you couldn't think critically?"

Simone sucked her teeth and continued to share her findings. "And look at what it says his approximate net worth is."

"I swear, this nigga's getting money," Stefan said. "I'm mad at that."

"Why?"

"'Cause I ain't get to him first."

"You'll get over it but, in the meantime, be happy for me. *He's gonna be my baby daddy,*" Simone sang as she bounced around on the counter.

Stefan put his index finger in front of his lips. "Shhh."

"Why?" Simone asked.

"I thought I heard somebody at the door."

"I ain't hear—"

Thump...thump...thump.

"What you waiting for? Go see who's at the door," Stefan said.

Simone slid down off of the counter and made her way to the door. The knocks became louder as Simone made her way downstairs.

"Goddamn, wait a minute!" Stefan shouted down the stairs.

"Who is it?" Simone asked.

"Paris."

Simone opened the door and Paris barraged past her, sniffling in a tissue, and plopped down on the living room sofa.

"What's wrong?" Simone asked.

Paris sat in silence for a few seconds before bursting into tears. Simone sat down beside him and threw her arm over his shoulder to comfort him.

Stefan made his way downstairs. "What's wrong?"

"I just left from over Michael's house," Paris said. "Today's his birthday. I made dinner for him and everything. I took a cab over to his house and who do you think he had over there with him?"

"Who?" Stefan and Simone asked in unison.

"Jewel," Paris said.

"What?" Simone squealed.

"Stop playing!" Stefan shouted.

"Shit, I ain't playing," Paris said. "Once he looked over his shoulder and saw Jewel standing behind him, he hurried up and slammed the door. Damn near slammed my finger in it."

"And, what did you do?" Simone asked.

"I was over there for about a half-hour trying to kick the door down to get in," Paris answered.

"I thought you had a key," Stefan said.

"I do, but it doesn't do me any good when he has a bolt on the door," Paris said. "I could strangle his ass for having me out there looking like a damn fool. All the neighbors were outside staring at me and shit."

"Okay, I've got a question for you," Simone said.

"What?" Paris asked.

"What happened to the food?" Simone asked.

"I just told you my man's fucking Jewel and all you can say is what happened to the food," Paris said.

"I wanted to know if you still have it; there's no need to let it go to waste," Simone said. "Goddamn, you act like I'm the one fucking Michael."

"Well, too late, it already went to waste. I slung them pots and pans at the windows, trying to get in," Paris said.

Simone and Stefan sniggered.

"I bet his front porch looks like a big-ass casserole," Simone joked.

"Y'all laughing; I'm ready to go back over there, wait for Jewel to come out, and fuck his ass up," Paris said.

"Shit, if that's what you're trying to do," Stefan said.

"Yeah, it's whatever," Simone agreed.

Paris jumped up off of the sofa. "Then let's roll."

[10]

Simone, Stefan, and Paris pulled up at the end of the block, three doors down from Michael's place. They scoped the block for any signs of Michael and Jewel.

"They're gone," Paris said.

"How do you know?" Simone asked.

"'Cause his car's not out here," Paris answered.

"So what are we still sitting here for? Ain't like we can do nothing if they already gone," Simone said.

"Since I can't get my hands on either one of them, I'm gonna go in here and fuck his shit up," Paris spat.

"I'm down with that," Stefan said as he got out of the car and started toward Michael's house.

"Wait a minute," Simone said. "It's still light outside. What if somebody sees us?"

"Who gives a fuck?" Stefan replied.

"It's not like we're breaking in. I've got a key," Paris added reassuringly.

"But what if the neighbors hear us busting his shit up?" Simone asked.

"So? Fuck them," Stefan snapped.

Simone and Stefan stood on the porch, waiting for Paris to unlock the door.

"Damn, I'm mad he ain't clean this food and shit off the porch before he left," Simone said.

"While we're in here, you should get a plate so you can scrape up what you want and carry it home with you, since you're so worried about it," Paris snapped.

"I don't want that shit," Simone said. "That's probably what it tastes like; some shit. That's why ol' boy's fucking Jewel. 'Cause he can fix a good meal. That nigga had to get tired of gnawing on that shit you be cooking."

Paris's face became red and Stefan chuckled.

"I ain't in the mood tonight," Paris said.

Simone laughed. "Well, I am, so don't dish it out if you can't take it."

"Awight, y'all," Stefan said. "Let's hurry up and get in here and do what we came to do before Michael pulls up and I have to whip his ass."

"Hold on; I ain't say nothing about y'all putting y'all hands on my man," Paris said. "I'd hate for us to be out this bitch rumbling."

Simone and Stefan gave each other one of those "he-doesn't-want-it-with-us" type of looks.

Simone, Stefan, and Paris stood in the middle of the front room taking in the beauty of Michael's place. The chandelier dangled from the ceiling elegantly and covered the paintings and family portraits that hung from the white walls with a light that rendered them flawless. The white living room set looked as if it had never been sat on and crystal figurines covered every space on the mantelpiece above the sofa. Across from the sofa sat a forty-two-inch, flat-screen TV and on each end of the room sat two black and white, checker-patterned crystal lamps.

"Oh, it's nice up in here," Stefan said.

"Wish I could live here," Simone added.

Stefan examined one of the crystal lamps on the end table. "I wish I could live here, too." Stefan snatched both of the crystal lamps off of the table and smashed them together. Remnants from the lamps scattered across the room and Stefan tossed what was left of the lamps onto the floor. "But after I get finished, ain't nobody gonna want to live here."

Paris looked down at what was left of the lamps and placed his hand over his mouth in disbelief.

"What's wrong with you?" Stefan asked.

"I didn't want you to break those," Paris said. "His grandmother bought those lamps for him."

"And your point is?" Simone asked.

"Good question," Stefan said. "'Cause I didn't understand that shit either. Is his grandma dead or something?"

Paris shook his head. "Naw but—"

"Good, then she can buy him some new ones," Stefan said. "Now I suggest we get to wrecking shit."

The three parted company and began their tasks. Simone headed to the back. She spotted four gallon containers of paint; two white and two black. She lugged the two containers of black paint to Stefan, who poured it over the living room furniture and everything that shared the space. Then Simone made her way back

to the back, passing Paris who was in the kitchen breaking up dishes and slinging food out of the icebox onto
the floor.

Simone grabbed the two containers of white paint
and carried them into the bedroom. She started by
smacking Michael's belongings off of the dresser and
then rummaged through the dresser drawers, tossing
the contents onto the floor, hoping to find something of
value. At the bottom of the drawer that held Michael's
undergarments, she found a pink Rolex watch, a tennis
bracelet, and a pair of three-carat diamond earrings. She
fastened the watch on her wrist and hid the bracelet and
earrings away in her bra.

Simone looked around the room, pleased with how
much damaged she had caused. She picked up one of
the containers of paint and splashed it across the floor
where Michael's clothing lay, then used the next bucket
of paint to cover the bedroom furniture.

Simone heard a scream and went racing into the front
room. "What's wrong?" she asked, as soon as she caught
sight of Paris.

Paris didn't answer. He stood there with his back
turned toward Stefan, holding his head down shaking it
back and forth. Simone looked over to see Stefan squatted
over Michael's family portrait, defecating on the figure
of the mother's head.

"Nigga, I know you ain't in here taking a shit!" Simone
shouted.

"You think he ain't; right in that man's mama's face. Talk about anal fixation," Paris said.

"You ain't lying," Simone said. "When that nigga gets here, he's gonna be heated."

Paris looked up at Simone and laughed and his attention went directly to Simone's wrist. "Where did you get that from?" Paris asked, grabbing Simone's wrist to examine the watch.

"It was in Michael's dresser," Simone said.

"That's mine." Paris took the watch off of Simone's wrist. "Michael gave it to me last year, then took it back that night we got into it at the bar. Did you run across any other jewelry?"

Simone thought about the bracelet and earrings that lay under her breasts, pinching her skin. "Naw, just that." There was no way in hell she was parting with the bracelet and definitely not the earrings; she already planned to wear them on her date.

"I'm mad; y'all standing in here with me talking about jewelry while I'm taking a shit," Stefan said.

"I'm mad you decided to take it in the front room," Simone said.

Stefan headed to the bathroom to clean himself up. Simone and Paris stood in the front room assessing the damage.

"Damn, I forgot that paint was here," Paris said. "He was going to use it to decorate the walls."

"Too late!" Stefan yelled from the bathroom. "We already

re-decorated for him. I even left him a little housewarming gift."

"Speaking of which, it's about time we bounce," Paris said.

"I know, right; it's starting to smell like a sewer up in here," Simone said.

"Awight, I'm coming," Stefan said.

"Yeah, hurry up so you can help us with this TV," Simone said.

"Help you do what with the TV?" Paris asked.

"Carry it to the car," Simone said. "Shit, that's going home with me. What you thought?"

"Girl, we can't be carrying a TV down the street; that shit looks suspect," Paris said. "Help me pick it up. I've got a better idea."

Paris grabbed one side of the TV and motioned for Simone to grab the other. "We're gonna throw this shit out the window, so it can be on the porch waiting for him when he comes home."

Simone and Paris stood in front of the window, prepared to toss the TV out.

"On the count of three," Paris said.

"Okay," Simone agreed. "One, two..."

"Oh, go ahead and toss that shit," Stefan said as he grabbed hold of the TV and helped Simone and Paris propel it through the window.

The high-pitched screams of a child echoed in their ears. Simone quickly peeked out of the window to see if someone was hurt.

A little boy stood frozen on the stoop, looking down at the TV that had rolled into the yard. "Mommy!" he cried. "Somebody threw a TV at me!" the little boy shouted as he ran up to his house.

"Oh shit!" Stefan yelled, and then bolted out the door, making his way to the car with Simone and Paris running behind him.

[11]

"Out of control," Simone muttered as she clasped Paris's earrings in her ears and fastened his bracelet on her wrist. She was thinking about the excitement she'd felt as she'd dashed out of Michael's place.

Simone sat in the car, primping herself until she looked as perfect as she possibly could. She was nervous about dinner. Sleeping with a man was one thing but sitting across the table and engaging in a conversation with one for thirty minutes or so, especially one who had some scruples, was totally different. She sat in the car, trying to figure out what she would tell Wayne if he asked about her parents, or what sort of education she had, and what she would tell him that she did for a living. She wondered if Wayne would frown down on the entry-level position she had just been appointed to at the bank, or if working at the bank as a branch manager for two years sounded like a more suitable career for a grounded young lady.

The text messages she'd sent Wayne kept popping up in her mind. She realized that it had him thinking about a little more than dinner and she didn't know if she would be able to resist. She didn't want to seem easy. She wanted Wayne to think of her as more than a one-night stand. She wanted him to think of her as a keeper. Someone he could talk to. Someone he was happy to have in his presence. Someone he would want in his corner. Not just somewhere to stick his dick when he had exhausted his options.

There was something about Wayne. She didn't exactly know what it was. The way he stood, the way he spoke. It subdued her and made her more willing to give into his request than money did. It was odd. Over forty men had fallen victim to Simone between the sheets since she was nineteen and she was sitting there brooding over dinner and the possibility of sleeping with a man that she actually wanted to sleep with. Then again, sex was her moneymaker. It could keep the money rolling in but it didn't seem to be successful when it came to snagging her love interest.

Before Simone started her infamous profession, she had hoped and dreamed to meet a man and fall in love. She had it all planned out. They would work part-time jobs as they both nickeled and dimed their way through college, where she would major in Fashion Design. And after they both graduated and got their careers off to a good start, they would get married and buy a house in Glen Allen, Virginia, where they would start a family. Simone wanted two girls and maybe a boy. She pictured herself on the treadmill, desperately fighting to regain her figure while her husband was gone on long business trips. But those dreams were crushed by her first love.

Simone met Danny while she was in high school. He was in the twelfth grade and a point guard on the basketball team. He was awarded a scholarship to play for Virginia Tech and the student body constantly praised him for it. He could have had any girl he wanted and he knew it by the way they threw themselves at him on a daily basis. Even the teachers would secretly flirt with him out of the sight of their colleagues. Simone was in the eleventh grade and a social misfit. So she was in disbelief when Danny parted company with his friends to approach her and ask for her number one day after school. Danny called her the same night. He told Simone how pretty she was. Danny said most of the girls at school were made up. Makeup pretty. But her, she didn't need that. She was naturally beautiful and she was someone he would love to have on his arm at the prom. Simone was flattered. She agreed to let Danny take her to the prom and they made plans to go to the movies the following day.

The next day when Danny pulled up at Simone's house, she was sitting on the porch waiting for him, wearing her black, low-cut, form-fitting shirt, a pair of jean capris, and a pair of strappy black sandals. Simone hopped in Danny's red convertible Mustang; his parents had recently purchased it for his birthday. She realized that she was the shit, riding down the street with Danny in his brand-new Mustang with her hair blowing in the wind. Simone pretended not to notice the neighborhood kids staring as they rode by. A lot of kids from school would be at the movies and she couldn't wait to see the looks on their faces when they spotted her with Danny.

Danny grabbed at his pockets. "Damn, I left my wallet at home."

Danny pulled up at his house and got out of the car. He asked Simone to come in the house with him. "I might be a while and I don't want to have to come back outside and fuck a nigga up for trying to holler at my girl," Danny said.

Simone was flattered by his comment and decided to accompany him inside.

Danny told Simone to have a seat on the sofa while he ran upstairs and searched for his wallet. When Danny came back downstairs, his shirt was off. Simone was embarrassed by how much the sight of the bulging muscles in his arms and chest aroused her and quickly looked away. Danny sat down on the sofa beside of Simone and grabbed her hand. Simone looked down at the shiny peach nail polish on her toes, not wanting to make eye contact with Danny.

"Simone," Danny said softly, placing two of his fingers on Simone's chin and turning her face toward his. "You're beautiful; you know that?"

Simone looked up at Danny as he leaned forward to kiss her.

"What's wrong?" Danny asked.

Simone shook her head.

"I told you, I'm going to take you to the prom with me," Danny said before he pecked her on her lips. "Next week, I'm going to take you to pick out your dress," Danny said before placing another kiss on Simone's lips. "I want you to be my girl. I ain't gonna let you turn me away that easily."

Danny bit down on Simone's lip and slid his tongue in her mouth. Simone lay down on the sofa as Danny ran his hands up her torso, feeling how plump her breasts were. He then made his way down to her waist, unbuckling her pants and sliding them off along with her panties.

"Turn around," Danny said, motioning for Simone to bend over the sofa. "I like doing it like this."

Danny eased his way inside of Simone until he fully occupied her body and she let out a faint cry.

"Don't worry," he said. "You'll like it."

The next thing Simone knew she was moaning at the top of her lungs while Danny squeezed her waist with his hands and plunged deep inside of her.

After what seemed to be about fifteen minutes, they were getting dressed and on their way to take Simone home.

As soon as Simone took a shower and got some rest, she swore that she was in love. Danny was all she could think about. First, she told herself that she wouldn't call him. She didn't want to seem pushy. But after not hearing from Danny the entire weekend, she decided to call. No one answered. She told herself to let it go. Maybe he was busy. She decided to wait an hour and then call Danny back. After an hour had passed, she called back but there was still no answer. She waited two more hours and called again. There was still no answer. From then on, she called Danny every hour. At first, she had no success. At about six o'clock, Danny's mother picked up and Simone could have sworn she heard Danny in the background telling his mother to tell her that he wasn't there.

"He's not here!" Danny's mother shouted before slamming down the phone.

Simone didn't talk to Danny until she got to school the next day.

"Where have you been?" she asked. "I've been trying to call you all weekend."

"Out, chilling with my girl," Danny said.

Simone was in total shock. "Oh, for real? I thought I was your girlfriend."

"Naw, I decided to work things out with my ex," Danny said before walking off.

Simone's eyes flooded with tears. She took refuge in the bathroom until she could control her emotions long enough to call a cab to take her home. She promised herself when she got home, she would crawl underneath her covers and die.

The day after the prom, pictures of Danny and his girlfriend, Tanya, the shapely chocolate chick all the guys put on a pedestal and regarded as the benchmark for beauty, were posted all over the school, congratulating them for being prom king and queen. All the chatter about how cute they were together ate Simone up inside. So she threw her book bag on her back and walked out of the front door. She rode the GRTC bus home and looked out of the window the entire ride, not wanting any of the passengers to see that she was a few seconds away from crying.

When Simone got home, she jumped in the bed and buried her face in her pillow. She replayed everything Danny had said to her since their first encounter in her mind. *How could he say all those things to me and then act like he doesn't even give a shit about me and ignore my calls like I'm some annoying groupie that's stalking him?* Simone asked herself.

After a few minutes, she became furious and built up the nerve to call Danny. She was going to ask him how could he do that to her. He was supposed to take her to the prom; she was supposed to be prom queen, the one in the picture with him that everyone around school was talking about. She thought he wanted her to be his girl; what happened to him not letting her slip away?

But when Danny picked up the phone, all Simone could say was, "How could you go to the prom with her? You said you were taking me."

"She's my fucking girl! Bitch, stop stalking me!" Danny shouted and then slammed down the phone.

Simone fell back down on her bed and cried.

A few weeks later, when Simone thought she was finally ready to put Danny behind her, she found out that what she had been buying tubes of yeast infection cream to treat, and what was so irritating that it had forced her to take a trip to the free clinic, was an STD. She was so pissed off that what she had kept secret from Stefan out of fear of ridicule she blurted out in front of Crystal, Jewel, and Paris as soon as she returned home from picking up her prescription at the pharmacy. She bent down and laid her head on Stefan's knee and cried.

"He did what?" Stefan shouted. "Oh, somebody's getting fucked up tonight."

Stefan stormed out of the house with his crew behind him. About thirty minutes later, the phone started ringing off of the hook. Simone looked at the caller ID and it displayed Danny's number across the screen.

"Hello," Simone answered.

"Let me speak to your grandmother!" Danny's mother yelled.

"She ain't here," Simone replied before hanging up the phone.

Danny's mother called right back.

"What?" Simone yelled into the phone.

"Little girl, put your grandmother on the phone," Danny's mother said.

Simone sucked her teeth. "I said, she ain't here."

"Child, you better stop playing games with me," Danny's mother said. "I know you sent them goddamn punks over here to fight my son. If you don't put your grandmother on this phone, I'm sending the police over there."

"Then send them, bitch!" Simone yelled and then slammed down the phone.

Simone walked into the living room and plopped down on the sofa, ignoring the sound of the phone ringing. She wondered what kind of damage the four of them had done to Danny.

Simone heard the door unlock and Stefan walked in with his crew behind him. All of them had bloodstains on their shirts, Paris's eye was puffy, and Stefan's shirt was torn.

"What happened?" Simone asked.

"What you think happened? We went 'round that nigga's house and whipped his ass," Stefan said.

"And you lucky I fucks with you," Paris added. "That nigga can throw and you know I bruise easily."

"Who keeps ringing the phone like that?" Stefan asked.

"That's Danny's mama," Simone said. "She's called damn near twenty times, asking for Grandma."

Stefan stomped in the kitchen and snatched the phone off of the base. "She's dead, bitch!" he shouted into the phone. "And don't call here no fucking more before I send somebody over there to whip your ass."

Despite Danny's run-in with Stefan and his crew, he still went on to do big things.

He attended Virginia Tech that fall and he became their starting point guard. He was all over the television during basketball season. Everywhere Simone went, Danny seemed to be the topic of conversation. *Did you see Danny play last night? I heard him and Tanya got engaged. That kid is doing big things. Yeah, that boy is going to the pros.* And her, she was still living at her grandma's house, hustling her body for money, and falling victim to every immature impulse Stefan and she had. Life wasn't in her favor because if it were, she would've been the one who'd gone to college. It would've been her clothing ads that everyone was admiring when they opened their favorite magazines. She would be engaged to some handsome guy and about to settle down and start a family. It wasn't fair.

[12]

Simone's eyes wandered nervously around the restaurant, following the sounds of laughter and clinking glasses as she waited for the waitress to bring their order to the table; she was sure their conversation would cease at that point.

"So what do you like to do?" Wayne asked.

"What most people like doing," Simone said. "I enjoy shopping, going out, being in the company of those I like. I'm not hard to please."

Wayne smiled. "It didn't seem that way earlier."

"You have to get to know me."

"I can't believe you don't have a man," Wayne said. "What's a pretty thing like you doing without a man?"

"I never said that I didn't have one."

Wayne rubbed Simone's hand. "Well, do you?"

Simone slid her hand away. "No."

"Why not?"

"I just don't; between school and work, I don't have time."

"Where do you work?"

"Wachovia."

"You're a teller?"

Simone looked away. She wasn't able to look Wayne in his eyes while she lied to him. "Naw, I'm the Branch Manager."

"Oh, you look too young to have a job like that. How old are you?"

"Twenty-two."

"Sounds like you're doing good for yourself, ma."

"How old are you?"

Wayne looked at Simone and grinned. "How old do I look?"

Simone shrugged. "I don't know, like you could be in your late-twenties or early-thirties."

"I'm twenty-six."

Simone giggled. "Okay, so I guessed right." *Lying bastard,* Simone thought to herself. "Do you have any kids?"

"Just one."

"Oh, is it a boy or girl?"

"A boy; he's a junior."

"Are you and his mother still together?"

Wayne laughed. "If we were, I wouldn't be here with you."

Simone thought about all of the lies that Wayne had spoken. "I'm not sure if I believe that one."

"Let me ask you something, ma; why are you so disagreeable?"

"It's a habit."

"Well, you need to break it or a lot of good things are going to pass you by."

"I appreciate your concern but let me worry about that," Simone said. "Now back to what I was saying."

"Naw, back to you," Wayne interrupted. "What are you taking up in school?"

Simone looked up like she was waiting for the answer to fall from the sky. "Fashion design."

"That's good. What year are you?"

"I'm a sophomore."

The waitress placed their plates in front of them and scurried away. Simone sighed. Now Wayne could stuff his mouth with food and finally shut up.

"So you design clothes, huh?"

Simone nodded as she took a bite of her food. She was in disbelief about how many lies she'd told since she'd been there and Wayne's questioning kept them rolling from her mouth. But she figured, what the hell? It wasn't like his mouth had been a prayer book.

"Can I get you to design something for me?"

"Like what?"

"I don't know; I want to see if you have skills. What do you think will look good on me?"

Simone smiled. "You're already wearing it."

"What? This," Wayne asked, tugging on his shirt.

"Naw, what's underneath it; the wife beater, boxers, and oh, you can keep on the Air Force."

Wayne grinned. "Oh, is that right? You know how I'd like to see you?"

"How?"

Wayne leaned forward and looked into Simone's eyes. "Bent over the bed in my hotel room, soaked in Dom Perignon, swarming around while I tickle your clit with my tongue."

The thought aroused Simone but she refused to give in. "Yeah, you and every other guy I run across."

"Do any of them luck up?"

"Let's just say you won't."

Wayne nodded his head. "It's all good; I can respect that."

Simone rolled her eyes. "Good, 'cause you really don't have a choice."

❖

Paris sat on the couch, eating out of a half-gallon container of chocolate chip ice cream while he watched TV. He was already feeling better about the incident with Michael; he hoped that by the time his spoon reached the bottom of the container, he'd feel like himself again. Paris was interrupted by a knock at the door. He peered through the peephole in his door and saw Michael standing outside.

He's crazy if he thinks I'm opening the door for his ass, Paris thought. Paris sat back down on the couch and finished eating his ice cream.

Michael banged on the door. "Paris, open this door. I know you're in there."

Paris turned up the TV to drown out the sound of Michael's voice.

"I know what you did to my apartment. If you don't open this door, I'm calling the police."

Paris sucked his teeth at Michael's comment and continued to watch TV.

"Awright, be like that. I've got something for your ass," Michael said before leaving.

It had been two hours since Michael had left. Paris was glad that he hadn't returned. He cut off his TV and prepared to go to sleep. Paris heard a fist pounding on his door. He peered through his peephole and saw Michael on the porch with two police officers.

And I thought he was bluffing, Paris thought.

Paris opened the door. "Can I help you?"

"That's him; that's the guy who broke into my apartment and damaged my furniture."

The police officer held up his hand to silence Michael. "I'm Officer Bradley; this man says you broke into his apartment and damaged some of his belongings. Do you know anything about that?"

"No, officer," Paris answered.

"Well, we have a witness that said they saw you running out of the house," Officer Bradley said.

"Ain't nobody see me running out no house," Paris said.

"This is a little boy; he'd have no reason to lie on you," Officer Bradley said.

"A little boy? Every man in a dress probably looks the same to him. And who knows how many be running out of his apartment?" Paris pointed to Michael.

"That's a lie!" Michael exclaimed. "That's why he did that shit, 'cause he's mad at me for putting him in his place. I told him that I don't mess around with no boys, to go on about his business and to stop stalking me. That's what's behind all this mess."

"Put me in my place?" Paris snapped. "Officer, if he put me in my place, it must've been in the bed beside him; it's hard to stalk somebody who spends most of their time lying on top of you."

Michael charged Paris and the two officers wrestled him down to the ground.

"I think we're done here," Officer Bradley said.

"Well, good night, officers," Paris said, before sticking his tongue out at Michael and going back into the house.

❖

"Ahhh," Simone moaned as Wayne forced her down on his robust chocolate dick. She couldn't believe she had given in so easily after giving him such a hard time at the restaurant.

Simone wanted to stake her claim to Wayne. She had to have him. He had money and he was gorgeous; not to mention that he was somewhat in the limelight. She was willing to do whatever she had to do to convince

Wayne to make her his woman. But she didn't want to seem easy. Men loved beautiful women who were easy, but the reality was, no matter how much money they spent on those type of women, or how often they liked to be in their company, they usually didn't make them *their* woman. Easy women were fads; here today, gone tomorrow. That's why she couldn't understand, for the life of her, how she'd managed to let Wayne persuade her into accompanying him to his hotel room and why, after a few minutes of pillow talk, she was straddled on top of him with her back toward him, her sweaty ass shining in his face while he grabbed her around her waist, forcing her down on his dick as hard as he could. She didn't want to deny him. If she did, he'd set his sights on another and she might not be given the opportunity to be with him again. If she broke him off right, he wouldn't be able to get enough of her and every time he came back for more, she'd have the chance to ease her way into his life.

After Wayne reached his climax, he gave Simone a long gentle kiss, despite the acts she'd performed on him with her mouth. Simone smiled. Wayne's kiss confirmed that she'd have no problem making him her man.

[13]

A month had passed. Simone and Stefan had started their jobs at the bank. Stefan excelled at his job. He never forgot to greet a customer and he was always polite, no matter how rude the customers were. He did nothing but work the entire time that he was there. He hardly ever took his fifteen-minute breaks; if he did, he took them to meet a customer outside that he was trying to get on board as one of his clients.

Simone hated working at the bank. Her shift couldn't go by fast enough for her. She hated the snotty-ass customers who came to her station acting like she owed them something other than the money they were withdrawing from their accounts. She hated the way that her supervisor pranced her hefty ass back and forth past her station, watching her every move. Most of all, Simone hated the Saturday mornings she had to spend there, looking in the customers' faces. She spent most of her time at work exchanging text messages with Wayne. When their messages became erotic, she put the closed sign in front of her station and went to the restroom where she would position herself on the floor in the stall and fondle herself while she snapped pictures with her phone. She'd send the pictures to Wayne and wait for him to send one back. Simone had been written up twice for her behavior. She didn't give a shit. As soon as her manager walked away, Simone tore up her disciplinary slip and threw it in the trash. She hoped the next time that her supervisor decided to write her up, she'd rethink it and fire her instead. She didn't want to quit. Stefan would be pissed and she would never be able to live it down. So she hung in there. In her mind, she had bigger plans.

Everything seemed to be going well between her and Wayne. Based on what she'd learned from her Internet search and their conversations, he had more than enough money to take care of the both of them. So if things went her way, there wouldn't be a need to lag behind Stefan to work, so-called planning for her future. Nor would there be a need to sex every clean-cut paycheck that crossed her path. Hell, the thought of it made her lazy. She went from servicing two clients a day to three clients a week and sometimes she would cancel. Instead of sitting at the kitchen table sketching designs when she got some downtime, she was sitting in front of the television talking to Wayne on the phone and that's if she wasn't somewhere laid up with him or sitting between his legs sipping Dom Perignon.

Simone was in love with the thought of being Wayne's lady. She would sit around and muse about sitting ringside at one of his fights. She could see herself on his arm after his fights as the reporters rushed him for his comments and the cameras zoomed in on them. She could picture everybody in town sitting at home watching in awe, and Danny eating his heart out, wishing he could trade places with Wayne. As far as she was concerned, Wayne was the best thing she had going for her. He was her future and she wasn't about to put him on hold for anyone or anything; not Stefan, a client, her sketches, and damn sure not her job.

⬧

Simone lay back in her seat with her arms resting above her head. She hummed the song that played on the radio while Stefan sat behind the wheel. The two were on their way to Ashland, Virginia, to meet Chris, a new client they'd met at work the week before, and his friend, Marvin.

Stefan was proud of all the new clients that he'd met at the bank.

Simone wasn't the least bit enthused; especially when it came to Chris. They had met with Chris the week before and the man was weird. He had a sly smile like a pedophile and his eyes appeared empty like his body wasn't occupied. He had some of the craziest requests Simone had ever heard.

Chris wanted her to penetrate him with a vibrator

while he penetrated Stefan. Simone didn't get it. Stefan was the one with the dick; why couldn't he penetrate Chris while Chris penetrated her? The whole experience rubbed her the wrong way. Not to mention that being in Chris's presence made her stomach turn. Simone expressed her feelings about Chris to Stefan and told him that she wanted to cross Chris off of their list of clients.

Stefan assured her that there was nothing to worry about; that nothing was wrong with Chris. He told her that she was paranoid and lazy. She wasn't used to playing the back, that was his position, and now that she realized how demanding it was, she didn't want any parts of it. She accepted Stefan's judgment and decided to ignore the gut-wrenching feeling that she felt whenever she got a mental image of Chris's face. She ignored the little voice in her head that whispered to her at every stoplight, telling her to admit to Stefan that she wanted out; to turn the car around and take her the fuck home.

Stefan grinned as he listened to Simone humming the song playing on the radio. "Damn, that nigga got you humming love songs. He must have some bumbiggiddy."

Simone giggled. "He sure does; he be tearing it up, from the front, from the back, and in the rear."

"Damn," Stefan said, snapping his friends. "I should've made that nigga mine."

Simone looked at Stefan and rolled her eyes. "Please, he wouldn't have your ass."

"That's what you think."

"That's what I know. He doesn't go that route."

"Shit, he went there with you."

"That's different."

"How is it different?"

"'Cause, I'm a woman, duh."

Stefan laughed. "Let me tell you something, if a man will fuck a girl in her ass, he'll fuck a boy in his ass, and that's real."

Simone huffed. "Whatever."

"You can say what you want. It might take a little more persuasion to get him there, but he'll go," Stefan said. "Don't ever underestimate what a man will do to get his dick down; especially if he thinks no one's looking."

Simone looked at Stefan and rolled her eyes. "You always got to find some way to rain on my parade."

"It ain't about raining on your parade," Stefan said. "I'm telling you some real shit."

Simone shook her head. "Naw, you're only saying that 'cause you wish it could go down like that."

Stefan burst out into laughter. "I don't have to wish. Give me an hour alone with him and I'll prove it."

"Naw, why don't you give me thirty minutes alone with Eugene and watch how fly he gets on your ass after I throw this pussy on him," Simone said.

"Not happening," Stefan said. "Eugene is strictly about the dick."

"Yeah, that's what you think," Simone said, rolling her eyes. "That's probably what he's been doing those six days out the week you ain't with him, getting some pussy."

"Shit, he might be."

"Ain't no might in it," Simone said. "He's fucking something."

"You know what, he might be. The difference between your naïve little ass and me is that I can accept the truth, move on with my life, and become wiser because of it," Stefan said. "Unlike you, who lives in a fantasy world and believes nothing is going to happen that you don't want to happen; then, when it does, you walk around like the sky is falling and all the forces in the universe are against you."

Simone sucked her teeth. "Oh, wow, I wish that I was as wise as you."

Simone's heart raced as they pulled into Chris's driveway. His house sat in the back of a wooded area about an acre away from his four neighbors.

Simone got out of the car and followed Stefan to the door. She was careful not to step in the animal feces spread across the walkway. She surveyed the yard, noticing that several cats hid under the two junk cars in the yard. "I'm gonna need him to get rid of some of these damn animals."

Stefan placed his index finger in front of his lips. "Shh, what's all the hostility for? I thought we talked about this."

"The man is a fucking weirdo and you can't deny it. Don't stand here and tell me you don't feel uncomfortable being around this muthafucka."

"I don't," Stefan said. "Even if I did, I came here to get some paper and then I'm out; I'm not spending the night with his ass."

"Well, I don't want to spend five minutes with him. Then he invited a friend, too. Who knows what that muthafucka—"

Chris opened the door and then turned around and headed toward his bedroom, not giving Simone or Stefan a second look. Simone and Stefan gave each other a puzzled glance, and then followed Chris.

The bedroom floor was covered with balled-up clothes, empty cigarette cartons, and paper plates with who knew what encrusted on them. Simone and Stefan kicked their way through the clutter and took seats in the two chairs sitting across from the bed.

Chris's friend, Marvin, lay in the center of the two disheveled king-sized beds that Chris had pulled together to increase the size of his playground, under a red satin sheet.

"Damn. He don't do nothing but eat, sleep, and fuck up in here," Simone mumbled.

Stefan looked at Simone with disapproval in his eyes. "Shh."

"Ladies, this is Marvin. Marvin, these are the two freaks that I was telling you about," Chris said.

Simone sneered. "Freaks."

Stefan snapped his fingers. "That's right; we aim to please."

"We'll see about that," Chris said.

Marvin shook Stefan's hand. "It's nice to meet you."

"Same here," Stefan said.

Simone turned up her nose, disgusted by the thought of having to fondle or be fondled by Chris or Marvin.

"Well, being that you both did such a good job the other night; I mean, Simone here literally blew my brains out," Chris said. "I thought we could put on a little show for the two of you and then you both can join in."

"Sounds fun," Stefan said.

Simone nodded her head in agreement.

Chris walked over to the vanity on the left side of the room and fumbled with the towels and clutter that lay on it. "Let's get started," Chris said as he made his way back over to the bed.

Marvin rose up on his knees and unfastened Chris's pants. Chris kissed Marvin, sliding his tongue in his mouth.

"Want me to turn off the lights?" Stefan asked.

"No thanks; I like the lights on. That way when I look back on it, I'll have a clear picture," Chris answered.

Marvin freed Chris's dick from his pants and slid his tongue around the tip before sliding it completely inside his mouth. Chris slapped Marvin's backside as he came close to reaching his climax.

"Stop," Chris said, freeing his dick from between Marvin's lips. "I don't want to cum yet; I'm saving that for our guests. Now turn around."

Marvin turned around and Chris bent over, balancing himself by placing his hands on the edge of the bed. Chris shoved his head between Marvin's hips and lapped him like he was a dog in heat.

Stefan sat on the edge of his chair, grinning from ear to ear with delight. Simone slouched down in her chair and kept her eyes on the floor, shaking her head, totally disgusted.

"Come on," Stefan said, nudging Simone. "Perk up and get with it. How often do you get to see a live flick? I don't know about you; I've been in a few but I've never seen one."

Of course he's enjoying this freak show. It's what he's into, Simone thought.

The sight of two men romping with each other in that manner made Simone sick to her stomach. She sat there counting the number of empty cigarette cartons on the floor, occasionally peeking up to see if they had put an end to their show.

"You ready for the dick?" Chris asked.

"Ooooh, give it here, Daddy," Marvin whimpered.

"You two ready to join us?" Chris asked, opening up the drawer to the nightstand and handing Simone his vibrator.

Simone and Stefan joined Chris and Marvin on the bed and waited for Chris to dictate their actions.

"This is how we're going to do this," Chris announced. "Stefan, you take Marvin's back, I'll take the front, and Mona, you handle my rear."

They got into their positions. Marvin knelt down on the edge of the bed; Stefan placed his hands on Marvin's waist and began to plunge him. Chris lay across the bed on his stomach, performing oral sex on Marvin. Simone straddled Chris, inserted the vibrator in his anus, and stroked it lightly.

"Harder," Chris muttered, with Marvin's organ still in his mouth.

Simone began to stroke Chris harder but he continued to demand her to use more force.

"You've got to do it harder," Chris said, removing his hand from Marvin's dick and grabbing the vibrator, forcing it harshly into his anus. "You've got to do it like this."

Chris focused his attention back on Marvin and Simone forced the vibrator into Chris's anus like he'd requested, nauseated by the impact.

"Oooh, I'm about to cum," Marvin squealed.

"Give it all here," Chris said and then held his tongue under Marvin's dick, stroking it rapidly.

Marvin closed his eyes and grunted as he covered Chris's tongue with cum. Marvin then leaned back on Stefan, panting heavily. Chris rose up on his knees, wrapped his arms around Marvin's neck, and kissed him.

"Woo!" Chris exclaimed, falling down on the bed and pulling Marvin on top of him. "Okay, now it's y'all turn."

Simone looked at Stefan and frowned. She wasn't eager to engage in any activity with Chris or Marvin that didn't involve one of them shutting the door behind her as she made her way out of the front door. She decided to let Stefan initiate the action and follow his lead. Stefan leaned over to kiss Chris on his lips.

"Uh uh," Chris said, tilting his index finger from side to side. Chris got up from the bed with his dick standing erect from his frail, pink body. "My friend and I put on a show for you; now it's y'all turn."

Stefan looked dumbfounded. "Our turn?"

"Yes," Marvin said. "It's time for you two to entertain us."

"Oh hell naw," Simone snapped.

"We're family; we don't perform on each other," Stefan explained.

"I know, you told me that last week," Chris said. "But tonight you said you aim to please and one of my fondest fantasies is watching two sisters go at it up close and personal, but a drag and his cousin will do."

"You sick sonofabitch. I don't know what type of shit you're into but that shit ain't popping off," Simone snapped with spit flying from her mouth.

"Hell naw; we're not doing that," Stefan said.

"Come on; let's roll," Simone said, nodding her head toward the door.

"Don't worry; we're leaving," Stefan said. "But first, where's our money?"

Chris chuckled. "Money, what money? As far as I'm concerned, you ain't do nothing worth a damn, so I ain't giving you shit. As a matter of fact, I still haven't gotten my money's worth out of you two from last time."

"I don't give a fuck about your concerns," Stefan said, pounding his fist in his hand. "I ain't leaving 'til I get my money."

"That's where you're wrong," Chris said, reaching underneath the bed and pulling out a shotgun. Chris walked toward Stefan and placed the shotgun against his forehead. "You're leaving here, one way or another. Pick one; either way, you ain't getting no money."

Simone's heart raced and she became dizzy. Her fear numbed her body.

The room became silent. Chris stood there with a smirk on his face, confidently holding the gun to Stefan's head and Marvin stood at Simone's side like he was preparing to attack.

"So what's it going to be?" Chris asked.

Stefan smirked. "You can give me my money and live or I can step over your cold dead body and take whatever I want."

Chris put his hand on the trigger. "You're one arrogant bastard, that's for sure, but arrogance never saved anyone's life."

Stefan quickly grabbed the barrel of the shotgun and snatched it from Chris's hand. Stefan smacked Chris across the face with the butt of the shotgun.

Marvin rushed toward Stefan and Simone pounced on his unyielding body. Marvin backhanded Simone and shoved her on the floor. Simone grabbed a handful of Marvin's hair, bringing him down to the floor with her. Marvin clutched Simone's face with his hand and banged her head against the floor. Simone dug her nails into Marvin's face until the blows to her head started to disorient her. Simone could hear Chris screaming, begging for his life, as Stefan continued to wallop him with the shotgun. Simone reached for the ice pick hidden away in her bra. She could feel her consciousness slipping away. If she didn't do something soon, she'd be out cold and the chances of her regaining consciousness were slim. Simone bit down on the palm of Marvin's hand, piercing his skin.

"Bitch," Marvin spat, holding Simone's head stable with one hand as he tried to pry the other hand from between her teeth.

Simone pulled her ice pick from beneath her bra and shoved it into Marvin's side. Marvin immediately removed his hand from Simone's head and grabbed his side. Simone raised her hand back up and shoved the ice pick into Marvin's throat. Marvin made a gurgling sound and collapsed on top of Simone. Blood trickled down Marvin's neck onto Simone's chest and she began to panic.

"Stefan!" Simone screamed.

Stefan didn't answer.

"And to think, for a minute, I actually thought I would

be leaving empty-handed." Stefan gloated before firing the gun.

Fragments of Chris's head flew across the room.

"Stefan!" Simone screamed louder. "Get this dead man off of me!"

Stefan searched Chris's pants pockets and pulled a knot of cash out of each one. "Damn, I hit the lottery."

Simone screamed louder, kicking and struggling to get from underneath Marvin's body.

Stefan kicked Marvin off of Simone and pulled her to her feet. Simone became weak, her knees buckled, and she fell back down to the floor.

Stefan grabbed Simone by her waist, holding her up. "Don't do this, Simone. Don't be a pussy. Get on your feet so we can get the fuck out of here."

❧[14]❧

Paris knocked at his parents' door. He took a deep breath and straightened up his dress. He debated with himself about turning around and going home.

His mother seemed to be on a mission to get their family back together but it wasn't going to happen. It was a lost cause. His father not only hated his lifestyle, he hated him also. Paris didn't think it was a progressive thing. Paris believed his father had hated him the moment he was born. And frankly, Paris didn't care for him either.

His mother was fickle. She didn't know whether she wanted to side with him, his father, or some article she'd read about raising gay children. But Paris loved her. He believed if it weren't for his father and his ignorant, judgmental, low-life ways, he and his mother could have a better relationship. But he wasn't bitter about it. It was the hand that life had dealt him and he played it well. He went with the flow of things and didn't stress shit. To him, life was a sick tale of loss, struggle, and disappointment. Its sole purpose was to break you so that you could realize how helpless you truly are. When he was born, the doctor might as well had slapped him on the ass and said "lights, camera, action" because the camera had been on him ever since and he performed as well as Josephine Baker had in her banana skirt. He made sure he did whatever he could to make life more interesting.

Paris's mother, Berniece, answered the door and gave Paris a hug. "Oh, it's so nice to see you, Paul, or should I say Paris? I know that's what you like to be called."

Paris smiled. "Hey, Mom; what you been up to?"

"Not much; taking care of your father. He can't get around like he used to."

Paris figured what the hell was the harm in telling one little white lie to please his mother. He had done worse things. "Oh…I'm sorry to hear that."

Paris walked over to the dining room table where his father, Glen, was seated. He looked down at his father's hands as he took his seat. His fingers were curled over and his hands were pink and swollen; they resembled pig hooves. Paris thought his body was starting to match his heart; crippled.

Berniece prepared his plate while his father looked him over with his nose turned up like he had raw chitterlings on his plates.

Paris decided to break the ice. "So, Dad, how are you?"

"That's Glen to you."

Paris smirked. *Old, contrary bastard*, he thought. "Well, how are things going, Glen?"

"Why would you waste your time asking me that?" his father said. "You know my life has been fucked up since the day you were born."

Paris's heart dropped. Why didn't the man like him? During his twenty-two years of life, the man never had one nice word to say to him. He wanted to tell his father how he was a miserable bastard and tell his mother how pathetic she was for not being able to stand up to him, and then he wanted to push the table over and leave. But he wouldn't dare let his father know that his insults bothered him.

"It brings joy to my heart to know I have that kind of effect on you," Paris said.

"Stop it," Berniece said. "I'm sure you're both happy to see each other."

Paris sucked his teeth. "Don't start me to lying."

Berniece slapped him on his shoulder. "Oh…stop it now."

"What he needs to stop doing is walking around here wearing dresses, high-heels, a weave, and a purse," Glen said.

Berniece took a look at Paris's alligator purse. "I love that purse; it had to be expensive. How much does a purse like that cost?"

"Money's not a problem when you're turning tricks for it," Glen said. "Besides, that bag is probably where he keeps all his voodoo shit."

"Naw, it's a big bag of dicks," Paris said.

"I'll bet; it's just like you," Glen said. "You can't stop playing with dicks long enough to see your mother."

"Actually, I brought them for her," Paris said. "I know she gets tired of having to pry yo' dick from underneath yo' big potbelly every time she wants to get laid."

"Come on, y'all; let's have a nice peaceful dinner," Berniece suggested.

"We could if this punk understood his place," Glen replied.

"I know my place," Paris said. "It's behind you with my foot up yo' ass. But I hate to get shit on my four-hundred-dollar shoes."

Berniece jumped in the argument again, trying to change the subject. "I noticed your shoes match your purse. You have to let me borrow them sometime, Paul. I mean, Paris. That's what you like to be called, right?"

"As long as he's in my house, he'll be called Paul," Glen said.

"My name is Paris."

Glen pounded his hand on the table. "Paul, Paul, Paul; that's what your mother named you and that's the name you'll go by in this house."

Berniece tried to change the subject again. "How is your friend, Charlie?"

Paris looked at his father and grinned. "You mean Crystal? I wouldn't know. I've only seen him once since he got out of jail."

"I heard him and Anthony, you know the one who used to live down the street from Stefan, I heard they were a couple."

"Stop playing!"

"I'm not; that's what's being said at church," Paris's mother said.

"Stefan; that's a faggot I can respect," Glen said. "No doubt he's the biggest queer of them all but he doesn't try to hide his identity and change his name to something dainty like Paris or Crystal."

Paris and his mother ignored his father and continued their conversation.

"His mother didn't take it too hard though," Berniece said. "But she's crushed about Anthony being strung out on crack."

"Anthony is on crack?" Paris said. "I would've never thought."

Berniece nodded. "Yeah, and they say Crystal also uses it."

"Well, that explains a lot," Paris said.

"Like what?"

"Like why I haven't heard from him," Paris answered.

Berniece placed her hand on top of his. "Sometimes, when people feel like they're doing something wrong, they cut themselves off from the people who love them."

Paris's father pounded his hand on the table again. "Stop gossiping about gay shit at my table. For God's sake, Berniece, don't encourage him. I know you want him to be your princess but, for crying out loud, he has a dick."

Berniece sighed as her husband ranted. Paris looked at Glen and shook his head. *What a dumb ass*, Paris thought.

"I know you're not dumb enough to think he's not using that shit, too," Glen said.

Before Berniece could answer, Paris decided to respond to his father's comment. "You just worry about how much crack you've smoked in your so-called joints."

"So-called?" Paris's father said. "They were joints; I don't smoke nothing but reefer."

"If you say so," Paris said.

"Well, one thing's for sure, I've never had another man's dick in my mouth," Glen said in disgust.

Paris couldn't take it anymore. His father had gone too far. Just because he'd helped conceive him didn't give him the right to disrespect him. "You've had the taste of dick in your mouth plenty of times and you seemed to enjoy it. Why else would you have Larry over every day so you could smoke with him?"

"You'd better watch your mouth," Glen warned. "Larry's a real man. He'd never take part in no shit like that."

"I have no objection to Larry being a real man," Paris said. "He sure did fuck me like one."

Berniece's eyes bulged.

"That's a lie and you know it," Glen said.

"No, but that's what you'd like to think," Paris replied. "Surely you're not dumb enough to think that he wanted me over his house every day so he could help me with my homework."

"That's a damn lie!" Paris's father exclaimed as he grabbed his cane and prepared to stand up.

"You wish it was," Paris said. "And I'll put something else in yo' ear; I remember plenty of times when he'd sucked my dick and then come right over here to smoke with you."

Paris's father stood up and walked toward him. "You might've fantasized about that shit but Larry wasn't thinking about you. He had a fine woman. He wouldn't dare stick his dick in some man's big, hairy ass."

Paris laughed. "Well, he did, and he loved it. That's why he went crazy. He realized that after he hooked up with that broad, he couldn't get no more of this."

"Boy, you better watch your mouth before I bash you in it," Glen said.

"You better go sit on yo' ass 'fore I knock you on it," Paris replied.

"Wait; this is serious," Berniece said. "I believe Paris. He was so young then. Your friend took advantage of him."

"Took advantage of him, ha," Paris's father said. "Larry probably went crazy because this boy worked a root on him."

Paris smirked. *I'm gonna get his ass*, he thought. "You mean like I'm going do to you?"

"I don't believe in that crap," Glen said.

"Well, that's good for you," Paris said. "It's too bad your beliefs won't help you." Paris took a handful of rice off his plate, said something inarticulate as he waved his hand over the rice, spit on it, and then threw it on his father.

Paris's father stumbled backward. "I can't believe it! The bastard worked a root on me!" he screamed. "Make him take it off, Berniece! Make him take it off!"

Paris grabbed his purse and made his way to the door. His mother followed behind him.

"I wish you would at least try to get along with your father," she said.

Paris kissed his mother on her cheek. "I've tried time and time again but nothing I do will ever please that man. He's a miserable creature and you dedicated your life to him; I didn't."

Paris's mother nodded. "See you around. Don't be a stranger."

But Paris planned to be a stranger. He promised himself that he wouldn't subject himself to his father's hatred. As long as his father was alive, he wouldn't step foot in that house again.

Berniece made her way out to the grocery store. "Are you sure you'll be okay until I get back?" she asked her husband.

"Yeah, Larry is supposed to stop by."

Berniece shook her head and shut the door. She was disturbed. *After what Paris told us last night, why would he invite that man into our home?* she thought.

Glen wondered if what his son had said was true and, if so, why he hadn't realized it. He didn't want to believe that he had befriended a homo. He hated all gay people. He didn't care what they had accomplished during their lifetime, how enlightening their paintings were, how great they were as conquerors, or how well they ran their countries. Whatever contributions they made to society would always be overshadowed by their disgraceful life-styles. He thought about Caesar and his legions. *I guess it's easy to be a great warrior when you go to bed with your boo and then wake up and fight beside him.* Their significant others weren't at home worrying about them and taking care of their hungry kids; no, they were beside them, keeping them in high spirits.

Glen remembered his father and his buddy, Vernon, whom he'd met while he was in the military. His father had told him that Vernon had saved his life many times and for that, he owed him his life.

Glen remembered walking in his parents' bedroom and seeing his father showing his gratitude to Vernon, on his hands and knees while Vernon straddled him. Glen quickly shut the door and ran to his room. He wondered had his eyes played a trick on him.

His father started bringing him candy home every day, taking him to the movies once a month, and giving him an allowance in an attempt to buy his silence. But Glen's conscience was getting the best of him. He realized that what he'd seen his father doing was wrong. The only person his father should've been in bed with was his mother. He felt sick when Vernon came over to eat dinner with his family and all of them sat around the table, laughing and smiling as if they were good friends without any secrets. It had all been a lie.

One day, while they were eating dinner, his parents

had discussed leaving him with Vernon while they went to the beach. Glen's mother asked him if he would be okay staying with Vernon for the weekend. Glen had trembled. He was scared Vernon would do to him what he'd witnessed him do to his father. "No, I want to go with you," Glen said.

"We want to spend some time alone," his mother said. "So you have to stay here."

Glen began to cry. "But I don't want to stay with Vernon."

"Why, what's wrong, honey?" his mother asked.

"I'm scared Vernon's going to do to me what he did to Daddy," Glen said.

"What are you talking about?" she asked.

"I saw Vernon and Daddy in the bed together and Vernon was hurting him," Glen said.

Glen's mother looked at his father. "What is Glen talking about?"

"I don't know," Glen's father said. "He's delirious." Glen's father reached over and touched Glen's forehead. "Maybe the boy's running a fever."

Glen's mother put him to bed. Glen cried himself to sleep. He thought telling his mother would make him feel better and there would be no more secrets. But it didn't. His father's words carried more weight than his. What else could he do? He had no power. He was a child; a six-year-old boy.

Later that night, Glen's father crept into his room. Glen woke up with his father's hands around his neck.

"I'm not going to let you ruin my life, boy," his father said. "What I do is none of your business. Keep your mouth shut about what I do," his father said, squeezing his neck tighter. "Or I'll snap your fucking neck."

Glen lived in fear for the next five years of his life. It wasn't until his father sat around slumped in his chair, looking like a brown, lesion-covered skeleton that Glen didn't fear him anymore. The same man that had saved his father's life had put it to an end.

Glen resented the fact that his mother had to take care of his father. He hated watching his mother cry day after day, anticipating his father's death. He couldn't understand how she nurtured and cried for such garbage.

Later, when his mother began to become sick, Glen was sent to live with his grandmother so he wouldn't have to watch his mother die from AIDS. He spent many nights wide awake, mourning the loss of his mother and worrying that the disease would spread through his family like locusts and kill everyone that he loved. It was his father's doing. Their protector had put them all in danger. Glen wanted to piss on his grave.

The day his wife, Berniece, gave birth to his Paul, Glen was happy. He wanted to do right by his family. He didn't want to be the deceitful bastard that his father had been.

As time went on and Paul started to grow into his looks, Glen was repulsed by how much he resembled his father. He swore Paul was his father's reincarnation and had come back to haunt him but he wasn't going to let him. He had the upper hand this time and he wouldn't let him destroy what he had worked so hard for; stability. He would mold him to be a better man this time around. He would do it by displaying the hatred he had toward him, hoping it would make him want to change his character so he could be someone a father could love and, if that didn't work, to hell with him.

No matter how hard he tried, he couldn't break Paul. Paul did what he wanted and lived how he wanted.

Glen opened the door for Larry.

"What's happening, man?" Larry asked. "How you been getting along?"

"Not good since I found out you were going behind my back and fucking my son." Glen balanced himself long enough to poke Larry in his chest with his cane. "What do you have to say for yourself?"

Larry wanted to tell Glen that he was insane for even thinking he would do such a thing. But Glen was set in his ways and when he believed something, there was no changing his mind. Besides, Glen had seen through every lie that he had told him during the thirty-five years they had known each other.

Larry decided to come clean. "There's nothing I can say. It just happened."

"How did you just happen to fuck my son?" Glen asked.

"We both were vulnerable," Larry said. "You never spent any time with the boy. He didn't have any friends. He was lonely and so was I."

"That's no excuse," Glen said. "I was your friend when no one else was. I got you a job when you were down on your luck and you repay me by fucking my teenage son."

"I repented for what I did," Larry said. "I put it behind me. It's the past. Let's leave it there."

Glen swung at Larry with his cane and Larry blocked the blow with his hand.

Glen huffed. "God may have forgiven you for it, but I never will. You're dead to me."

"You're blowing this out of proportion," Larry said.

"Get off my damn property," Glen said before shutting the door.

Larry walked away, trying not to display how hurt he was. Just when everything in his life was finally starting to get better, his past had popped back up to dismantle it.

Simone lay on the sofa balled up in a knot with her head hanging over the trashcan that she'd spent the night vomiting in. She hadn't moved from the sofa since she'd arrived home.

Stefan stood in the kitchen cooking breakfast, unfazed by the incident. After a hot shower and a good night's sleep, he'd decided to put the incident behind him and do what he did best; move on with his life.

That wasn't the case with Simone. Killing two people and leaving them in the house to decompose wasn't something she could put behind her that easily. She couldn't stop looking at the dried-up blood on her chest. She was worried that guilt wouldn't be the only repercussion from the incident. *What if someone saw us?* Simone wondered. She imagined that some nosy old lady had heard the gunfire and stayed glued to the window, waiting to see someone flee the scene.

The phone rang. Simone sat up and looked at the caller ID on the phone.

"Who is that?" Stefan asked.

"It's the job."

Stefan sucked his teeth. "Don't answer that shit; the hell with them."

Simone lifted the phone off of the receiver and slammed it back down. She wasn't about to complain.

Keep thinking like that and maybe one day you'll redeem yourself for that bullshit last night, Simone thought. She turned on the TV and flipped through the channels until she came across the local news.

Stefan walked out the kitchen and handed Simone a plate full of pancakes and sausage. "What you watching?"

"The news."

"For what?"

Simone rolled her eyes. "'Cause."

"'Cause what?"

"I like knowing what's going on."

"Since when?" Stefan asked with a mouthful of food.

"Damn, Stefan, I'm gonna need you not to talk with your mouth full," Simone said. "That shit makes me sick to my stomach."

"And I'm gonna need you to grow the fuck up." Stefan grabbed the remote and flipped through the TV channels.

"I was watching that."

"Well, you shouldn't be."

Simone squinted. "Why is that?"

"'Cause if something as simple as me talking with my mouth full upsets your stomach, I can't imagine what watching the news will do to you."

"Whatever; I just don't get off on other people's misfortune."

"You could've fooled me," Stefan said. "'Cause you damn sure don't mind taking part in it."

"That's bullshit!" Simone shouted. "I do what I have to do, usually 'cause I find myself caught up in some shit with you."

"Is that right?" Stefan asked wryly.

"Yeah, like last night."

"I'm not trying to hear that shit," Stefan said. "I ain't start that shit, them niggas did, and you just happened to be there."

Simone sighed. "Whatever you say."

Stefan frowned. "Oh, it's whatever I say, huh?"

Simone rolled her eyes and directed her attention back to the television.

Stefan sniggered. "Maybe I've got you wrong. Maybe you were willing to roll around in the bed together for those fools. But let me tell you something, I might be down with a lot of shit, but I do have boundaries. That shit right there wasn't hopping off."

"You know damn well that's not what I meant," Simone said. "We could've counted our losses and left."

"If you thought I was leaving without my money, you're a lot dumber than I thought."

Simone jumped to her feet and slapped his plate of food on the floor. "Fuck you."

Stefan smirked. "Aw, are we gonna throw a tantrum?"

"Don't sit here and act like I was down with that shit!" Simone shouted. "I didn't want to go in the first place!"

"Then why did you?"

"'Cause you kept saying nothing was wrong with the muthafucka; I was being paranoid and shit," Simone said.

"Grandma always used to say, you can't depend on other people's judgment," Stefan said. "Maybe if you would've listened to her instead of sitting in front of the TV plucking the dirt from under your fingernails all the time, you wouldn't be in this predicament."

"Naw, I'm in this predicament because you put me in it," Simone said. "This shit was your idea from jumpstreet. I wanted to go to college, stay on campus, and make some friends, to have my own clothing line. Not be some high-class hooker."

Stefan leaned back on the sofa smugly and looked Simone up and down. "First of all, you're a low-class hoe so don't go and get it twisted. And college?" Stefan chuckled. "How the hell you get from eleventh grade all the way to college? You don't even have a GED."

"It doesn't matter; I can get it."

"Yeah, and I would love to be a fly on the wall when you march into VCU and hand them your GED," Stefan said. "They'll laugh your dumb ass out the door."

"That shit doesn't matter now," Simone said on the verge of tears. "All that does is you ruin my life."

"Wrong, just 'cause I had an idea, didn't mean you had to go along with it," Stefan said. "You ruined your own life."

"Well, I'm through ruining it," Simone said. "I'm getting the fuck out of here, away from you."

Stefan giggled. "How? Who's going to take you in? You're too big of a baby to stay by yourself."

"Please, I've got plenty of places to go."

"Ha, I hope you don't think that nigga you're so fixated with is going to let you move in with him," Stefan said. "You probably ain't even been to his house."

"He'd let me move in with him, if I asked him to."

"Bitch, please, that nigga probably got at least forty more of you who can do what you do just as good or better," Stefan said. "I'd be surprised if that nigga would let you camp out in his garage."

"You don't know shit about him, so keep his name out your mouth."

"And if I don't, what you gonna do?" Stefan teased. "Close it for me?"

"I wouldn't waste my time putting my hands on no shit like you."

Stefan laughed. "That must mean you ain't ready to take the ass-whipping that's gonna follow."

"I ain't thinking about your ass," Simone said. "You're mad 'cause you're only allowed over Eugene's house once a week."

"That's the hater in you talking."

"If that's what you want to believe," Simone said. "The truth hurts, doesn't it?"

"I don't know about all that," Stefan said. "What I do know is if I needed a place to stay, Eugene would put me up. I wouldn't be standing on his porch with my bags in my hand, looking like a damn fool and praying it's the right address 'cause I looked it up on the Internet."

"You don't know shit and I'm not staying with him," Simone said. "I'm going to stay with my daddy, so you can shut the fuck up."

"Yo' daddy? I forgot you even had a daddy," Stefan said. "How are you going to find him? Are you going to run a people search on him, too?"

"Unlike you, I know where my daddy lives," Simone said.

Stefan clapped his hands. "Well, I'll be damned. Wonders never cease."

"Too bad you can't say the same about your dad."

"Please, your dad doesn't want anything to do with your ass," Stefan said. "If he ain't been around in this long, what the fuck makes you think he wants to be bothered with your ass now?"

"At least my daddy did send me money and stuff for my birthday," Simone said gloatingly. "What did yours send you? Hold on, I can answer that one myself; nothing. Guess he hasn't gotten over you peering at him through the peephole, huh?"

Stefan jumped up and shoved Simone's head with his index finger. "Keep listening to that doped-out bitch you call Mama. She wasn't here for me to whip her ass when she said that shit but you are. You must've forgotten about that ass-whipping I gave her up in here. I guess you're ready for yours."

Simone grabbed the ashtray off of the table and swung it at Stefan's head. Stefan blocked the ashtray with his forearm, then fastened his hands around Simone's neck and choked her. Simone slid on the plate she'd slapped on the floor and fell backward onto the sofa. Stefan stood over Simone gritting his teeth, tightening his grip on her neck. Simone gathered up all of the saliva she could and spat into Stefan's face. Stefan removed his hands from Simone's neck and wiped the spit off of his face. Simone kicked Stefan in his stomach. Stefan stumbled backward and Simone sat on the sofa, trying to catch her breath.

"Oh, we like to spit," Stefan said. "Well, I can do better than that."

Stefan grabbed the trashcan Simone had been vomiting in all night and threw its contents on her.

"Arrrgh!" Simone screamed, hopping to her feet and charging Stefan.

Stefan grabbed Simone's arms and pinned her against the wall. "Calm down, Simone; don't make me hurt you."

Simone kicked and screamed obscenities at Stefan until she became exhausted and slid down to the floor. She didn't bother to try and get up. She sat there and cried.

Stefan reached under the sofa and pulled out a pack of cigarettes and a lighter. He lit a cigarette and plopped down on the sofa. "Simone, what happened last night was fucked up but I didn't want that shit to go down like that; Chris did. I'm not gonna spend my life walking around feeling like a jerk because of it and neither should you."

Simone looked up at Stefan and wiped her eyes. "But..."

"But what?" Stefan asked. "Grow up and let it go. You can start by taking a shower."

Simone looked down at the blood, vomit, and sweat that covered her body. She must've been out of her mind. Any sane person would've been anxious to take a shower. She got up from the floor and headed upstairs.

"I wonder what Paris has been up to," Stefan said.

"When's the last time you heard from him?"

"That day we went with him over to Michael's house," Stefan answered. "You trying to go over there and see him?"

"Sure, why not."

Stefan puffed on his cigarette. "Good, 'cause being in this house is driving our asses crazy."

❧[16]❧

Simone sighed as they pulled up at Paris's house. It had begun to rain. She didn't have an umbrella and didn't want the rain to mess up her hair. She wished that she were somewhere cuddled up with Wayne instead of out in the rain. She would rather sweat the curls out of her hair pleasing him than let the rain wash them out. "How do you know Paris is here?"

"He never goes anywhere," Stefan said. "If I had to bet my life on it, I'd say he was still in the bed sleep."

"What! It's damn near eight o'clock."

"What does that mean?" Stefan asked. "I've known Paris to stay in the bed from one day clean into the next."

Simone giggled. "Now, that's lazy."

"Who are you telling?" Stefan said.

"I wonder if Michael ever confronted Paris about what happened to his place."

Stefan shrugged. "Who knows; ask him when we get in there."

Paris opened the door and stood in the doorway, wearing a scarf around his head, a wife beater, and a pair of blue spandex capris.

Stefan leaned against the rail on the porch and grabbed his chest. "Oh Lord, somebody call the police."

"What's wrong?" Paris and Simone asked in unison.

"Somebody done robbed Paris!" Stefan shouted.

Simone flipped her cell phone open to call the police.

"What are you talking about?" Paris asked. "Ain't nobody robbed me."

"Then what the fuck happened to yo' ass and titties?" Stefan asked. "Don't tell me you've worn down all your breast and butt pads already."

Simone squealed to the top of her lungs with laughter.

"Oh, go to hell!" Paris snapped as he turned around and walked back into the house.

Paris took a seat on the sofa and Simone and Stefan sat on the loveseat across from him.

"What it is, hoes? Long time, no see; what's been going on?" Paris asked.

"Ain't nothing; the same old shit," Stefan replied.

"I was starting to wonder if I'd ever see y'all asses again," Paris said. "Seems like ever since y'all got them little jobs at the bank, don't nobody hear from y'all."

"How you know we were working at the bank?" Stefan asked.

"Crystal told me that he seen y'all one day when he was up there waiting for one of his clients to get some money," Paris answered.

"Well, you know our number and where to find us," Simone said. "It doesn't look like your fingers or feet are broken to me. Why you ain't call or come over?"

"I went over there one day when I was coming from the pizza parlor but your car wasn't outside," Paris said. "I even sat on the porch and ate my pizza while I waited for y'all to come home but y'all never showed up. And after I finished eating, I was out."

"What has Crystal been up to?" Stefan asked.

"I don't even see his ass no more," Paris said. "He's been running around getting high with some nigga."

"What you mean, getting high?" Simone asked.

"Smoking crack," Paris said.

"What!" Simone exclaimed. "Get the fuck out of here!"

"Hell yeah, we all fuck with a little powder every now and then," Paris said. "But this nigga done bit the bullet and him and his man is straight hitting the pipe."

"Who is his man?" Stefan asked.

Paris grinned. "Anthony, you know the one that used to live down the street from y'all."

"You're shitting me," Simone said. "I didn't know he was like that."

"Girl, please," Paris said. "That thing tried to holler at me about a year ago. They say he's bi or something and I don't swing that route. I'm gonna need a nigga to make up his mind if he wants to be with me."

"I hear that," Stefan said in agreement.

"I wonder what his mama had to say about it," Simone said. "She's supposed to be in the church and everything."

"She probably knew all along," Stefan said. "See, that's what the problem was back in the day; his peeps knew that nigga wanted me," Stefan said, nudging Simone.

"Oh yeah, did Michael ever confront you about what happened to his apartment?" Simone asked.

Paris nodded. "Yeah, you mean to tell me, we haven't talk since then?"

Stefan and Simone shook their heads.

"Well, let me tell you about that," Paris said.

Simone squirmed around on the loveseat, anxious to hear what Paris had to say.

"Don't you know he had the nerve to bring the police around here," Paris said.

"You're lying," Simone said.

"Shit, no I ain't," Paris said. "And had the nerve to tell them I be stalking him."

"No, he didn't," Simone said.

"Oh yes, he did," Paris replied. "And get this, he told them that he met me through a friend of his and ain't know I was gay until I tried to come on to him and he put me in my place right then and there and cut ties with me and ever since then, I had been stalking him."

"Ol' boy was straight shitting," Stefan said.

"Humph, wasn't he," Paris replied. "I started to go to the bathroom and toss his ass a roll of toilet paper."

"Well, what did you say, Paris?" Simone asked. "'Cause I know you ain't let that shit go down like that."

"I told them if that muthafucka put me in my place, it must've been in his bed and it's hard to stalk somebody if they lying on top of you every night," Paris said.

Simone laughed and stomped her feet on the floor with excitement.

"I know he ain't like that shit," Stefan said.

"You know he didn't; he went off," Paris said. "He even tried to attack me. I could've sworn he was gonna knock the shit out me, but them officers grabbed him and threw his ass on the ground just in time."

"I know you were happy they held that nigga down," Simone teased.

"Hell yeah, I had just gotten my micro-braids touched up. I wasn't trying to fuck with him," Paris said.

"Did you and Jewel ever make back up?" Simone asked.

"Hell naw," Paris said. "Don't be asking me no stupid shit like that."

"You ain't lying; you'd be a damn fool to kick it with him again," Stefan said.

"I know, right," Paris agreed. "He called here though."

"And what did he have to say?" Stefan asked.

"He was talking all this shit about how Michael was his man now and how he was gonna fuck me up for what I did to his place," Paris said.

"What did you say?" Simone asked.

"I told him to bring that shit; he knows where I live," Paris said. "You know he wasn't trying to do that, so he tried to play it off, talking 'bout I was lucky he had somewhere to go 'cause if he didn't, he'd be over here whipping my ass."

"Damn, he was talking shit, wasn't he," Simone said.

"Hell yeah," Stefan agreed. "That nigga must be eating his damn Wheaties."

"King Vitamins or something," Simone added. "That muthafucka done got bold."

"I ain't thinking about his ass," Paris said. "He's still the same scared-ass nigga."

"Yeah, I think so, too," Simone said.

"Naw, ain't nothing changed," Stefan said. "The nigga always been telephone hard; he'll talk all types of shit on the phone. Tell you he'll fuck you up, talk about yo' mama, and some more shit."

"But when it's time to go to blows, his ass can't follow through," Paris added.

"Hell yeah, that nigga be hiding behind trees, rolling underneath cars, and some more shit," Stefan said.

Paris nodded. "Exactly, just like he was that day we went to fuck Danny up for Simone. His ass straight disappeared. Stefan ain't told you about that, Simone?"

Simone shook her head. "Naw."

"The whole time we was out that joint rumbling, Jewel was under Danny's car on some stop, drop, and roll shit," Stefan said.

"Why y'all ain't call him out on it?" Simone asked.

"I was too busy laughing at his ass," Paris answered.

"I was too ashamed to say anything," Stefan answered.

"Well, he got to know y'all bound to cross paths sooner or later," Simone said.

"All I got to say is he better hope we don't," Paris said. "'Cause I'll kill his ass."

"Why bother when you can get Stefan to do it for you?" Simone said.

Stefan cut his eyes at Simone and decided not to respond

to her comment. "Speaking of Danny, Simone found her another one."

"Another what?" Paris asked.

"Jock," Stefan said.

"Go head on, not another high school basketball player," Paris said. "Don't you think you a little too old for that?"

"Naw," Simone said.

"I heard that," Paris replied. "Take it any way you can get it; I ain't mad at you."

Stefan looked at Simone and chuckled.

"That's not what I meant," Simone said. "He's not in high school, he's—"

"Thirty-seven and a professional boxer," Stefan announced.

"Go 'head; what's his name?" Paris asked.

"Wayne," Simone answered.

"You can't be talking about what's his name...Wayne Jasper," Paris said.

Simone nodded. "That's him."

"You're lying," Paris said.

"Naw, she ain't; she met him at the detail shop," Stefan replied.

"I'll tell you one thing, that nigga was always taking a beating in the ring," Paris said.

"Wasn't he?" Stefan agreed.

"How y'all know?" Simone asked.

"'Cause we've seen his fights," Paris said.

"You're lying," Simone said.

"No, I ain't," Paris said. "How the hell you think he got them dimples?"

"Hell yeah, a nigga drilled them joints in," Stefan joked.

"Naw, for real, he is gorgeous," Paris said. "I'd love to get my hands on him. Shit, I'll drink his bath water. Can you get me a cup?"

Stefan laughed. "Now, that's nasty."

"Hell naw, I ain't bringing you a cup of his bath water," Simone said. "And you don't have to worry about getting your hands on him 'cause he's mine."

"Aren't we possessive," Paris said.

"Not to mention defensive," Stefan added.

"I'm simply claiming what's mine," Simone said.

"I heard that, but make sure he's yours before you start making claims to him," Paris said. "You don't want to end up looking like a damn fool."

Simone sucked her teeth. "Whatever."

"There's no need to get mad," Paris said. "I'm merely running it past you. I remember how heartbroken you were over Danny."

"Yeah, she was going through it," Stefan said.

"I know," Paris said. "I don't want to see her go through that again. It took her months to get over that shit."

"Months? Try damn near a year," Stefan said. "She dropped out of school behind that shit."

"Whatever; I ain't trying to hear that shit," Simone snapped.

"Okay, I'm just saying; you've got to watch them jocks," Paris said. "They usually have plenty of women."

"And STDs," Stefan added.

"Well, the only thing Wayne has is me," Simone said.

Stefan and Paris looked at each other and rolled their eyes.

"Don't hate," Simone said.

Stefan felt his cell phone vibrating on his side. It was Eugene. He quickly flipped his phone open to answer it. "Hey, boo," Stefan sang into the phone.

Paris looked over at Simone. "We both know who that is."

Stefan threw his finger in the air to silence Paris and went on with his conversation. "Baby, I ain't doing nothing but sitting here talking to Simone and Paris. Okay; that's what's up. See you in a little while."

Stefan flipped his phone closed and stood there with a huge grin on his face.

"Where you going?" Simone asked.

"To see my man," Stefan answered.

"How you getting there?" Simone asked.

"Oh, somebody's shitting," Paris joked.

"I'll walk if I have to," Stefan said.

"You sound a little desperate to me, but I'll take you," Simone said. "You lucky I don't want to see you walk in the rain."

Simone and Stefan made their way to the door.

"Awright, Paris, see you later," Stefan said, unlocking the door.

"What you doing for the rest of the night, Simone?" Paris queried.

"After I drop Stefan off to his man, I'm going to see what's up with mine," Simone said.

"I heard that," Paris said. "Do me a favor and ask him do he have a friend I can get with."

"You haven't found a new man yet?" Simone asked.

"Girl, please; when you're as fine as me, you can replace a man immediately," Paris said, snapping his fingers.

"You're a mess," Stefan said as he and Simone made their way out of the door.

[17]

Simone lay on Wayne's chest twisting the coarse brown hair that hung from his chin as she drifted off to sleep.

"Damn, ma, you're not falling asleep on me, are you?"

"My bad; I'm a little tired," Simone said. "You wouldn't believe all the shit I've been through this week."

"Oh, is that right?"

"Yeah, but I'll tell you one thing; being with you has made me feel a hell of a lot better."

Wayne smiled. "I'm glad that I could do that for you."

Wayne lifted Simone's head up and softly kissed her lips. "Maybe you can help me with something."

"What might that be?"

"The little surprise that's going to be here in a minute."

"Surprise? What are you talking about?"

"Just a little something special I had planned for us tonight."

Simone laid her head back down on Wayne's chest, pondering what the little something special he spoke of might be. *Maybe it's flowers. I hope not. Maybe it's a mink. Naw, it's probably some type of jewelry. Maybe I'll give Paris his stuff back after all.*

There was a knock on the door. Wayne slid from underneath Simone, put on his boxers, and went to answer the door. Simone got out of bed, slid on her skirt and top, and followed Wayne to the door. Wayne opened the door and a tall, thin, leggy, mocha-colored woman, wearing a sultry, low-cut red dress, walked in and closed the door behind her. Simone stood there with her arms folded across her chest, watching as Wayne kissed the woman. Wayne placed his arm around his visitor's waist.

"What is this supposed to be?" Simone asked.

"Surprise," Wayne said as he swatted his visitor's backside. "Simone, this is Michelle. She's going to be joining us tonight." Wayne kissed Michelle on her neck. "Damn, Simone. Her skin is almost as soft as yours. Come see; I think a kiss would be the perfect way for you two to get acquainted."

Simone's eyes flooded with tears and she immediately charged Wayne and Michelle, not yet knowing whom she planned to take her anger out on. Michelle grabbed onto Wayne. Simone grabbed a handful of Michelle's long brown hair and snatched her off of Wayne. Simone clawed Michelle's face, and then drew her hand back to smack Michelle.

"Hold on!" Wayne yelled as he pulled Simone off Michelle and pinned her against the wall. "What the fuck is wrong with you?"

"How you gonna bring this bitch up in here like this? Huh?" Simone screamed. "I thought—"

"You thought what?" Wayne shouted, spraying Simone with saliva.

"Just get the fuck out of my face!" Simone screamed, kneeing Wayne in his groin.

"Bitch!" Wayne snapped, squeezing Simone's jaw and slamming her head into the wall. "Don't do that shit again. Fuck is you thinking 'bout."

"Let the fuck go of me!" Simone screamed.

"I swear," Wayne said, squeezing Simone's jaw tighter. "You lucky I ain't one of those grimy-ass niggas off the street 'cause I'd break your fucking face."

"Please, you don't have it in you," Simone said.

"You just like every other hoe. Dumb; don't know shit. You lucky I gave your ass the time of day." Wayne turned around and looked at Michelle. "Look at her. That's what kind of woman I'm used to having on my arm; models and actresses. Not a loose-pussy, flabby-ass tramp that works at a bank."

Wayne looked at Michelle and nodded toward the door. Michelle walked over and swung the door open.

"Now get the fuck out!" Wayne snapped.

Wayne pushed Simone out of the room and slammed the heel of her foot in the door. Simone banged on the door. She wanted to retaliate but, at that point, she was more concerned about retrieving her undergarments and shoes. She didn't want to be subjected to the stares and whispers of everybody in the lobby who would wonder why the hell a woman was fleeing the hotel without her shoes.

"Give me my shit, Wayne!" Simone yelled.

"Fuck you! I ain't giving you shit!" Wayne shouted.

Michelle's high-pitched giggles echoed throughout the hallway. "Where the hell did you get her from? That bitch is crazy."

"Oh, you ain't seen shit yet! Trust me on that!" Simone yelled.

A hotel attendant walked by, staring at Simone and wondering what all of the commotion was about.

Simone looked the hotel attendant up and down as she made her way to the elevator. "What the fuck are you looking at? Don't you have a room to clean or something?"

Simone peeked out of the elevator before stepping out into the lobby. Relieved that the lobby was fairly empty and she only had to endure a few humiliating stares, she pushed her way through the exit and walked out into the rain.

The rain soaked into her clothes in a matter of seconds. Her skirt became heavy and the concrete pinched the bottom of her feet as she made her way across the parking lot.

Simone rummaged through her trunk, grabbed her crowbar, and approached Wayne's car, envisioning the damage she would cause. *I'm gonna give this nigga an automatic air conditioner*, she thought as she cocked back the crowbar, ready to strike the windshield. Simone paused. *He's right*, she thought. *He's not one of these niggas on the street.*

There was no doubt he would be peeved when he walked

outside and saw the broken glass scattered across the pavement, looked up, and realized that it came from his car, but it wasn't anything he couldn't rectify. Hell, he could buy a new car if he wanted to. She could see him sitting around with his friends after he'd managed to cool down, telling them how he had this bitch so gone that when he cut her off, she went ballistic and busted up his car. That wasn't good enough for her. She needed to see Wayne suffer. She had something better in mind.

Stefan lay under the covers cuddled up with Eugene. *Maybe things will work out between us after all*, Stefan thought. Eugene had made love to him so passionately, Stefan regretted ever thinking that Eugene was only using him for his money. Maybe Eugene had been under a lot of stress. *I can't believe I was so insensitive*, Stefan thought. It had to be hard for Eugene to come home from prison and start over. He was proud of how quickly Eugene had found a job. *Eugene's just been tired from all the hours he's put in at work; that's all*, Stefan told himself.

Eugene got out of bed to take a shower. "You coming?"

"Naw," Stefan answered. "I'm going to lie here a while longer."

"Oh, I have something I want you to take a look at." Eugene reached in his dresser drawer, pulled out a piece of paper, and handed it to Stefan.

Stefan looked down at the piece of paper. "What the fuck are you doing with an eviction notice?"

"I should be asking you that," Eugene said. "You're the one who's supposed to be paying the rent."

"Is this why you called me over here?" Stefan asked. "I ain't talk to you since who knows when and you call me over here, fuck me, and hand me an eviction notice."

"But why you ain't been paying it though?"

"'Cause you got a job."

"But I'm saying though, I don't get enough to do what I want to do for myself and pay the rent."

"Oh, so you use your money for partying and impressing bitches, but it's my job to keep a roof over your head?"

Eugene gritted his teeth. "I don't mess with no bitches."

"Please, you're fucking somebody other than me."

"She ain't no bitch."

"Oh, now the truth comes out," Stefan said. "Who is she? What's her name?"

"That's not important."

"You're right," Stefan said. "But why can't she pay the rent?"

Eugene shrugged. "'Cause."

"'Cause what, muthafucka? I'm good enough to pay your bills and help you get on your feet but when it's time for you to go fuck something, I ain't enough; you need to weigh your options," Stefan said as he got out of bed and started to get dressed.

"It's not like that."

"Well, I just hope she's healthy and you ain't give her nothing."

"What's that supposed to mean?"

Stefan grabbed his purse off of the table and made his way out the door. "What it means is fuck you, do what you want. I'll have the last laugh."

"If you're gonna carry it like that, then you don't have to worry about me no more," Eugene said. "Just like I found you, I'll find someone else that's willing to do for me; it's all good."

Stefan wanted to walk back in the house and beat the hell out of Eugene but he kept walking. He refused to let Eugene see the tears rolling down his cheeks.

❧[18]❧

Simone lay across the bed in her robe watching the news, eating a slice of the homemade coconut cake that Stefan had made to help comfort her after her misfortune.

Stefan walked in the room and handed Simone her prescription. "Did they say anything about Wayne yet?"

"Naw, not yet."

"Don't worry; it'll be on there," Stefan said reassuringly. "That reporter I tipped off seemed just a little too interested not to pursue it."

"I hope so," Simone whined.

"I can't wait to see them expose his ass," Stefan said. "It's gonna take him a long time to redeem himself after this."

That's what Simone was hoping for. If Wayne wasn't thrashed by the media, thrown in jail, tormented, and frowned upon, she would never be able to live down what she had put herself through.

Simone paused and thought of what she had done after she'd left the hotel. After leaving the hotel she'd driven down the street to the gas station, bought a lighter, a pack of cigarettes, and a forty-ounce bottle of beer. She'd parked her car in a nearby alley, lit five cigarettes one by one and held her breath so she wouldn't scream as she placed them on her clitoris and labia. Afterward, she'd screwed the top off the forty-ounce and drenched herself with beer. Thirty minutes later, she'd walked into the ER, limped over to the triage area, and told the lady behind the desk that she had been raped. She was immediately escorted to the back where she'd stood naked under a florescent light, crying like a baby. She didn't know whether her tears were from humiliation or the joy she felt as she thought about how Wayne's comfortable life was about to turn into a living hell. As far as she was concerned she had been raped and no one knew otherwise, except for Wayne and Michelle and their words would carry very little weight. She had two orifices full of Wayne's semen and plenty of burns to go along with it. Not to mention the panties and shoes she was forced to leave behind in his room. As far as she was concerned, it was her little secret. The only people on earth who knew the truth were the three of them and she was taking it to the grave with her.

"In local news, former middleweight champion…," the reporter announced, standing in front of the hotel where the incident had taken place.

"Here it goes," Stefan said, grabbing the remote and turning the volume up on the TV.

A feeling of dizziness came upon Simone as the reporter continued to relate her story.

"…was arrested here at the Hyatt hotel along with his significant other for the assault and rape of a twenty-two-year-old female." Simone sat there in awe that her plan was actually coming to fruition. "Sources say that after refusing to participate in sexual activities with the two, she was held against her will, raped, and repeatedly burned."

Simone snatched the remote from Stefan and cut off the TV.

"Damn, I don't even want to hear any more."

Stefan hugged Simone, attempting to console her. "It's going to be awright, I promise."

Tears began to stream from Simone's eyes. "I can't believe this shit. I swear shit like this only happens to me."

Stefan was saddened by Simone's reaction and his inability to comfort her. He pulled the sheets back from the bed and patted his hand on the mattress. "Come on, Simone; lay down and take a nap. Everything will be awright. It hurts but you need to give yourself time to get over this."

Simone slid under the covers and pulled them over her head and continued crying. She wanted badly to confide in Stefan, to tell him the truth about what had happened. She wasn't sure whether she could do so without being told how stupid she was, without being told that she'd made a huge mistake, without being taunted by him about what really happened for the rest of her life.

Stefan flicked off the light on his way out the room.

"Where are you going?"

"To pack my stuff."

"For what?"

"My trip's tomorrow, remember. Southern Decadence; I told you a little while back."

Simone remained quiet as Stefan made his way out of the room. She couldn't help but think about Wayne, his smile, how good he had made her feel up until that point. The thought of him lying with Michelle and enjoying her body made Simone's blood boil but she assured herself that they were both in jail regretting their night together.

Stefan packed his suitcase. He was feeling guilty for not canceling his trip and leaving Simone alone to mope. He reflected back on the argument they'd had the day before. He considered that Simone may have been right. Maybe he did ruin her life. She had vested him more influence over her life than she realized and he had taken advantage of it, not wanting to be in his trade without company, not wanting the only family he had left to leave him behind. Simone had become helpless. She wasn't capable of governing her life.

Stefan was fearful of what would happen to her when he was no longer around to look out for her. She would fall victim to degenerates and victimizers. They would prey on her like vultures until there was nothing left of her. He couldn't let that happen. He couldn't leave Simone alone to suffer for any reason. Not even death. How would he be able to rest in peace if he did? He took the necessary steps to make sure that he didn't leave Simone in the world to suffer after he was gone. She might not go with him but she wouldn't be far behind him.

Stefan stopped packing his suitcase to answer the phone. "Hello," Stefan said.

"You still going?" Paris blurted out.

"Damn, not hi, how you doing, what you doing, kiss my ass, nothing; just are you still going."

"Naw, I asked 'cause I talked to Crystal and he said he ain't going."

"What!" Stefan exclaimed.

"Yeah, that's what he said; guess he can't pull himself from under that nigga he be fucking with."

Stefan shook his head. "I can't believe this."

"You can't believe it," Paris said. "I paid for his reservations; how you think I feel?"

"That's fucked up."

"I know, right," Paris said. "Do you think Simone might want to go? I'd hate for my money to go to waste."

Stefan plopped down on his bed and took a deep breath. "I don't know. She's going through it right now."

"What you mean?"

"You haven't seen the news?"

"Hell naw; you know I don't watch that shit," Paris said. "Just tell me what's going on."

"You know she went to see ol' boy the other night, right," Stefan said. "Well, when she got there, he tried to get her to have a threesome with him and this other chick. When she said no and tried to leave, they held her down and raped her."

"What!" Paris exclaimed.

"You heard me," Stefan said. "They held her down, burnt her with cigarettes, and some more shit."

"Is she okay?"

"Yeah, for the most part," Stefan said. "She's real hurt behind it though. You know, going through the motions."

"Well, this might be a good opportunity for her to get out and get her mind off things."

"True, I'll check and see how she feels about it."

"Well, hurry up," Paris said. "Ain't like she's got a lot of time to decide."

"Awright, I'll hit you back in a minute."

Stefan pulled his extra luggage bag out of the closet and dragged it toward Simone's room. *I guess I better get her shit packed.*

▸[19]◂

S imone had been in high spirits ever since she stepped off the plane into New Orleans. She was embarrassed about how nervous she was when Stefan announced that she would be accompanying him on his trip.

She was taken in by the rainbow colors that lined the street and the banners hanging in front of the clubs and restaurants with "Welcome to SDGMs XXXVII" displayed on them. She started to feel a bit over, as well as under dressed, as she took notice of those around her. People were wearing everything from cabarets to cow customs with udders dangling from their crotches. Stefan wore a blue headdress and a black cabaret with silver ostrich feathers. Paris wore a short zebra-print, halter-style dress and black glitter covered the exposed parts of his body. Simone felt out of place, wearing a skirt and a tank top.

She was amazed at all the different types of men that she saw displaying their gay pride. Big, brawny men wearing tall wigs and leather jumpsuits; tall, slinky men wearing short, sheer dresses and long, crisscross, glittery eyelashes; and hard-body men she would have sworn were straight if she hadn't seen them parading around in bright-colored Speedos, carrying huge, penis-shaped balloons.

Simone had never known of an event like Southern Decadence, where people could walk around barely dressed to relieve themselves of the sauna-like heat, where cocktails were served and drunk on the street in twenty-four-ounce cups, where people could engage in sexual acts and seemingly go unnoticed, where those who weren't heterosexuals could be themselves without being ridiculed.

It was after twelve o'clock when Simone, Stefan, and Paris decided to venture into the Bourbon Pub to join the party and dance events. Despite how crowded it was, the three managed to find seats at the bar. They ordered their drinks and directed their attention to the festivities. Simone was exhausted. Her feet hurt from all the walking they had done and she was tipsy from all the drinks she had consumed. Just as she was about to get out of her seat and tell Stefan and Paris that she was going back to the hotel to call it a night, a woman stood in front of her, reaching out her hand.

"Hey, I'm Jana."

Simone looked the woman up and down, before shaking her hand. "Hi."

"And your name is?" Jana asked.

Simone sighed. "Mona."

"Oh, that's cute."

Jana stood there and continued to talk, hoping Simone would warm up to her.

Paris tapped Stefan on his shoulder and nodded toward Simone. "Look, Simone made a friend already."

The two giggled, catching Jana's attention.

"Hi, how are you doing?" Stefan asked.

"Are you three together?" Jana asked.

"Um hmm," Simone muttered.

"Oh okay; my name's Jana."

Stefan and Paris both reached out to shake Jana's hand.

"I'm Stefan."

"And I'm Paris."

"Is this y'all first time here?" Jana asked.

Stefan nodded. "Yeah."

"I thought y'all look new," Jana said. "I've been coming here for a few years, so I recognize a newcomer when I see one."

"Yeah, we're first-timers," Paris said sarcastically.

"Well, I'll tell you what; I'm here with a couple of friends that I'm sure would like to meet you," Jana said. "We can all get together the next five days and we can show y'all around."

"Okay, that's what's up," Stefan said.

"Where are they?" Paris asked.

Jana looked puzzled. "Excuse me?"

"Your friends; where are they?" Paris asked.

Jana pointed toward the back of the club. "They're over there; I'll go get them."

Jana eased her way through the crowd to where her friends sat.

"Damn, that was strange," Simone said. "I've never met a woman that friendly."

"Yeah, I bet," Paris joked.

Stefan laughed. "Don't worry; she seems like good people."

Jana came back over to the bar with her two friends. "These are my friends, Jamal and Kenneth. Jamal, Kenneth, this is Stefan, Paris, and Simone."

Stefan immediately took a liking to Jamal. Jamal was about six feet tall, with dark brown skin and a muscular frame. He was definitely Stefan's type. "That one's mine," Stefan whispered to Paris.

"That's fine with me," Paris said. "Shit, I'll take either one."

Jana turned around to Jamal and Kenneth. "I told them they could chill with us for the next five days."

"That's if you two don't mind," Paris said, eyeing Kenneth, already making plans to run his tongue over Kenneth's chocolate-colored body.

Kenneth smiled, revealing his gold fronts. "Naw, I don't mind; I'd love to."

"Same here," Jamal said, rubbing his hands together as he eyed Stefan.

"Good," Jana said. "Then we'll meet back here at one o'clock this afternoon."

"Sounds good," Stefan said. "We'll see you then."

◈

Simone walked out of the bathroom, dressed in a sheer skimpy black dress and a headdress with fuchsia, black, and silver ostrich feathers. Her headdress reflected the colors of that year's decadence celebration.

Simone walked over to Jana and stood in front of her. "You like?"

"Yes, you look stunning."

Simone explained to Jana how out of place she felt in her everyday clothing while everyone else flaunted about the French Quarter in their showy costumes. So Jana decided to take Simone to the Hit Parade to pick up some suitable clothing for the event; her treat.

Simone had only known Jana for a few hours and Jana was going out of her way to make her happy, taking her to buy suitable clothing so she wouldn't feel uncomfortable, constantly saying things to flatter her. It wasn't anything Simone couldn't do for herself. She had money and when she looked in the mirror every day, she realized that she was pretty but it was something no one had ever done for her; something that made her feel special as if she was worthy of love and consideration.

Simone looked in the mirror, fascinated by her appearance.

Jana gazed at Simone's reflection in the mirror, thinking about how young she looked, even though she wore a revealing dress and a dark-colored headdress. "You know what you need," Jana said, pulling a makeup case out of her purse. "You need some of this."

Simone frowned. "I don't know about all that."

"Why not?" Jana asked.

"I don't know," Simone said. "It might make me look funny."

Jana laughed. "No, it won't. Makeup looks good on everybody."

"I wouldn't know," Simone said. "I've never used any."

"You've never used makeup!" Jana exclaimed. "Are you serious?"

Simone nodded.

"It'll look great on you," Jana said. "We don't have to use anything heavy. Maybe a little foundation, some eyeshadow, mascara, some lipstick to bring out that mold on your lip."

Simone looked at Jana doubtfully. "I don't know. I don't wanna be walking around here looking like a damn clown."

Jana giggled and slid the chair from underneath the desk and sat it in front of the mirror. She then placed her hands on Simone's shoulders, motioning for her to sit down. "Trust me; you'll look gorgeous."

Stefan and Paris sat in the back of Club Oz waiting for Jamal and Kenneth to come back with their drinks.

"I'm telling you, they've got some. When we met up with them this morning, that nigga, Kenneth, still had some stuck in his nostrils," Paris said. "I swear to God."

Stefan laughed. "Awright, we'll see."

"But how?" Paris asked. "Ain't like they gonna offer it up."

"Don't worry; I'll mention it," Stefan said.

Simone walked over to the table and sat down. "Hey, y'all; what y'all been up to?"

"Well, look at you," Stefan said.

"You like?" Simone asked. "Jana bought it for me and she did my makeup, too."

"Yeah, you look exactly like a little drag queen Barbie doll," Paris joked.

"Well, I'll take that as a compliment," Simone said.

"That's how you better take it," said a guy wearing a high-blonde wig and a yellow dress with fringes, eaves-dropping on their conversation from a table nearby.

The three laughed and continued with their conversation.

"What y'all been doing?" Simone asked.

"Not too much," Stefan answered. "Just getting to know the area and having a little fun; that's all."

"Well, I hope y'all ain't having too much fun without stopping by the AIDS taskforce booth to pick up some condoms," Simone said.

"Yeah, make sure you stop and pick up some dental dams," Paris joked.

"Dental dams; why would I need dental dams?" Simone asked.

Stefan looked up and saw Jana heading to the table along with Jamal and Kenneth, and decided to put an end to their conversation. "Don't pay Paris ass no mind; he doesn't know what the hell he's talking about."

Jana placed Simone's glass in front of her and sat down. "What are you three talking about?"

"Oh, nothing; just trying to educate Simone," Paris said.

"If he was, he did a poor job of it, 'cause I still don't know what the hell he's talking about," Simone said.

"Well, I'll tell you what," Paris said. "I'll holla at you in a couple of days and see if you're still singing the same tune."

"Shhh…the impersonations are about to start," Jana said.

Simone looked at Paris and rolled her eyes and Paris sipped his drink, giggling to himself about how naïve Simone was not to consider that Jana might have more than a friendly interest in her.

Stefan rested his head in his hand while he sipped his fifth drink. He noticed Simone and Paris seemed equally as bored. "What else is up for tonight?"

"Yeah, 'cause this shit is not what's up," Paris said.

"Don't tell me y'all are bored already," Kenneth said.

"Out our damn minds," Simone answered.

"No problem; we could do something else," Jana said.

"They have nude swimming at the country club," Jamal said. "Y'all want to see what's up with that?"

"Naw, I'll pass," Simone answered.

"I'll tell you one thing; my nose is getting a little wet," Stefan said. "I sure would love to get my hands on some powder."

Jamal's eyes widened. "Excuse me?"

Stefan smiled. "You know yay, white."

"I prefer the term nose candy myself," Paris added.

Simone held her head down, embarrassed that Stefan had shared their recreational activity with their new acquaintances. She was sure they didn't share their interests and would frown down on them for engaging in it.

Jamal looked at Kenneth and Jana, and then grinned. "No problem; we can go back to my room and take care of that."

"You want to go, Simone?" Jana asked.

Simone nodded her head.

Paris gulped down the remainder of his drink and then led the way out of the club. "Who would have thought we had so much in common?"

◈

"Damn, I haven't sniffed anything this good in a couple years," Stefan said.

Simone sat back on the sofa across from Stefan, rubbing her fingers across her nose. "You ain't lying."

Stefan stretched out across Jamal's lap, moving his legs back and forth nervously. "I remember the first time I used this shit. I was thirteen, my grandma was in the middle of a card game and asked me to run upstairs and get her pocketbook. When I went in the kitchen, I saw the empty sandwich bag on the table beside her; it still had a little residue on it so I set her pocketbook in front of it and slid it off the table. As soon as I got out the kitchen, I ran upstairs to the bathroom, locked the door, and sat there on the toilet, sniffing the residue off the bag."

Jamal smirked. "Damn, you started early."

Stefan slapped him on his arm playfully. "When did you start?"

"To tell you the truth, I didn't really care for the shit 'til about two years ago," Jamal said. "It was my hustle and that was about it, until I met up with this big-time cat I was copping from. It seemed like every time I saw the nigga, he was sniffing the shit. One day, I went to holler at him and he was sitting at the table with a gang of other niggas, sniffing lines. I tried to conduct my business as fast as possible and be out but, for some reason, this nigga was on some friendly shit. He asked me to come sniff a few lines with him and his people. I ain't want to be like naw, 'cause I ain't want to offend the man, so I sat down at the table with them and snorted some of that shit. Man, I swear, when that shit went up my nose, I thought my head was about to explode."

"Amateur," Paris joked.

Kenneth laughed. "Oh shit."

Jamal giggled. "Yeah, that's what that nigga called me; an amateur. He thought it was the funniest shit."

"Did you still cop from him after that?" Stefan asked.

"Yeah, we tight as a bitch now," Jamal said. "Matter of fact, there the nigga go right there," Jamal said, pointing at Kenneth.

Jana rested her hand on Simone's thigh. "What about you, Simone? How did you start using?"

Simone pointed to Stefan. "That's who turned me on to it. He turned Paris on, too," Simone said, paying no attention to the hand Jana had rested on her thigh.

"He sure did," Paris said. "He called me over there one night so I could sit on the porch with him and sniffed residue off one of them damn sandwich bags."

Jana reached under the cushion on the sofa and pulled out a blunt stuffed with dro, grabbed a lighter from her purse, lit it, and then took a few puffs. "I tell you one thing though; I still love this shit right here."

Jana passed the blunt to Simone. Simone took a few deep pulls and handed it to Stefan.

Paris looked over at Simone, whose eyes were red and narrow. "Damn, Simone, that shit getting to you already. That must be some good shit; hurry up and pass it, Stefan."

Stefan passed the blunt to Jamal and he took a few puffs and handed it to Paris. Paris took a few puffs and then he and Kenneth took turns blowing each other guns. The blunt made its way back to Jana and she took a few puffs and leaned over and blew Simone a gun. Simone could feel her body become numb with every passing moment and before she knew it, she drifted off to sleep.

20

S imone didn't make it back to her hotel room until five o'clock that morning. She slept late into the evening.

She was awakened by a knock on the door. She couldn't help but think about how awful she felt. Her lips were parched and her stomach seemed to be trying to reject something she'd consumed the night before. Her back was hot and itchy where the sun had burned her through her dress. She reached for her cell phone to check the time. *Damn, it's seven o'clock*, she thought. She wondered had Stefan and Paris overslept, too. Simone grabbed her robe from the foot of the bed, slid it on, and made her way to the door. "Who is it?"

"It's Jana."

Simone cracked the door open.

Jana greeted her with a smile. "Can I come in?"

Simone nodded. "Sure."

Jana took a seat on the bed and Simone stretched out on the bed beside of her.

Jana looked Simone over, taking notice of the dark area underneath her eyes. "Are you feeling alright?"

Simone shook her head. "I feel like I'm about to pass out."

"You think you might have a hangover from yesterday?"

"Naw, I think it's all that time I spent outside in the heat," Simone answered. "Plus, I've only eaten once since I've been here."

"Damn, I wish you would've said something," Jana said. "We could've grabbed something to eat."

"We still can."

"There's a Ruth's Chris on Fulton Street; we can go there," Jana said.

"That's what's up." Simone reached for her suitcase and grabbed something to wear. "Just give me some time to shower and get dressed and we can be on our way."

Paris pulled the key card out of his pocket. "You sure they ain't here?"

"Yeah, I'm sure," Stefan said. "They're at the club, waiting for us."

"Well, call Jamal and make sure, 'cause the last thing I need is for them to come up in here whiles we stealing their shit," Paris said. "I'm too tired to be fighting for my life."

Stefan sighed. He flipped open his phone and called Jamal.

"Hello," Jamal answered.

"Where y'all at?"

"Down here at Body and Soul, waiting on y'all."

"Oh my bad; we got tied up," Stefan said. "Paris wanted to get a tattoo; we ain't think it was gonna take this long."

"So are y'all coming or what?"

"Yeah, we'll be there in about an hour," Stefan said. "Don't go anywhere."

Jamal sighed. "Yeah, awright."

Paris slid the key card in the door and swiped it. "You think he knows it's missing yet?"

Stefan shrugged. "I don't know. Even if he does, he probably figures he misplaced it."

Paris gazed around the room, wondering where to search first.

Stefan snapped his fingers to get Paris's attention. "You search the dresser and I'll search the closet."

Paris slammed the last dresser drawer. "Well, it damn sure ain't in the dresser. All the drawers are empty."

Stefan dragged two suitcases out of the closet. "Come over here and look through one of these suitcases."

Paris sat down on the bed beside Stefan. He grabbed the suitcase that had Jamal's name on it and searched through it. "Damn, there's nothing in here either. We probably came up in here for nothing. We probably helped them sniff the last of that shit last night."

Stefan continued looking through Kenneth's suitcase. "We won't know until we finish looking, will we?"

Stefan couldn't help but think about what Jamal had said about the big-time cat that he used to cop from; Kenneth. He refused to believe Jamal and Kenneth's trip was purely for pleasure. It was a business trip as well. He was damn near sure of it.

Stefan pulled two neatly coiled shirts that lay side by side out of Kenneth's suitcase and unraveled them. Stefan held up his findings so Paris could see; a twelve-ounce bag of powdered coke and a stack of hundred-dollar bills four-inches thick, held tightly together by rubber bands. "We came in here for nothing, huh?"

Paris couldn't believe his eyes. He reached for the money.

Stefan snatched it away. "Naw, this mines right here."

"What!" Paris exclaimed.

"I stole the key, I found the shit, and this was my idea in the first place, so this is my lick." Stefan handed Paris the bag of coke. "That's yours."

"Come the fuck on," Paris said. "How the hell am I gonna get that shit on the plane?"

Stefan caught sight of a large baby powder bottle on the dresser and gave it to Paris. "Pry the top off of this and put the powder in here."

Stefan zipped both suitcases up and put them back in the closet while Paris stared at the bottle of baby powder, unsure about Stefan's suggestion.

Stefan nodded toward the door. "Aight, let's dip."

Paris peeked out the door, making sure no one was in

the hallway as they made their way out. "I wonder if we could catch an earlier flight."

Stefan nodded. "Yeah, we need to leave as soon as possible 'cause when that nigga realizes his shit's gone, he's gonna be ready to kill something."

◈

Jana squeezed aloe vera gel in her hand, preparing to rub it on Simone's back. "Take your shirt off. I don't want to mess it up."

Simone took her shirt off and lay down on the bed. Jana rubbed lotion on her back. The coolness of the lotion soothed Simone and she cried out with pleasure. "That feels good."

Jana smiled. "Oh, you like that?"

Simone nodded.

Jana unhooked Simone's bra and kissed her on her neck. Simone opened her eyes, wondering whether Jana had actually kissed her. Jana slid her hands underneath Simone, clutching her breasts.

Simone sat up and hooked her bra. "What are you doing?"

"What I've wanted to do since I laid eyes on you."

"Jana, I'm not gay."

Jana frowned. "What?"

"I'm not a dyke! I'm not a lesbian! I'm not gay!" Simone exclaimed.

Jana slapped herself on her forehead. "I can't believe this shit. So, what was all this, me taking you out, treating and shit? You used me."

"I ain't do nothing," Simone said. "You were the one who approached me, who offered to do that shit for me. If I knew you were trying to fuck me, you wouldn't have gotten far enough to know my name."

"Well, if you aren't gay, what are you doing here?"

"Chillin', with my cousin; that's what. Stefan asked me to come; ain't like I've been anticipating this shit all year."

"And you're telling me that you didn't think, for one moment, that I was gay? That I might be trying to get with you?"

"Naw, I mean people do shit like that for me all the time," Simone said. "How was I supposed to know?"

Jana shook her head. "I can't believe this shit."

Simone grabbed her purse and pulled out her money. "Want me to give you your money back? How much did you spend? Maybe five or six hundred dollars?" Simone handed Jana the money.

Jana stared at the money in Simone's hand and shook her head. "Naw, it's all good."

Simone put the money back in her purse. *I know it is, 'cause you weren't getting shit.*

Jana leaned back on the headboard and sighed. "I just wish I would've known."

"Oh, so if you knew you couldn't have your way with me, you would've never said a word to me?"

"I probably wouldn't have," Jana said. "I came here to put some notches under my belt; not to make friends." Jana placed her hand on top of Simone's hand. "But I'm glad that I did."

Jana made her way for the door.

"Where are you going?" Simone asked.

"I better leave."

"Don't leave," Simone said. "We can chill and watch TV or something."

Jana agreed. She spent the night with Simone watching TV. When Simone fell asleep, Jana held her and took in her scent until she drifted off herself.

❖

The ringing of Simone's cell phone woke her up. She answered the phone, breathing deeply into it. "Hello."

"What you doing?" Stefan asked.

"I was sleep."

"Look, our plans have changed," Stefan said. "I thought our flight left at five o'clock this evening but, actually, it leaves at five o'clock this morning. So hurry up and get your stuff together and meet us downstairs."

"Okay, I have to wake up Jana."

"Jana?" Stefan looked at Paris and smiled. "Naw, don't wake her up."

Paris giggled. "Bet she knows what she needed the dental dam for."

"I can't just leave her here."

"She'll be awright," Stefan said. "Hurry up and get your shit together so we can leave."

Simone sighed. "Awight."

"And do me a favor," Stefan said.

"What?" Simone asked.

"Lock the bathroom door."

"For what?"

"Just do it and hurry up," Stefan said, before hanging up the phone.

Simone stuffed her belongings into her suitcase. She picked up the headdress Jana had bought for her and took a deep breath. She didn't want to go home. She wanted to stay in the carefree city of New Orleans, away from family and the bad relationships she had managed to develop. She didn't want to take a chance on not ever seeing Jana again. But she knew that everything had its proper place. Soon, she would be home in Virginia, and Jana would shortly after make her trip home. She had a good time, but nothing lasted forever and it was the good times that were often short-lived in her life. Simone kissed her hand and placed it against Jana's forehead. She then grabbed her suitcase and made her way out of the door.

◈

Kenneth shut the door to his hotel room. "Damn, man, I can't believe they left us hanging like that."

"Fuck them. It's their loss," Jamal said. "Now go grab us some of that powder so we can end the night right."

Kenneth opened his suitcase to retrieve his stash. "Fuck, my shit is gone, and my money."

Jamal got up from his seat and helped Kenneth search through his suitcase. "You sure you had it in here?"

"Yeah, I'm sure," Kenneth said, kicking his suitcase.

"Nobody could've stolen it," Jamal said.

"What the fuck you think happened to it?"

Jamal shrugged. "Who would've known you had the shit?"

"I'll tell you who, the two muthafuckas that stood us up a few hours ago."

Kenneth called Paris and didn't get an answer. He then called the hotel where Paris and Stefan were staying and was told that they had checked out. Next, he called Jana.

"Hello," Jana answered.

"Hey, is Simone there with you?"

"Yeah, I'm in her room."

"Ask her if she's heard from Stefan and Paris."

Jana scanned the room for Simone and noticed the bathroom door was locked. "I'll ask her when she comes out the bathroom."

"I'll ask her myself when I get there."

"Is something wrong?"

"I'll let you in on it when I get there," Kenneth said, and then hung up the phone.

Jana knocked on the bathroom door. "Kenneth says

he's on his way up here. I think he's looking for Stefan and Paris."

Jana waited for Simone's response but never received one.

Jana sat on the bed and waited for Kenneth and Jamal to arrive. She hoped nothing had gone wrong between Kenneth and Stefan or Paris. She didn't want Simone to get caught in the middle. She didn't know whether she could help Simone, if she did.

Jana heard Kenneth pounding on the door. She opened the door and let Kenneth and Jamal in.

"Where's she at?" Kenneth asked.

Jana pointed toward the bathroom. "In there."

Kenneth knocked on the bathroom door. "Simone, I know what y'all did. Just give me my shit back and everything will be awright."

Jana stood there, clueless. "What are you talking about?"

"Simone and her little friends stole all Kenneth's coke and his money," Jamal answered.

"I've been with Simone all day so she couldn't have had anything to do with it," Jana said.

"Why she ain't answering me?" Kenneth asked.

"I don't know; she's been in there for a while," Jana said. "Maybe something's wrong with her."

"Maybe she knows she fucked up," Kenneth said.

Kenneth kicked the door open.

Jana was shocked to see that the bathroom was empty. *Damn, I can't believe she played me like that*, Jana thought.

Kenneth pounded his hand against the wall. "They said they're from Virginia, right?"

Jana nodded her head.

"Yeah, I'm gonna find these muthafuckas," Kenneth said. "Ain't no way I'm gonna take a loss like that and let it ride. They're gonna pay out their asses for this shit."

imone stood back, looking at the outfit she had designed for Paris to wear to the beauty pageant. She was so in-spired by her trip that she'd stayed up all night working on it. She was sure Paris would be pleased. It was a jumpsuit that flared out a little below the knee and it was zebra print, like the dress he had worn their first day at the decadence celebration. It had a deep plunge in the front and a red tie across the back and Simone had taken a red belt from one of her outfits for Paris to wear along with it. She hoped Paris hadn't gained any weight since she had taken his measurements.

Stefan made his way up the stairs. He had just gotten back from the beauty salon and wanted to jump in his bed and take a nap.

Simone caught sight of Stefan out the corner of her eye and screamed. She paused to look at him for a moment, taking in his new hairdo.

"What the hell is wrong with you?" Stefan asked.

"My bad; I ain't know who the hell you were, walking through here like that." Simone ran her fingers through Stefan's long, layered auburn weave. "Why didn't you tell me you were taking your dreads out?"

"I hadn't planned on taking them out," Stefan said. "It was a last-minute thing. I was getting tired of the same ol' thing."

"But you had those things for years and they were long, too," Simone said. "I can't believe you cut them out just like that."

"It's only hair," Stefan said. "It's not hard to come by. If it were, I wouldn't have a head full of it right now and neither would you."

Simone laughed. "Yeah, it's amazing what you can buy."

Stefan caught sight of the outfit hanging on the door of Simone's closet and shoved her aside to take a look at it. "Oh, what is this?"

"That's Paris's outfit for the pageant."

"I didn't know you had started on it."

"I started working on it last night."

"You're shitting me!" Stefan exclaimed.

Simone shook her head.

"You mean to tell me, you started working on this last night and you're already finished."

Simone nodded.

"What prompted that?"

"I got the idea for it when I saw him wearing that zebra print dress," Simone said. "All I had to do was put it together."

"I ain't trying to be funny or nothing, but that dress Paris had on was ugly as all hell." Stefan turned the jumpsuit around to look at the back of it. "But this right here is the bomb."

Simone smiled, happy that the first comment about her creation was positive and the fact that it was coming from Stefan, who usually had a mouth full of negative comments about everything she did, meant a lot to her.

"Let's go out for lunch to celebrate, my treat," Stefan said.

"That's something you don't hear come out your mouth too often," Simone said. "I can't pass that up."

"I suggest you hurry up before I change my mind." Stefan giggled. "I'm having second thoughts already."

The doorbell rang as they were on their way out.

Stefan pulled down the blinds and peeked out the window. "Aw damn."

"Who is it?" Simone asked.

Stefan looked at Simone and rolled his eyes. "Mrs. Sandra."

"Who?"

"Mrs. Sandra, you know, from down the street; Anthony's mama."

Simone frowned. "What the hell she want?"

"I don't know," Stefan said. "Open the door and see."

Simone walked out of the door and Stefan walked out behind her and locked the door, not bothering to look Mrs. Sandra's way. Simone looked Mrs. Sandra up and down. The long, lavender floral print dress that hung down to her ankles was out of the ordinary for her. Simone was used to seeing Mrs. Sandra wearing tight booty shorts or mini-skirts. She couldn't help but wonder what had prompted the change in Mrs. Sandra's attire.

"How have you two been doing?" Mrs. Sandra asked.

"Fine," Simone answered.

Mrs. Sandra smiled. "That's good. I just wanted to make sure you were okay."

Stefan smirked. "You wanted to make sure she was okay. Why? Since when are you concerned about her well-being?"

Mrs. Sandra paused for a moment, trying to think of what she could say to smooth things over. "Come on, don't be like that. I know some things have happened between us in the past but I can't change that. All I can do is try to make things right with you two now."

Stefan and Simone looked at each other and rolled their eyes.

"Come on, you two. Don't give me such a hard time," Mrs. Sandra pleaded. "I came over here with the best intentions. I know what you've been going through the last few years since you lost your grandmother and I see you two over here taking care of yourselves and watching out for each other and I am so proud of you."

Mrs. Sandra reached in her purse and handed Simone a pamphlet.

Simone looked at it and turned up her nose. "What is this?"

"It's a handout about how to deal with a crisis."

Simone looked down at it and took a deep breath.

"You don't have to read it now; you can wait to you get alone and look through it," Mrs. Sandra said.

Simone sucked her teeth. "I don't know how it'll help me, but awright."

"Simone, I know there's been a lot of disappointment in your life but sometimes you have to give things a chance," Mrs. Sandra said. "By the way, do you two attend church?"

Simone and Stefan shook their heads, anticipating what was coming next.

"I'd love to have you two attend service with me one day," Mrs. Sandra said. "As a matter of fact, your father is a member of my church, Stefan. I'm sure he'd love to see you. Just think about it."

Mrs. Sandra smiled and then walked off toward her house.

Simone got in the car and sighed. "I thought she would never leave."

"You should've told her to take her ass up the street," Stefan said.

"Why you couldn't tell her?"

"She ain't come to talk to me. She came to talk to you," Stefan said. "Besides, the shit was so touching, I didn't want to interrupt."

"I wonder when she started wearing long dresses and going to church."

"Probably around the time she found out Anthony was gay."

Simone sucked her teeth. "I hate people like that."

"Like what?"

"People who walk around downing people, being all trashy and shit, but as soon as they got a problem and people start criticizing them, they want to hide behind a Bible like it's a bulletproof vest or some shit."

"Girl, you better watch your mouth," Stefan said. "The Lord hears all."

"So what," Simone said. "He ain't gonna do shit. If He had as much clout as everyone says He does, there wouldn't be a Hell and you damn sure wouldn't have on that dress."

"You can talk all the shit you want but don't underestimate God," Stefan said. "Just 'cause you feel like He didn't save you from some of the shit that happened to you doesn't mean He doesn't have any say-so in the scheme of things."

Simone sneered. "Yeah, whatever."

Stefan folded up his menu and slid it to the side. "You brought me to the most expensive restaurant you could find."

"Jana took me to the one in New Orleans and she didn't have a problem with it," Simone said. "So I didn't think you would have one either."

"Jana probably didn't mind 'cause you gave her some butt."

Simone rolled her eyes. "You know I didn't sleep with Jana."

Stefan chuckled. "Then why was she in your room asleep at two o'clock in the morning?"

"You know what? I'm going to the bathroom on that note."

Simone was shocked to see Wayne standing against the wall waiting for her as she walked out of the bathroom. She tried to sidestep him and head back to the table but he stood in her way.

"I've got one question for you," Wayne said. "What the hell is this about?"

Simone was intimidated by the rage in Wayne's eyes. "I don't think it's a good idea for you to talk to me."

"I don't think it's a good idea for little girls to run around saying things that aren't true," Wayne said. "We both know what happened in that room."

Simone nodded. "Yeah, you raped me and if you haven't heard, the state has all the evidence they need to prosecute you."

Simone turned around to walk off and Wayne yanked her by her arm.

"Let go of me," Simone snapped. "I would hate to have to call the police and let them know I had another run-in with you."

Wayne released his grip on Simone's arm.

Simone smiled. "Yeah, that's what I thought."

Wayne reached in his pocket, pulled out five hundred dollars, and handed it to Simone. "Is this what you want?"

Simone's face turned red; the nerve of him offering her five hundred dollars as if it was the solution to his problems. It would take a lot more than that to persuade her to drop the charges. "You've got to be kidding me."

Wayne reached in his pocket and pulled out three hundred dollars and raised his offer. "Here, it's my final offer."

"Your final offer?" Simone giggled. "Don't worry; I'll get whatever money I need through civil court after the trial."

Simone stomped off, leaving Wayne in the hallway, mad as shit.

Simone sat down at the table and sipped her drink.

"What took you so long?" Stefan asked. "I was starting to get worried. I thought you'd flushed yourself down the toilet. I'm too cute to be running around the James River looking for yo' ass."

Simone sucked her teeth. "Naw, I'm awright. Guess who I saw leaving the bathroom."

"Who?"

"Wayne."

"What? He's here?"

"Yeah, he's here."

Stefan stood up from the table, scoping the restaurant for Wayne. "There he is, over there." Stefan grabbed his butter knife off of the table. "I'm gonna whip his ass."

Simone reached over and grabbed Stefan's arm. "Ain't no need for all that; calm down."

"Hell you mean, calm down?" Stefan snapped. "This nigga had you all beat and burned the fuck up and you're telling me to calm down."

"This is not the time or the place," Simone said. "Besides, what you gonna do with that?" Simone nodded toward the butter knife Stefan held in his hand. "Rub it across his neck and hope you break his skin?"

Stefan paused for a moment. Simone was right for once. There was no need to mess up his lunch by causing a scene and getting thrown out of the restaurant. Although he was willing to run up on Wayne, Wayne had a few others with him that may not let him fight alone and Stefan didn't think he would fare well against the four of them. Stefan sat back down and sipped his drink. "That's awright, I've seen the nigga here, so there's a good chance I'll run into him again and when I do, I'm whipping that ass."

Simone shook her head. "No, I've got a better idea."

[22]

Stefan flipped his cell phone closed and glanced in the direction of Wayne's table as he scribbled a message on a napkin:

Want the charges dropped? Meet me at the Hyatt hotel, room 223 in two hours.

Stefan gave the napkin to a waitress to pass on to Wayne and hurried out of the restaurant.

He looked at Simone and smiled as he got in the car. "We need a camcorder."

Stefan lay across the bed in the hotel room on his stomach, wearing a purple corset and a matching G-string. Simone stood in the closet focusing the camcorder on the bed through the opening in the door. Her fingers were crossed. She hoped that Wayne would show up and everything would go as planned. She touched the gun on her side, recalling what Stefan had said when he handed it to her. "Don't look at me like you don't know what it is. If something goes wrong up in here, you might have to use it."

Wayne slid the key card, which was left at the front desk for him, into the door. He walked in, checking out the curves on the body that lay across the bed. He smiled, pleased by what he saw.

Simone's palms became sweaty and she closed her eyes. *Please, please let this work.*

Wayne moved closer toward the bed, taking off his shirt and laying it in the chair. Stefan sat up in the bed and stretched, leaning his head back.

Wayne came to a halt, looking at Stefan's Adam's apple, noticing how round and prominent it was. He then moved his eyes down to Stefan's chest, staring wildly as if he was confused. "What the fuck is this?"

Stefan reached his hand out, wanting Wayne to grab it so he could pull Wayne into the bed with him. "Your get out of jail free card."

Wayne grabbed the phone off of the table beside the bed and threw it at Stefan.

Stefan blocked the phone with his forearm and jumped to his feet. "Nigga, what the fuck is wrong with you?"

"I don't know what you thought when you wrote your little note but I ain't no fucking punk!" Wayne shouted, spraying Stefan with saliva.

Stefan wiped the spit from his face. "What I was thinking was you could use a favor." Stefan smirked. "And from what I heard, you like going in the rear too much not to be."

"Watch how you come off at me," Wayne said. "I'll hurt you."

Stefan grabbed his clothes off of the bed. "Fuck this; I ain't about to waste my time standing here arguing with yo' ass. I'll put on my clothes and leave."

Wayne looked at Stefan with disdain in his eyes. "You ain't hurting me."

"After they sentence your ass and you get to pulling that time, you'll wish you'd taken me up on my offer," Stefan said.

"Do you know who I am?" Wayne asked. "I ain't fitting to do no time for that bullshit."

Stefan smirked. "You mean, do I know who you *were*. Nigga, that shit is old news. With the evidence they have, your fate is as good as sealed. But, on the other hand, if you let me work this out for you, I'll get her to say everything that happened that night was consensual. It's y'all usual thing; she likes rough violent sex and that's how she wanted you to give it to her. Hell, depending on how good you are, I'll get you a public apology."

An uncomfortable silence filled the room. Stefan glanced over at the closet, wondering if Wayne agreed to go along with it, was Simone ready, was she able to get a good view of them through the opening in the door, and was she ready to stomach the fact that what he had told her about Wayne was true. Wayne put up such a fight that Stefan started to question whether he was right about Wayne's sexuality.

Wayne moved closer to him. "What makes you think this would be an option for me?"

"If it wasn't, you wouldn't still be here."

Wayne grabbed Stefan by his arms and threw him down on the bed.

Stefan looked up at Wayne as he unbuckled his pants. Stefan smiled at the sight of Wayne's erection. "I knew you'd change your mind."

Wayne let drool fall from his mouth onto his fleshy chocolate tool and began to stroke it with his hand, lubricating it, preparing to enter Stefan. "Shut the fuck up and bend over."

❖

Simone sat on the couch, twirling a lock of her hair and watching the DVD of Stefan and Wayne as she made copies. She pinched herself. *I can't believe Stefan was right.* Why would Wayne be interested in guys? It was hard to believe it was the first time he had been with another man. If he had never considered being with, or had never been sexually active with a man, he wouldn't have been coerced so easily. A man's pride is hard to break and when you insult it, you put yourself in harm's way. They will fight, kill, die over it. So it was hard to believe a jail sentence that wasn't exactly etched in stone would cause Wayne to go against his morals. Then again, as her grandmother used to say, they don't make men like they used to.

On the other hand, Wayne seemed too damn comfortable not to have done it before. Nonetheless she took pleasure in having her goal accomplished and prepared to go to the post office where she could have a copy of the DVD mailed to Wayne overnight.

❧[23]❧

Wayne picked up the envelope he had signed for earlier that day. He wondered who it could be from. The sender had only written "guess who" on the envelope and drawn a smiley face beside of it. He debated about opening it. He thought of the possibility of it containing anthrax or something else that may be hazardous to his health. He fiddled with the envelope for a moment, trying to get some idea of what was inside. He felt something round and thin that only took up a small portion of the envelope. Right away, he realized that it was a CD or DVD. He tore open the envelope and pulled it out.

He read the label: *Did I ever tell you I always get the last laugh?*

Wayne smiled. He knew it was from Simone. He would bet every last cent he had on it. He stared at the DVD for a moment, wondering what could be on it. Why would she have sent it to him? Maybe she had made a recording, ranting and raving about how she knew about what had happened between him and her cousin, enraged about the idea of him giving his dick away again.

Crazy-ass bitch just can't get over me. Wayne looked in the mirror, flexed his muscles, and then smiled. *Shit, I can't blame her. Just look at me.*

Then he thought maybe it was what Stefan had promised. Maybe it was a video of Simone admitting that he didn't rape her and apologizing to him.

Wayne put the DVD in the player and sat down on his bed to watch it. He grinned with anticipation. He was ready to laugh, ready to see Simone make a fool out of herself. But his grin quickly left his face. There was no yelling, no screaming, no confession, no apology, no Simone; just a lot of panting and him and Stefan going at it. Wayne jumped off of his bed and shoved the TV on the floor, and then stomped it when it didn't cease playing. He yanked the DVD player out of the wall and slung it into the mirror. He fell down on his bed, holding his chest, trying to calm himself down. He couldn't believe it. No one was there but Stefan and him. He didn't remember seeing a camcorder. He couldn't believe they'd set him up. What was more unbelievable to him was that he fell for it. How could he? He considered himself to be smarter than that. But he let his desire get the best of him. Not his desire to get the charges dropped against him. He had a good chance of that anyway. He had a good lawyer and there was also the maid that had overheard their dispute.

If he couldn't get the charges dropped, then he would accept a plea. He didn't care what others thought as long as he knew he didn't do it. He had done a few things that he was ashamed of during his lifetime but that one wouldn't go on his conscience. He could honestly say that he didn't do it. There was no miscommunication between them. She was more than willing. Knowing that she was the type of person who would conjure up such a story to attempt to take away his freedom and ruin his image made him let go of the little bit of guilt he had for the way he'd treated her that night.

It was something about seeing Stefan lying across the bed with the line of his G-string disappearing between his firm hips that had raised a passion in Wayne that he thought he had left behind him and promised himself that he would never acknowledge again.

He was sixteen when the feelings started. He had been friends with Jason ever since they were in first grade but he had never thought of Jason that way until that day on the basketball court. Jason had taken his tee shirt off and poured his bottle of water over his head to cool himself off. It was then that Wayne noticed Jason's body. He noticed how Jason's body was different from his and the other guys. Jason's shoulders were broader and his body robust. His developed chest brought attention to how prominent his nipples were and the way his shorts sat low on his round, chocolate hips aroused Wayne. When Wayne got home that evening, he tried to dismiss Jason's image from his mind and forget about what he'd felt earlier that day on the basketball court. He thought of all the times they had played together and the times they had fought, trying to convince himself that he only thought of Jason as a friend; a good friend and nothing more.

His memories became twisted as he thought about the wrestling matches they'd had and the fights they'd gotten into. The thought crept into his mind of what may have happened if they would've gotten a little closer, or paused for a moment when their eyes made contact, or when one of their genitals accidentally rubbed against the other's body, and took advantage of the situation. He became aroused and masturbated to relieve himself, hoping it would cure his lust. He was disgusted by his actions so much it nauseated him to even think about it. He decided to avoid Jason and began sitting as far away from him in class as possible. Wayne decided not to go to the basketball court anymore and not to answer Jason's calls. It worked for about a month.

Wayne missed his bus one Friday evening and decided to walk home from school. Jason pulled up beside Wayne in his car and offered him a ride. At first Wayne declined, not knowing if he could stomach being in Jason's presence for the ten minutes it would take to get to his house. But Jason was persistent and made Wayne feel foolish, asking him did he plan to cry on his way home or something, and didn't want anyone to see him. Wayne got in the car, figuring he could find it in himself to deal with Jason for that short period of time. They took a shortcut through the wooded area behind the school that had a dirt road that led to the street that Wayne lived on. After a few seconds of quietness, Wayne started to feel awkward, turned on the radio, and started flipping through the stations.

Jason looked at Wayne and smiled, seeing how dissatisfied he was. "Nigga, what is you doing?"

"Trying to find something to listen to."

"I've got some tapes in the glove compartment."

Wayne opened the glove compartment, started looking through the tapes, and found one that he'd loaned Jason the year before. It was one of Wayne's favorites. Jason had told him that he'd lost it and changed the subject every time he asked him to replace it. It wasn't like Wayne couldn't replace it himself. It was the principle of the matter.

Wayne held up the tape, showing Jason that he had found it. "I thought you lost it."

Jason glanced at the tape, reading the title. "Naw, man, that one is mine."

"Well, it's mine now."

"Yeah right," Jason said. "You better put my shit back."

"Hey, just think of it as you replacing mine."

Jason pulled to the side of the road and grabbed for the cassette tape. Wayne quickly put it in his pocket. Jason reached over and grabbed Wayne's pocket, his hand rubbing against Wayne's dick.

Wayne grabbed Jason's hand, removing it from his pants. "Come on, man; stop playing."

Jason snatched his hand away from Wayne and reached

for Wayne's pocket again. Wayne could feel Jason's breath on his neck and his dick stood at attention. Wayne became frightened. He was afraid of what his feelings might cause him to do. Wayne shoved Jason into the car door. Jason became infuriated and swung on Wayne, landing a punch on Wayne's jaw. Wayne wrapped his hands around Jason's neck and began to choke him. Jason struggled to lift his leg off of the floor and kicked Wayne, but there was not enough room for him to do so. Jason tried to pry Wayne's hand from around his neck.

Wayne leaned in closer to Jason. "How the fuck you start some shit and can't even handle yours? I should throw your ass out your own car and make you walk home."

Wayne's rage made him want to follow through with his threat but he was captivated by Jason's eyes; even in rage, they seduced him. He wanted to act on his impulse to kiss Jason but before he could, Jason kissed him and all his reservations disappeared. He caressed Jason's hips like he had fantasized about. It didn't take two minutes for them to begin fogging up the windows.

Sweaty, embarrassed, and ashamed, Wayne and Jason were silent the few minutes it took them to get to Wayne's house. When they pulled up, Wayne didn't say bye, see you later, or nothing. He got out of the car, slammed the door, and went inside the house, not saying a word to his parents who greeted him when he walked in. He made his way to the bathroom and showered. He scrubbed so hard that his skin became red. He wanted it to go away, what he had done and the sensation he'd felt when he was doing it. He could still hear Jason's voice in his head. He could still imagine the feeling he'd gotten when their lips had touched.

Wayne could hear his father's words; his hatred of anyone who wasn't heterosexual. He could see the scornful look on his father's face when he said homosexuals shouldn't be allowed to share the same space with those who weren't sexually immoral. His father would preach about how homosexuals should be jailed because their crime was one of the worst types, a crime against nature and a crime against God. Wayne's father always told him that homosexuals infested the world the same way roaches did a home and they shouldn't be allowed to breathe the same air as everyone else. Wayne's father thought all homosexuals should be shipped off to the same place they dumped the world's garbage because they were nothing but trash polluting society. That way they could wallow in garbage until the day they died off and their souls burnt in eternal fire.

As soon as Wayne got dressed, he got a trash bag to put his clothes in. Not wanting to touch his soiled clothes, he wrapped them in a towel, put them in the trash bag, and went outside and stuffed them in the garbage. He went back to his room and knelt down beside his bed and prayed. He spent hours repenting for what he did, crying with a wail that came from deep down in his soul. Afterwards Wayne asked for a sign that he was forgiven and that his soul would not burn in the fire that his father had talked about. He lay in bed crying the rest of the night, afraid of what would become of his soul. He waited for a sign but one never came.

The next morning Wayne's mother went into his room to wake him up for school. Wayne wouldn't get up; he just lay there looking at her with his teary bloodshot eyes. Wayne's mother placed her hand on Wayne's chest to see if it would rise and fall, to see if Wayne was still among the living. She was relieved that there was still breath in his body but frightened by the way he lay there. Not knowing what to say or do, Wayne's mother asked him why he wasn't up and getting ready for school. Wayne didn't answer. He just lay there, staring blankly as tears fell from his eyes. Wayne's mother called to her husband, who was on his way out to work.

Wayne's father came in the room and looked Wayne over. "The boy looks fine to me. Get him up and send him to school."

Wayne's mother shook her head. "He ain't going to school. Something's wrong with him. Look at him; he's just lying there, not saying nothing."

Wayne's father took off his belt and shook it at Wayne. "Boy, get up 'fore I come over there and get you up myself."

Wayne didn't move; he just looked at his father. Wayne didn't care about his father's threat. In his mind, his soul would perish in a lake of fire on Judgment Day and he would cease to exist. Nothing his father or any-one could do would hurt him; he was already doomed.

Wayne's mother called the ambulance and, about ten minutes later, Wayne was being carried out the house on a stretcher.

After a day of running tests on Wayne and examining him, the doctor advised Wayne's mother that he was suffer-ing from a nervous breakdown and then committed him into a mental institution. Wayne's mother wondered what had happened to him, what had caused him to lay there speechless and to have a break with reality. Her precious child was in so much misery that she never wanted to see him like that again.

She visited Wayne every week and watched him sit there and stare at her. It was after her tenth visit with Wayne that she went home and sat in her living room and cried. She wondered if Wayne would ever be his energetic, good-natured self again. She longed for him to be able to come home.

Wayne's mother heard a knock on her door. She dried her tears, went to the door, and cracked it open. Jason was standing there with his head down and his shoulders slouched.

Wayne's mother took a deep breath, trying to keep her composure long enough to tell Jason that Wayne was in the hospital. She looked at Jason and smiled. "Sweetheart, Wayne isn't here. He's in the hospital and won't be home for a while."

"I know," Jason said. "That's what I wanted to talk to you about."

"Oh?" Wayne's mother said, stunned by Jason's nerve. Who did he think he was? Where did he get the nerve to come over and pry into her family's business? "What is it that you want to say?"

"What's wrong with Wayne?" Jason asked. "I mean, does he have some kind of disease or something?"

Her eyes widened. "Little boy, I don't know who you think you are, coming here and asking me some mess like that. You better do yourself a favor and run on home before you get your feelings hurt."

Jason's voice began to crack. "But Mrs. Jasper—"

"But nothing!" Mrs. Jasper screamed. "Run on home! It's none of your business!"

"It *is* my business."

Mrs. Jasper tried to shut the door. Jason pushed the door open and forced his way inside.

"Child, if you don't get out of my house, I'll beat two years off your life."

Jason stood there, unyielding. "Does Wayne have AIDS?"

Mrs. Jasper gritted her teeth. "What did you say, boy?"

Jason tried to repeat his question. "Does Wayne have—"

Mrs. Jasper slapped Jason on his cheek. "How dare you come in my house and make an accusation like that?"

Jason began to cry. He was getting nowhere with her. He needed to know that his health wasn't in jeopardy. He'd skipped school and gone to the free clinic as soon as he'd heard about Wayne. But it was taking too long to get his test results and his paranoia had increased every day. All he'd heard around school was that Wayne was sick but no one could tell him what ailed Wayne. He had to know. He was on the verge of losing his sanity.

Mrs. Jasper's face was the color of blood and her eyes swelled with tears. "Boy, you should be ashamed, coming in here with that nonsense. If you don't get out of my house right now, I'm calling the police."

"But you don't understand."

Mrs. Jasper huffed. *This boy must take me for a joke.*

Mrs. Jasper picked up the phone to call the police.

"We had sex," Jason blurted out.

Mrs. Jasper dropped the phone and grabbed her chest. "What?"

Jason began to cry. "The last time I saw Wayne, we had sex."

"You stupid, stupid boy," Mrs. Jasper said. "How could you do such a thing? You probably can barely get yourself ready for school in the morning. What makes you think you're ready for the consequences of sex; especially the type you're having."

Jason tried to speak but he was too shaken for Mrs. Jasper to understand his dialect. Mrs. Jasper made Jason sit on the sofa with her and attempted to calm him down. Jason told Mrs. Jasper how sorry he was. How he and Wayne were playing around and it just happened. Mrs. Jasper rubbed Jason's back while he wiped his tears. She assured Jason that Wayne did not have AIDS or any STDs. She told him how Wayne had had a break with reality and was in a psychiatric hospital.

Jason expressed his regret about what had happened. He asked Mrs. Jasper to tell Wayne that he wanted to put what happened behind them and be friends again. Mrs. Jasper promised that she would tell Wayne and then sent Jason on his way.

Mrs. Jasper was relieved to know what had caused her son's condition. Her husband could never find out. She would have to kill him. She refused to let him degrade Wayne for what he had done. She would see her husband dead before she would let him poison Wayne's mind with his ignorance.

Mrs. Jasper didn't plan to give Wayne Jason's message. She wanted to keep Wayne as far away from Jason as possible. They needed to move but she needed her husband to agree to it. She had no money. Her husband was the wage-earner in the family and she took care of their home.

When Mr. Jasper came home that evening, she did everything she could to seduce all of his senses. She fixed her hair and wore his favorite perfume. She fixed his favorite meal for dinner. She didn't even complain when he sat in front of the TV with the volume turned up as high as it could go, gorging himself with beer.

When they retired to the bedroom, she did things to please him that she had never done for him or any other man. She licked and sucked every crevice on his body. During sex she would usually lie on her back with her legs spread apart while her husband did all of the work. She was forty years old and had never been able to build up the nerve to be in the lead role during sex. She was too timid to be on top, gyrating and bouncing around on her partner while he watched her flesh jiggle. But that night she took charge. She wanted Wayne to be able to start over when he came home. She couldn't be self-conscious. She needed her husband to agree to move her and Wayne away from there and it would take some persuasion.

After a few nights of her routine, Mrs. Jasper laid in the bed exhausted. Her husband looked over at her tired body and smiled and then pulled her onto his chest. She looked up at him and closed her eyes, trying to build up the nerve to ask.

"What's wrong?" her husband asked.

Mrs. Jasper swallowed before she answered him. It was the moment she had been waiting for. "I'm thinking about Wayne; that's all."

"He'll be all right," her husband assured her. "Some girl probably broke his heart."

"I wish we could move," Mrs. Jasper said. "You know, to get him away from whatever made him this way."

Her husband nodded. "Would be nice, but we can't afford to."

"Well, haven't you been saving up? What about your

retirement plan; can't you take a loan from that or something?"

Her husband frowned. *I know this bitch didn't just ask
me to withdraw from my retirement. That's my money*, he
thought. "Like I said, we can't afford it."

"But I think it would be good for Wayne."

"That's enough," her husband snapped. "I don't want
to hear anymore."

Mrs. Jasper turned around in the bed and sobbed. *He
is so insensitive*, she thought. She felt her husband's hand
on her hip, got out of the bed, and went to Wayne's
room to sleep. If he wouldn't move them away from
there, she would. She could go back to North Carolina
to live with her parents. They had plenty of room. Her
husband could keep his money and kiss them goodbye.

The next day, Wayne's mother confronted him during
their visit. She told him that she had talked to Jason and
he'd told her all about what had happened. Wayne began
to cry. That was the first time that Mrs. Jasper had heard
a sound out of Wayne in over two months. She promised
Wayne that she would not tell his father. She told him
that she could move him away from there if he wanted.
He could start over and forget about what happened but
he had to promise her that he would work on getting
better. Wayne nodded his head in agreement.

When Mrs. Jasper left her visit with Wayne, she called
her parents. As soon as she got their approval, she began
to pack their belongings.

Her husband came home from work and noticed that the closet in his room was half-empty. He confronted his wife and asked her what was going on. Mrs. Jasper explained that she was moving back with her parents and taking Wayne with her.

Her husband laughed. "You'll never make it," he said. "You don't have a job and I damn sure ain't sending you any money."

"I can get a job," Mrs. Jasper said. "And if not, I'm sure I can survive on what you'll be paying me for child support and alimony."

Her husband didn't think she had the nerve to leave him but he realized that she would do almost anything for their son. Since she had already taken action by packing her and Wayne's belongings, he thought he'd better take action himself. He hurried down to the personnel office at his job to see what needed to be done to withdraw from his retirement.

❖

Wayne stayed to himself at his new school. He went to class and went to the gym and sparred every day as he had done since fifth grade but didn't utter a word to anyone. He would hear his peers whispering amongst each other, asking if he was mute, saying something was wrong with him. "That boy ain't right," they would say. Wayne didn't entertain their comments. They were foolish to be so hung up on him when they had issues of their own that needed their attention.

It wasn't until the day Wayne saw his wife, Nicole, that he considered putting an end to his rut and begin socializing. Nicole was new to the school like he was and she always sat in the far right corner of the back of the classroom. Wayne couldn't help but stare at her. She was beautiful. Wayne loved her smooth brown skin and high cheekbones. Nicole was five-six and weighed about 140 pounds. Wayne blushed when he thought to himself about how Nicole's butt was composed of fifty pounds and her breasts twenty pounds and the other seventy pounds made up the remainder of her body. She was soft-spoken but no matter how soft she spoke, he heard every word she uttered. Wayne wanted to approach Nicole but he couldn't build up the nerve. He needed to find a common ground, something they both had in common, to spark up a conversation about.

One afternoon after school, Wayne saw Nicole walking outside to the spot where she waited for her ride. As Nicole walked over to wait, her necklace fell from around her neck.

Wayne picked up Nicole's necklace and walked over to her. "You dropped this."

Nicole looked at Wayne and smiled. "Thanks." Nicole took her necklace and continued to gaze out at the street, waiting for her ride to pull up.

Wayne looked at Nicole's necklace. "That symbol on your necklace; what does it represent?"

"It represents Scorpio; my Zodiac sign," Nicole explained.

"Are you a Christian?" Wayne asked.

Nicole shot Wayne an awkward look but didn't answer him.

Wayne felt himself about to break a sweat. He cleared his throat and tried to keep his composure. "I only asked because, you know, God says that stuff is an abomination."

Nicole fixated her gaze on Wayne, now more interested in what he had to say than seeing her ride pull up. "What stuff?"

"You know, horoscopes, reading the stars, trying to read rocks and stones, that type of shit."

"When did God tell you that?"

"He didn't," Wayne said. "But it's written in the Bible."

"You shouldn't believe everything you read."

Wayne became irritated. He regretted starting up a conversation with her. He wanted to walk away but the conversation had gone too far for him to end it at that moment without seeming rude. "Are you calling God a liar?"

Nicole sighed. "The last time I checked, God didn't write the Bible."

"But the people who did were dictating the word of God."

"And people have been known to lie," Nicole said. "So like I said, don't believe everything you read."

"Well, do you believe in God?"

"Obviously not in the same sense you do," Nicole said.

"So, what if you're wrong and you keep wearing your symbols?"

Nicole shrugged. "Then I'm wrong?"

"And you're going to hell," Wayne muttered.

"I don't believe in such a place," Nicole said. "And even if I did, I'd rather spend eternity in hell than with your God that the Bible describes who is just as petty and judgmental as the people we share the earth with."

"So you don't believe in God," Wayne concluded.

"What I believe is God is love and will not cast His children that are a part of Him into a lake of fire to be destroyed."

Wayne shook his head, disagreeing with Nicole's comment. "Well, if you don't live right, that's what happens."

"If someone loved you, how could they do that to you?" Nicole asked. "If you did something your mother didn't like, do you think she would throw you in a lake of fire and destroy your soul if she could?"

Wayne shook his head. "No."

"So what makes your mother better than God?"

Wayne considered Nicole's statement. He'd never thought about it that way. If his mother could forgive him for what he had done with Jason, then God would indeed forgive him.

His conversation with Nicole made him appreciate her more. Nicole had given him what no one else could; solace. From that day forward, Wayne had a different view about life. He lived his life to the fullest. He accepted all the blessings God gave him, including Nicole's hand in marriage. Through the years his profession and infidelity drove them apart. Despite their differences, Wayne always thought of Nicole as his angel. He wouldn't let her want for anything. Nicole meant more to him than his parents, the kids she had given him, his money, and his life.

Wayne never told Nicole what had happened to him before they'd met and never wanted to have to explain it to her. Nicole was forgiving but Wayne felt she had forgiven him for too much already. He'd never divorce Nicole. He hoped they would work things out in the future. Wayne couldn't stand the thought of the pain Nicole would feel when their kids came home from school, telling her that the other children had called their daddy gay, a pole smoker, or whatever awful term they would think of to describe him. When he saw Stefan's oiled body lying across the bed in the hotel room and heard his offer, he had become weak. Now he had to pay for his weakness, but he couldn't. He had too much to lose.

24

Paris plopped down on his bed and sighed. He was having second thoughts about the pageant. He went to the club where the pageant was going to be held to pick up tickets for Stefan and Simone. He also went to get a look at the other contestants to see what he was up against. There were three that bothered him. They were sitting at a table, not talking to anyone outside of their circle. They began eyeing him the moment he walked in the club, whispering and giggling amongst themselves as they sized him up. The one who eyed him first seemed to be the leader of the three. He was loud and obnoxious. Every obscenity that came out of his mouth was followed by a chuckle from his two cronies along with the phrase: "You ain't never lied." They had trouble written all over them. Even if they didn't cause trouble for him directly, Paris was sure they would cause trouble for the pageant. But they were the least of his worries.

Michael frequented the club and Paris was sure he would be there to check out the pageant and to scout for his next victim. Paris mentioned to Michael that he was thinking about entering the pageant but never told him about his final decision. *What if Michael shows up with his new lover? What if Michael shows up with Jewel on his arm?* Paris doubted if Jewel would come to the pageant. Jewel knew that he'd entered and after what he had done, Paris would be stunned if Jewel had the guts to be in the same room with him, but as the saying goes, wonders never cease.

Paris knew if his attitude about the pageant didn't become more positive, he would have to drop out; otherwise, he would be the cause of his own failure.

Paris emerged from the shower and put on his robe. He invoked Isis, lit the white candle on his dresser, and then sat in front of the candle, focusing on the flame. He slowly breathed in and out of his nose. With each breath, his eyes became heavier. The scent from the candle relaxed him.

Paris closed his eyes. "Success is upon me. Blessed is my life; I will not endure pain or strife," Paris chanted.

In his mind's eye Paris saw himself surrounded by clouds. The clouds dispersed and he stood naked in a circle. He noticed his anatomy and the restriction he felt being encased in a body that was not of his choosing; a body that wasn't compatible with what he lusted for. He wanted to be free from his body, free to be what he wanted to be, free to have the visage of his choice. He let his outward breath free him of his negative thoughts. He then envisioned the body of his dreams. A white light shined down on him. He now stood naked inside a wreath, looking down at his body, admiring his curves. He had a thin waist, full breasts, and shapely hips. All the bushy hair that plagued his body was gone. He danced, celebrating his nakedness. He was filled with happiness and it pulsated throughout his body and brought a smile to his face. A rose fell from the wreath, a gift from Isis. Paris grabbed the rose and put it in his hair. A hand reached into the wreath and Paris grabbed it. He was led out of the wreath and stood on stage at the nightclub where he would compete in the pageant. The club was dim but a bright light showcased him. His eyes glistened as a crown was placed on his head and he was handed a bouquet of flowers and the first-place, five-hundred-dollar cash prize. He basked in his success and pictured a ray coming from his third eye, carrying his thoughts out into the world where they would manifest. "So shall it be," Paris said. "So shall it be."

❖

Paris stood in front of the mirror, admiring his outfit. No one at the pageant would be wearing anything like it. That was good for him; he strived to be different. In that respect, his outfit not only flattered his body, it also complemented his personality. He doubted that any of the competition had the body or the swagger to pull off such an outfit. If they tried to flaunt the way he did wearing a similar outfit, they would look like an ass;

foolish and unconfident. So it was to their benefit that his outfit was an original.

Paris couldn't believe how nervous he was before. The thought of him not winning was now absurd. He was psyched after his visualization and ready to take on the world.

Paris smiled. "Damn, Simone, I knew you would hook me up, but you've really outdone yourself this time."

Simone shrugged. "Yeah, don't mention it."

"Damn, what's wrong with you?" Paris asked.

"Don't pay her any mind. She has her own issues," Stefan joked. "Maybe it's moon time; who knows."

Simone sucked her teeth. *Why is it taking Wayne so long to call me?* She knew the package had been delivered. She began to think that maybe the address she had gotten from her online search was bogus. She hoped no one had signed for the package and viewed the DVD before Wayne did, and had taken it to the tabloids. If that happened, her power over him was nonexistent. She wished that Wayne would call her. She needed to know where she stood in the scheme of things. She needed confirmation that she had the upper hand.

Stefan looked at Paris, who was studying himself in the mirror and playing with his hair. Paris was trying to get some idea about how he would wear his hair for the pageant.

Stefan looked Paris up and down and then nudged Simone so she could observe Paris. "Don't get up in there tomorrow with your outfit and your hair pinned up and act like you don't know us."

Paris laughed. "I wouldn't do anything like that. I might be one of the finest things down here in Virginia, but I'll never be too fly for y'all bitches."

Simone sucked her teeth. "That's bullshit. Let this nigga get his hands on a million dollars today or tomorrow. Shit, let him get a half-million dollars; he'll forget all about our asses."

The smile on Paris's face disappeared and his eyes were full of anger. "Just 'cause you would carry it like that doesn't mean I would."

Simone sniggered. "Oh, so you gonna break bread and the whole nine?"

"I sure would."

"Well, we know you wouldn't get far," Simone said. "You'd give your money away and let other people party it up until you were broke again."

"And you would take your money and run with it," Paris said.

"Damn right."

"People like you never get anywhere."

"Bullshit," Simone said. "People like you never get anywhere."

"Stefan and I have been cool as rocks since day one," Paris said. "So it doesn't matter. We can be rich together and we can be poor together. Money ain't everything. The people you love are."

Stefan clapped his hands. "Aw, that was sweet. I feel so special. Are you trying to say you love me?"

"I love both of y'all," Paris said. "Simone just gets on my fucking nerves."

Simone jumped out of her seat. "If that's the case, give me my shit back."

Paris looked at Simone and grinned. "What are you talking about?"

"My outfit, bitch."

Paris looked Simone up and down and laughed. "Yeah, right." Paris turned back around to examine himself in the mirror. "If you think you're getting this back, your ass is crazy."

"I'll rip it off your back."

"And I'll stomp a hole in your ass."

Stefan threw up his hands. "Hold up, y'all need to drop this shit now before it gets out of hand."

Simone gritted her teeth. "Out of hand; it's already out of hand. You've got your friend up in here disrespecting me. You need to handle that."

"What the fuck you mean, he needs to handle that?" Paris asked. "You act like he's pimping me or some shit."

"He might as well be," Simone said. "You're exactly like a little bitch, following him everywhere he goes."

"Naw, that's your cry-baby ass." Paris began to whine, attempting to mimic Simone. "Stefan, don't leave me at home by myself, although you have a life of your own. I can't think for myself. If you leave me behind, when you come back, I might have a black eye and an ass load full of STDs. I might even burn the house down."

Simone looked over at Stefan. "You see this shit," she said, pounding her fist in her hand. "I'd never let one of my friends come up in here and talk to you like that."

"You don't have any friends!" Paris shouted.

Simone grabbed a catalog off of the table and threw it at Paris.

Paris looked over at Stefan and pointed to Simone. "Stefan, you better get her ass, for real."

Stefan lit a cigarette. *Always the same old bullshit*, he thought. Simone and Paris had been going back and forth with each other for a while, making sly comments to one another. Stefan figured he would let them get it out of their systems. They wouldn't hurt each other. They would only talk shit and maybe pass a few licks. Stefan puffed on his cigarette and watched them go at it.

"What the fuck you gonna do if he doesn't?"

"Don't let my appearance fool you," Paris said. "I might look like a girl but underneath my clothes are a dick and two balls and I fight like it, too; I'll whip your ass."

"Do it then."

"Make me."

Stefan took a deep breath. They were so childish. He didn't know why they took themselves so seriously.

Simone grabbed the cordless phone off of the base. "If you don't shut up, I'm gonna toss this phone upside your big-ass forehead."

"Then do it, bitch."

Simone motioned her arm like she was going to throw the phone at Paris, psyching him out. Paris flinched, not knowing whether Simone was actually going to throw the phone at him. The phone rang and Simone paused to look at the caller ID.

Simone ran out of the room, not wanting the phone to stop ringing before she could get somewhere private. "You're lucky the phone rang or you would've been wearing a knot on your forehead to the pageant tomorrow."

"Naw, you lucky," Paris said. "If you would've thrown that phone, I would've beaten your ass." Paris looked over at Stefan. "Come on, Stefan; help me decide how to wear my hair tomorrow."

"Hello," Simone answered.

Wayne was irritated by the pleasure that he heard in Simone's voice. "You don't know when to quit, do you?"

"Oh, I guess you liked the package I sent you."

"Bitch, you don't know who you're playing games with."

"I'd hold my tongue if I were you," Simone said. "You don't want your video to make it to the tabloids but, then again, I don't think you're important enough for anyone to give a shit. I mean, your glory days are long gone, but I'm sure it'll ruin what's left of your career."

"All this 'cause I don't want you?"

"'Cause you don't want me!" Simone exclaimed. "Do you think that's all this is about? You humiliated me and now it's your turn."

"Damn, I'm sorry. What the fuck do you want from me?"

"Five hundred thousand dollars," Simone said. "You can start by giving me one hundred fifty thousand tomorrow and the rest within the next two weeks."

"What? I don't have that type of money," Wayne said. "I have bills to pay like everyone else."

"I don't care; that's your problem," Simone said. "Sell your house, the house you got your parents living in, the house you got your baby mama living in. Put them out on the street or take out a loan. I want my money."

"Yeah, keep dreaming."

"Well, I'll tell you this," Simone said, "If I can't get it from you, I'm sure I can sell the video and make a profit. I'll sell it to the tabloids for a lot less than what I'm asking you for, so you decide."

"You know, if you weren't such a silly little bitch, we could've had something special," Wayne said. "I would've given you the world."

"If you can't come up with five hundred thousand dollars, I doubt you have the world to give."

"You're in over your head, baby girl," Wayne warned.

"Fuck what you think; I'll tell you what I know," Simone said. "I better have the money I asked you for by nine o'clock tomorrow night; end of discussion."

Simone hung up the phone and went to her room. She took her copy of the DVD from underneath her mattress and smiled. She got a magic marker and wrote "Jackpot" in big letters on the DVD. *Finally, I'm going places*, she thought.

Wayne walked back and forth through his house, shivering. *I can't believe she's doing this to me*, he thought. He was sorry. He wished that he hadn't been so arrogant and demeaning. He wished that he could take back everything that had happened at the hotel that night. God knew his life had been hectic since that night, but what could he do? There was no reasoning with Simone and he couldn't let her ruin him. She had already taken him through enough. He had no choice. It was time to call in a favor.

25

P aris put on his makeup. He could hear the laughs of the three troublemakers he had seen previously. One would make an obnoxious remark about one of the other contestants and the others would laugh and holler so loud that they could've been mistaken for dogs howling at the moon. Paris decided he wasn't going to let them bother him and he wasn't going to worry about whether Michael was there and who he was with. That night was about him. He didn't care what any of the other competitors thought about him or who would be there that night. The only thing that mattered was that he was pleased with himself, and he was. He was sure when he walked out onstage, the crowd would love him.

Paris lined up with the rest of the contestants and walked onstage to be introduced. He glanced out into the audience and almost lost his balance. Michael was sitting upfront with Jewel. Jewel grinned when Paris looked over at them. Paris took a deep breath. *Everything is fine*, he told himself. He wasn't going to panic or get flustered but he would strut a little bit harder and be extra charming. When Michael looked at him, he would not see odium but the value of what he'd lost and would never have again.

All the contestants stood onstage, ready for the first part of the competition. They would all walk up to the podium and answer the question: "Why did you decide to be gay?" Paris knew the question would be asked but had no idea how he would answer. Hell, he didn't remember deciding to be gay. He only remembered the moment he realized, in his heart, that he was gay and embraced it. All the contestants had the same tired answer: "Because you can't help who you love."

Paris decided to switch it up a bit. When it was his turn, he walked up to the podium and said, "I decided to be gay because you can't choose who you fall in love with, but you can choose who you have sex with."

The crowd cheered and Paris walked back to his spot onstage, grinning from ear to ear.

Next was the swimsuit segment of the competition. Paris wore a red halter bikini. The glitter from his lotion made his skin sparkle under the stage lights. As he watched the other competitors wobble out onto the stage like ducks, he realized that he would be the victor.

For the dance segment, Paris did a choreographed segment to Destiny Child's song "Bootylicious." As he danced and gyrated across the stage, he became exhausted. He heard Stefan and Simone in the audience cheering for him, along with the rest of the crowd. The sound of their voices gave him the strength to go on.

For the talent segment, Paris performed a spoken word piece that he had written himself. He walked up to the podium and gave his introduction. "This goes out to all the haters, all those who choose to spend their whole existence spreading negativity, disturbing the natural order of the earth; this one's for y'all."

Bitch, ho', slut, tramp, these are the things you say about me. So miserable you have to stroke your ego by bad-mouthing me. Jealous because I do things you only have the nerve to do in your dreams.

"I know that's right!" a voice yelled from the crowd.

Fag, queer, homo, gay, you spend so much time trying to think of words to classify me. Going out your way to expose me but don't know who you are, or who you want to be, or is it you want to come out the closet and be like me.

The audience applauded. "Tell it!" they screamed. "Tell it like it really is!"

Syphilis, herpes, HIV, these are the rumors you spread about me.

"You ain't never lied!" a member of the audience shouted.

So scared your man wants me, you couldn't give a damn about your integrity, as long as you can convince him my body is diseased, so you can have reassurance he won't come near me.

The audience applauded. Paris, out of breath, took advantage of the opportunity and paused to catch his breath.

Heathen, savage, heretic, if I don't share your beliefs you choose to demoralize me, but will look in my face and smile at me, even hand me your Bible and try to convert me. All the while gossiping about the people you claimed to have helped and their families.

The audience applauded once again. "Amen to that."

Did creation spur from you? Did you create the universe, the elements, the sun or the moon?

"Hell naw; they didn't create a damn thing!" a voice sounded from the audience.

Who are you to place judgment on me? You cover your ears, too proud to listen to me. It's time someone informed you, you are the lost one; not me.

The audience stood up and applauded him. Paris walked behind stage and got a drink of water. He got a washcloth to wipe the sweat from his body and took a seat. He was pleased with himself. He thanked Isis for his confidence and courage.

All the contestants stood onstage, ready for the winners to be announced. Paris was anxious. He prayed silently, and held his hands behind his back with his fingers crossed.

The host commented on the wonderful job all of the contestants had done and began to announce the winners. "For third place, give it up for Diva Delight."

Paris watched Diva Delight walk up and get his prize, a single red rose and fifty dollars. He was one of the three who were stirring up trouble backstage. Paris told himself that he wasn't going to get upset. He was going to take the high road and be happy for him. He refused to let jealousy sneak up on him. Jealousy was one of those emotions that could change you, for the worse. Besides, Diva Delight might've come in third place but Paris was certain that his name would be announced for first.

The host looked at his card and announced the winner for second place. "In second place, give it up for Paris."

Paris's jaw dropped. He stood there, frozen in his spot. *You've got to be kidding me*, he thought to himself. How was that possible? He saw the other contestants and none of them were as good as he was.

"Come on, Paris," the host said. "Don't keep us waiting too long."

Paris walked over and got his prize, a dozen red roses and two hundred dollars. Paris walked back to his spot onstage. He wanted the contest to be over. He wanted to get offstage and get a few drinks to lessen his disappointment.

The host announced the winner for first place. "First place goes to Cocoa Queen."

Cocoa Queen walked over to receive his prize, a dozen white roses and five hundred dollars. He was the ringleader of the three troublemakers. Paris rolled his eyes. *How the fuck could he win?* Cocoa Queen stumbled across stage the entire time, not able to walk in his shoes. He didn't even care enough to shave his legs for the swimsuit competition. His dancing was lousy. It looked more like he was having convulsions than dancing. When Cocoa

Queen went up to the podium to speak, he said, "umm," and smacked his lips so much, it seemed like he was waiting for a fuse to come on in his brain so he could recall the words that he needed to complete his statement.

Cocoa Queen began to blow kisses at the crowd and the crowd booed him. "Well, fuck y'all, too!" Cocoa Queen shouted, and then flung his roses out into the audience.

A shoe flew back at him, then a wig, a bottle of lotion, and more shoes. The host and the contestants covered their faces with their arms, trying to block the flying objects. Paris fled backstage and the others followed.

Cocoa Queen ran backstage, teary-eyed. He held his head down to avoid the stares. His cockiness was gone and his two friends laughed at him. Cocoa Queen grabbed his belongings and left out of the back door.

While the other contestants sat there discussing Cocoa Queen's misfortune, Paris thought about how amazing it was, that everything might not work out the way he'd expected them to but whenever he called on Isis, things did work out. He had to be conscientious not to take too much delight in Cocoa Queen's misfortune.

When the music in the club started to play, Paris joined his two friends and enjoyed himself, forgetting all about Cocoa Queen.

26

Simone drove down the street as the sun crept into the sky, illuminating the world. As she watched the transformation of the horizon from the deep darkness of midnight, to purple, to rose, she felt like she was part of it. She looked at Stefan and Paris through her rearview mirror. They had had their fill of drinks and now a look of boredom had settled on their faces. Simone smiled at the sight of the two. She could never remember a time that she'd felt so close to them. The feeling scared her. It was the quiet before the storm. Whenever she felt peace or happiness, God would reach out and shake the ground underneath her, causing everything she'd worked so hard for to tumble down. It was the same feeling she'd had when she left her grandmother at the hospital that day and went home with Stefan to cook, clean, and prepare for their grandmother to come home. God was about to strike again. She did not know what the result would be but the anxiety she felt warned that it would be nothing she could do to prevent it. She would be severely punished for her happiness. She couldn't conceive it as anything else but a punishment. God didn't want her to be happy. She was the one creature on earth God wouldn't allow pleasure. She never considered that her happiness was based on falsehoods that needed to be torn down so she could rebuild with new awareness, awareness of truth. Nor could she admit to herself that she had taken advantage of the familiar. She'd used it as her security blanket and it had stifled her growth. It was time for her to grow up.

Simone wished that she could take a picture of the moment so she would always remember that feeling of happiness. She never wanted to lose that feeling. She recalled her grandmother telling her that she didn't need a camera to take a picture. If she wanted to capture the moment, all she had to do was close her eyes and picture all that was going on at that moment in her mind for a few seconds. That way she would not have to fumble through photo albums searching for a photo. She could always recall it because it was inside of her and could never be destroyed. Simone pulled to the side of the road and closed her eyes tightly, remembering that moment, remembering the now.

"Where are we going now?" Stefan asked.

"Home. Why? Do you have something else in mind?" Simone asked.

"Well, now that you brought it up, I have this sudden urge to take Mrs. Sandra up on her offer."

"You want to go to church!" Simone exclaimed.

Paris giggled. "Church? What the hell has gotten into you?"

"I don't know," Stefan said. "It might be because I heard somebody yell 'amen' when we were at the club. They said it with such passion, I just feel compelled to go to church."

"You're so full of it," Paris said.

"I think the real reason is because his father goes to Mrs. Sandra's church and he wants to see his daddy," Simone said.

"Oh shut up," Stefan said. "I just want to go; that's all."

"I know one thing," Paris said. "I wouldn't mind seeing the look on Sandra's face when she sees y'all walk through the door."

"Why you say that?" Simone asked.

"You know damn well she really don't want y'all to come," Paris said. "The only reason she asked y'all to come is 'cause she figured y'all wouldn't and she could feel good about herself for inviting y'all."

"Well, I hope she's feeling mighty Christian-like, 'cause we're gonna surprise her ass today," Stefan said.

They all went to Simone and Stefan's house to wash up and change clothes. They hurried to make the service. Stefan and Paris jumped in the shower together and Simone washed up in the sink, spot-checking, only washing the parts of her body that were prone to odor.

Simone put on a summer dress and wore a shawl to

cover up her shoulders and back. Paris borrowed a pair of slacks, a dress shirt, trouser socks, and a pair of dress shoes from Stefan. Stefan wore a brown V-neck dress that tied in the back, a pair of sandals, and a big brown hat with a black bow on the side that had once belonged to his grandmother. Stefan had kept his grandmother's hat for such an occasion.

Stefan looked himself over in the mirror. "Okay, y'all, let's go."

Simone looked at Stefan and covered her mouth. "Are you really going to church like that?"

"They say come as you are and this is who I am."

Paris looked at Stefan and smiled. "I'll tell you one thing, your boldness has no boundaries."

❖

The three walked up the church steps. Simone's cheeks turned cherry red. She felt the embarrassment she thought that Stefan should have felt. She took a deep breath and prepared herself for the reaction of the congregation.

Stefan held his head high as he walked through the door. He nodded his head, acknowledging everyone who looked his way. The ladies smirked and the men looked at him with disdain. The congregation began to whisper among themselves. One of the men hurried over to get one of the ushers.

By the time Simone, Stefan, and Paris made it to the pew, the entire congregation was eyeing Stefan.

The usher walked over to Stefan as he was taking his seat and grabbed his arm. "Come with me."

"Excuse me?" Stefan said.

"Come on," the usher said, squeezing Stefan's arm.

Stefan snatched away from the usher. "I'm not going anywhere. I'm here to praise the Lord like everyone else."

The commotion grabbed Mrs. Sandra's attention. She slid past the people who sat on the pew with her and made her way over to Stefan.

The usher grabbed Stefan's arm again and demanded that he come with him.

"Come on, man; I told you, I'm not going anywhere," Stefan said. "Now go sit down. You can't keep groping on me in the house of the Lord."

"What?" the usher exclaimed.

"You heard me," Stefan said. "If you've got to have me that bad, I'll give you my number and we can get together later, but now ain't the time."

Mrs. Sandra tapped the usher on his shoulder. "Excuse me, Brother Thompson, he's with me."

The usher huffed and walked back to his post.

Simone sighed. She felt like she had been rescued from embarrassment.

Mrs. Sandra sat down on the pew with Simone, Stefan, and Paris and waited for the sermon to start. She looked around the church to see if Stefan's father was there. She spotted Stefan's father sitting three rows up from them. She tapped the lady in front of her on her shoulder and asked her to get his attention. The lady passed the message up the next row and soon Stefan's father turned around. Mrs. Sandra motioned for him to come to the pew where they sat but as soon as he saw Stefan, he turned away.

Stefan's father hadn't seen Stefan in over ten years. No matter how much Stefan had changed, it was impossible to forget his eyes. Stefan's father was shaken; he had seen a ghost.

The pastor asked the congregation to bow their heads for prayer. As the congregation prayed, Stefan looked over at his father, who took advantage of the opportunity. Stefan's father looked back at Stefan and then grabbed his hat and made his way out of the church.

Stefan's father tried to convince himself that he'd left because he was angry at what Stefan had become, but his soul knew the truth. The anger he felt when Stefan was a little boy was gone. This time he left because he feared how the congregation would perceive him when they found out that Stefan was his son. He also feared having to explain to Stefan why he was too weak to be a gay boy's father. He fled the church with his head held down like a coward with no intention of ever coming there again.

Mrs. Sandra looked up and noticed Stefan's father was gone. "I'm sorry, Stefan," she said, patting Stefan on his knee.

Stefan looked up at Mrs. Sandra and faked a smile. "It's okay; he did exactly what I expected him to do."

The pastor's voice shook the church as he sermonized about the love God had for all of His children who fell short of His glory. His children the sinners, whom He loved so much that He sent His only son down to earth to suffer all of the discomforts and limitations that came along with inhabiting a physical body and to be persecuted to give mankind the opportunity to be saved from the torment of hell.

Tears filled Stefan's eyes. They misrepresented God. They made Him petty and vengeful toward His children who didn't follow the laws set in place by officials. God wasn't the one that was petty or vengeful; it was men and they used the professed word of God to excuse their actions. Men lied, misconstrued words, and spoke falsely of people and situations for their benefit. The victors of wars and the thieves of continents wrote history to their liking, making fairytales out of notorieties. It was their practice all throughout time. Officers of the law inflated situations, lawyers twisted words, and the judges adhered. All in the name of collecting fines from the citizens they so-called protected, the same citizens who had to jump through hoops or perform other circus tricks, or be beaten nearly to death to get a restraining order. A lot of religious organizations had similar practices. They could tell you how to live and what would happen to you if you didn't adhere to their rules. Pay the church; follow our rules; break them and God will punish you; if you oppose us you're a heathen and heathens go to hell. They could tell you that but rarely nurtured the destitute or lent any physical help to those in need. As far as Stefan was concerned, they could take all of their rules, talk of sin and abomination, and hell-fire and shove it up their asses. If there was such a thing as sin it would be telling fibs about God, giving the masses a feeling of inferiority from the day they were old enough to comprehend the dogma drilled into their heads by religious groups. If sin did actually exist, it would be no more than guilt and inhibition. He didn't spread dogma. He didn't have any inhibitions. Nor was he guilty about how he lived his life.

Stefan wished his father would have accepted him for who he was and been a part of his life but he had chosen not to. If he could change how his father felt about him, he would, but he lacked the power to do so. He wasn't going to pretend to be someone he wasn't to court his father's acceptance; it was hard enough being himself. Stefan could not imagine the strain of acting as if he was something that he was not. He would be enslaving himself and he loved his freedom. Despite his father's feelings about him, Stefan wished him the best. He only wanted to lay eyes on him once more.

Simone lay in bed hugging her pillow with her sheet strung between her legs, only covering the front of her body. A breeze came through her window and blew across her face. It was a heavy smell in the air, the kind of smell that filled the air before a thunderstorm. Simone welcomed the storm. She planned to sleep into the next day and the sound of rain would induce a heavy sleep.

The phone rang. Simone dragged herself across the bed and grabbed the phone off of the nightstand. "Hello."

"I'm sorry," Wayne muttered.

Simone sighed. "Do you have my money?"

"Can't we talk about this?" Wayne asked. "Damn, give me a chance to make things right."

"I am," Simone said. "All you have to do is give me my fucking money."

Wayne did not want to go through with his plans. He did not want to have to take such extreme measures to put an end to the situation. He wanted to call his guy back and call the entire thing off, but Simone was so adamant about getting her way, she had left him no choice.

"Fuck it; if you want your money that bad, then meet me at the detail shop where we first met in an hour," Wayne said. "I'll have it."

"Are you going to have your down payment or are you going to have all of it?"

"All of it," Wayne answered.

"Oh, at first you said you didn't have it," Simone said. "So who got the boot? Mom and dad or was it the baby mama?"

"Do you want the money or not?"

Simone sucked her teeth. "Of course I want it."

"Then meet me in an hour," Wayne said, and then hung up the phone.

Simone stood up on her bed and jumped for joy.

"What the hell are you doing up there?" Stefan yelled from downstairs.

"Nothing," Simone answered. "Getting ready to meet Wayne."

"Why?"

"'Cause he's got my money."

"Oh, that's what's up," Stefan said. "What's my cut?"

"You ain't getting shit," Simone mumbled.

"I didn't hear you say anything."

"We'll talk about it when I get back," Simone said.

"Awright, but come here for a minute."

"For what?" Simone asked.

"I want you to see something."

Simone sighed. "What, Stefan?"

"This guy that's been sitting outside in this Impala," Stefan said. "He's fine. He's light-skinned and has curly hair. It looks like he has hazel eyes. He's been sitting in his car looking like a damn fool for about twenty minutes, but he sure is fine."

"How you know how long he's been out there?"

"'Cause I've been going back and forth to the window looking at him," Stefan answered.

Simone stopped ironing her clothes and went downstairs to humor Stefan and look out of the window at the fine man that he talked about.

Simone peeked through the blinds. "I don't see anybody."

"You don't see a gray Impala out there?"

"Yeah, but ain't nobody in it."

Stefan walked to the window and peeked through the blinds to confirm if what Simone had said was true. The car was still outside but the fine man that was sitting inside of it was gone.

Simone sucked her teeth. "I can't believe you called me all the way down here for nothing."

"Damn, you act like you ran down the block or some shit."

Simone rolled her eyes and stomped back upstairs to iron.

"Stomp your ass up the stairs then," Stefan said. "That's the last time I try to include you in something."

Simone sighed and continued on her way.

Stefan walked in the bathroom while Simone was putting on her earrings. "I'm about to step out for a minute."

"What you telling me for?"

"I need to use your car."

Simone squinted. "Why?"

"What do you mean, why?"

"You've been getting where you need to go without my car," Simone said. "Why can't you walk?"

"Well, aren't you a bitch."

"Whatever."

"I was only going to the drugstore to pick up my prescription."

"Damn, Stefan, you better hurry up," Simone said. "I have to meet Wayne in an hour."

Stefan went into Simone's room and grabbed her keys off of the nightstand. "I'll be right back."

"You better be."

Stefan started up the car and drove out of the backyard into the alley. He was on a mission. He had to go to the drugstore, swing by a fast-food restaurant to get something to eat, and get back home in enough time for Simone to meet up with Wayne.

Raindrops fell on the windshield. Stefan turned on the wipers and adjusted the rearview mirror. He caught a glimpse of someone sitting in the backseat as he was directing his attention back to the road. He looked back into the mirror and a pair of hazel eyes looked back at him, but they weren't his own. It was the guy that he'd seen sitting in the Impala across the street from his house. The guy looked back at him with a menacing grin. Stefan slammed on the brakes and grabbed for the door. Before Stefan could bail out of the car, the guy forced a plastic bag over his head. Stefan lost control of the car and ran into a neighbor's fence. He tugged at the bag, trying to rip a hole in it to get some relief but it was too thick. Stefan grabbed the metal fingernail file Simone kept between the seats and stabbed the guy in his forearm. The guy screeched and then he tightened his grip on the bag. Stefan jerked forward, hoping to make the guy lose his grip. He almost pulled the stranger over the front seat.

The guy was flustered. He couldn't believe how strong the woman that he'd come to kill was. He had to end things quickly before the situation got out of hand. He braced himself by planting his feet on the back of Stefan's seat and held a tight grip on the bag. All of a sudden, the struggling stopped. Stefan was slumped over with sweat dripping down his lifeless body. The guy sat there for a few seconds, trying to gather himself. He then got out of the car and rushed down the alley and around the block to his car. The guy got in his car, wiped the sweat off of his forehead, and then drove off. He called Wayne on his cell phone to tell him that the job was done.

28

The clock ticked past nine. Simone paced the living room floor. She'd told Stefan that she had to meet Wayne and he said he'd be right back. She wondered did the phrase "right back" have a different meaning to Stefan than it did to her. It had been three hours since he'd left and he wouldn't even pick up his cell phone when she called. Simone was tired of Stefan's shit. She was tired of him undermining her and taking advantage of her kindness. It was going to stop. As soon as Stefan walked through the door, she was going to tell him off and she didn't care how he felt about it. She was about to get a half-million dollars. If Stefan was going to carry it like that with her, she didn't need him. She could pack her bags and go about her business without him. *He's doing this shit on purpose*, she thought. He didn't want her to be better off than he was.

That was the problem with all the hating-ass bitches on the planet. They wanted it all for themselves, so they could scoff at the ones who were not as fortunate as they were. Like the chick with the new shoes and fresh hairdo that would poke fun at the woman whose shoes were worn out and whose hair wasn't done. The woman could be smarter, more lady-like, and have her priorities straight while the woman with the new shoes and hairdo could be unconcerned about expanding her mind, vulgar as hell, behind on her rent, and have no food in her refrigerator but knew she was better than the other woman because she had a nice pair of shoes and her hair was done. Then you had the ones who didn't do anything but sit around and complain about how bad things were for them. *If so and so can have that, why can't I have it, too? That bitch ain't no better than me; it's not fair.* They'd hold a grudge, not because someone harmed them or had taken something that belonged to them, but because someone had something they didn't have but felt entitled to.

Simone could not wait to get away from there and build a new life. With a half-million dollars she could make things work for her. Stefan was not the only one who could make friends.

She planned to make a lot of friends, friends that could introduce her to important people, friends who could teach her things and help her go places. Maybe she would be able to have her own line of clothing one day and Stefan would be somewhere strung out on drugs when he caught a glimpse of someone wearing something from her clothing line and he would eat his heart out.

Simone plopped down on the sofa and folded her arms over her chest. *I need to get the fuck away from here*, she thought.

Simone heard a knock on the door. *Damn, who the fuck could this be!* Simone swung the door open. Paris stood in front of her with tears in his eyes, and the smell of vomit covered his clothes and his breath. Simone wanted to give him the third degree; ask him had he heard from Stefan. If he knew where he was, he better call him and tell him to bring her car back, but she didn't want to seem insensitive when he appeared to be in so much distress.

Paris stooped down, resting his hands on his knees, trying to catch his breath so he could break the news to Simone.

"What's wrong?" Simone asked.

Paris's face scrunched up and tears begun to flow from his eyes.

Simone didn't understand Paris at first. His moaning and crying distorted his speech. The only word she understood was "Stefan." Paris's emotional state worried her.

Simone laid her hand on Paris's shoulder. "What did you say?"

Paris took a deep breath and repeated himself.

All Simone could decipher were the words "Stefan," "alley," and "dead." Simone ran down the porch steps, through the backyard, and down the alley. Paris staggered behind her, his vision blurred by grief.

Simone saw the coroner and medical examiners lift Stefan's body out of her car and lay him on a stretcher. She didn't want to believe that it was him but she couldn't convince herself otherwise. Although the bag still covered Stefan's head, she was too familiar with the sight of his arms and legs, the shoes on his feet, the dress on his body, and the necklace that dangled from his neck.

Simone's screams echoed throughout the neighborhood.

The neighbors, who had not come outside to snoop, opened their windows and backdoors to look outside and see what was going on and then made their way to the scene.

Simone ran over to the stretcher.

A police officer grabbed her. "Ma'am, you can't go over there."

"The hell I can't," Simone snapped. "That's my cousin."

Simone wiggled from the police officer's grasp and ran over to Stefan. She pulled at the bag on Stefan's head.

"Get her!" one of the medical examiners yelled.

The police officer grabbed Simone and tried again to restrain her. "It's going to be alright," the police officer said, trying to console her.

"What do you mean, it's going to be awright? Take the fucking bag off his head! He can't breathe!" Simone shouted. "He can't breathe!"

The neighbors stared at Simone. Some had tears in their eyes and some of their eyes were only filled with amusement.

"What the fuck y'all looking at?" Simone yelled. "Y'all bitches don't ever have two words to say to us but when something happens to one of us, y'all want to come and be nosy!" Simone kicked gravel on them. "Get the fuck out of here!"

Her comments filled the neighbors with guilt and they made their way back to their homes.

Mrs. Sandra stepped out of the crowd and put her arms around Simone and Paris. "If there is anything I can do, just let me know." She kissed them both on the cheek.

Paris's cries became more intense. "I love you, Stefan. I can't believe you're gone," he cried out.

Mrs. Sandra held Simone and Paris tightly, hoping to comfort them.

The detective walked over to them. "Excuse me."

Mrs. Sandra looked up at the detective. "Can I help you?"

"I'm Detective Warner; I heard one of these girls say the victim was her cousin."

"I'm a *woman* and he's my cousin," Simone said.

"And I'm a man, you bitch," Paris snapped.

Detective Warner's face turned as red as a garnet. "I suggest you two watch your tone. I'm the law and you need to show me some respect."

"No, you're not the law. That's scribed on paper," Mrs. Sandra said. "You're an officer of the law; try not to forget that. And anyone with decent sense could appreciate that these two have been through a lot tonight."

The detective huffed. He did not care what they had been through; he had some questions and he wanted answers right that second. He looked around and saw the police officers at the scene looking in his direction and decided to settle down. He had made an ass out of himself too many times, dealing with lowlifes. He would disrespect them to attempt to make them feel worthless or throw off on them because he'd had a bad day; in return, they would tell him how much of a joke he was, how fat and worthless he was. He'd roughed a few of them up and had taken them to lock up, but he could not live down the stories the officers carried back to the precinct. He was not about to give them any more ammunition for their jokes. So he nodded his head and agreed with Mrs. Sandra.

"Yes, I can understand that," Detective Warner said. "Maybe we got off to a bad start. All I want to know is whose car was he driving."

"Mine," Simone answered.

"So your name is Virginia Simmons?" Detective Warner asked.

"No, that's my grandma's name," Simone answered.

Detective Warner nodded. "What's your name?"

"Simone Simmons."

"And your cousin was Stefan Brown?" Detective Warner asked.

Simone sighed and nodded her head.

"Well, that's all I need to know right now," Detective Warner said. "I'm going to let you all go home. We'll have to take your car because it was involved in the crime, but we'll let you know when you can get it back."

"We understand," Mrs. Sandra said.

"Goodnight," Detective Warner said as he made his way to his car.

Detective Warner was sure that he'd overheard one of the detectives that he worked with describe the car. A 2010 pink convertible Saab registered to a deceased woman. He had to get back to his office and refresh his memory. He was sure he had found the culprit of another crime. It had been seven years since he had solved a case. He had become the butt of his coworkers' jokes. He was tired of hearing them whisper amongst each other, asking why he still had a job. This was his opportunity to redeem himself. It was his chance to show the arrogant bastards at work what he was made of.

There was a chance that the case was outside of his jurisdiction. He had heard talk of it but had never heard of it being assigned to anyone. He shrugged his shoulders. No matter, if it wasn't in his jurisdiction, it would only make the fact that he found the perpetrator that more plausible.

A dark cloud formed over the city as the news of Stefan's death spread. Rain poured from the sky as if the universe itself was mourning Stefan's death.

Simone and Paris sat on the sofa, holding each other as they cried, attempting to console one another.

Eugene flicked through the channels on his TV while

his new female friend gyrated on his tool, making her best effort to please him. Eugene thought he heard Stefan's name when skipping past the nightly news and flipped back to that channel. He couldn't believe it. The murder scene was in the alley behind Stefan's house. They showed Simone's car and once again the news reporter said his name; Stefan Brown. Tears ran down Eugene's face. He sat up and pushed his friend off of him.

"What's wrong?" his friend asked.

Eugene didn't answer. He was ashamed of how he had treated Stefan. How on the day of his death he had spent his time trying to woo some woman when he could have spent Stefan's last day on earth with him. And because he was sharing his body with someone else as he heard the news of Stefan's death, his guts churned with guilt. He wondered if Stefan's spirit had come to visit him as it made its exit and, if so, was him having sex with someone else the last thing he witnessed before he left the world. What type of person was he to inflict pain on someone who loved him as much as Stefan?

Mrs. Sandra thought about her son, Anthony. Life was too short and sometimes came to an end without warning. She didn't care how Anthony lived his life or what others thought about it. They could all burn in hell as far as she was concerned, including her husband. She wanted to be in her son's life, no matter what was going on with him. She picked up the phone and called Anthony. Maybe she would invite him to breakfast in the morning. The least she could do was call him and see how life was treating him.

Across town, Anthony sat on his bed with Crystal, smoking out of his crack pipe. They planned to get high and then make love.

Anthony saw his cell phone glowing in the darkness of the room. His mother's number appeared on the screen. He handed his crack pipe to Crystal and then stepped outside of the room.

"Hello."

"Hey, baby," Mrs. Sandra answered. "How have you been?"

Anthony paused for a moment. He was in shock. He hadn't heard his mother's voice in years. "I'm good," he answered. "How are you?"

"Oh, I'm fine."

"You sure?" Anthony asked. "I mean, nothing's wrong, is there?"

"It's funny you asked that," Mrs. Sandra said. "A lot has happened today. Have you heard about Stefan?"

"Naw, what about him?"

"He was killed."

"*What!*"

"He was murdered in the alley behind his house."

"Damn, I'm sorry to hear that," Anthony said. "That just fucked up my whole night."

"Mine as well," Mrs. Sandra said. "I stayed with Simone and Paris for a while. They are really hurting."

"Damn, I forgot all about those two."

"This incident really made me realize how much I miss having you in my life."

"I miss you, too," Anthony said.

"Who the fuck you talking to?" Crystal yelled.

"Look, Mom, I've got to go. I kind of have company."

"I see…I wanted to ask you to have breakfast with me tomorrow."

"I don't know," Anthony said. "What about I call you in the morning and let you know if I feel up to it?"

Mrs. Sandra paused. She had so many things that she wanted to discuss with Anthony. She wanted to tell him that she didn't care if he was dating Charlie and if he wanted, he could bring him along for breakfast. She wanted Anthony to understand that she realized that he and Charlie were junkies and she would do anything she could to help them break their addiction. She wanted to ask him had he and Charlie considered going to rehab. But she decided to take things slow. "Well, just let me know. Charlie is welcome to come."

"Okay, Mom, take care."

"You, too."

Anthony went back into the room with Crystal.

"Who the hell were you taking to?" Crystal asked.

"That was my mother."

"Your mother? What made her call out of the blue like that?"

Anthony looked at Crystal; he seemed to be in a good

mood and tonight was their night. He didn't want to spoil it by making Crystal cry. He kissed Crystal on his forehead. "We'll talk about it in the morning."

❖

Thomas lay in bed with his wife. As his wife slept, he stared up at the ceiling thinking about Stefan. He couldn't believe that he was gone. Stefan was more than a hooker to him. He was more beautiful than any woman could ever be and his beauty brought him joy. Every time he thought of Stefan, he felt like the sun was shining on him and life was fine, everything was just fine. He didn't care what anyone said, Stefan was a treasure, a jewel that shined his light on the world and now he was gone.

❖

Stefan's father, who hadn't heard the news yet, lay in his bed having a fitful dream. The angel of death had come for his soul and he struggled to break free from its grasp. He wasn't ready yet. He had so much more to do with his life. He hadn't finished making his contribution to the world. As he cried and struggled in his dreams, he managed to come out of his tee shirt. He heard a voice in his head say, "Be still and know that I am God." Was it God or was it the Devil toying with him? "Oh, please help me!" he screamed at the top of his lungs. It was the sound of his screams that woke him from his sleep. He sat in the bed sweaty and terrified, trying to catch his breath.

⬦

Tessa sat in the alley by a Dumpster as she waited for Tony to score. Not only did Tony come back with some smack, he also came back with the news of Stefan's death. Tessa squealed and danced around with joy. "It's about time," Tessa said. "It's about damn time."

29

T he sunlight peeked through the blinds, waking Paris. He turned his back to the window and pulled the covers over his head. He'd spent the night with Simone. He was not up for the walk home and neither he nor Simone wanted to be alone. He'd slept in Stefan's room. He could smell Stefan's scent on the sheets that covered the bed and all throughout the room. He had dozed in and out of sleep, dreaming that Stefan was still alive. He dreamt that Stefan walked into the room and had asked him what he was doing in his bed, and they had both stayed up all night reminiscing about old boyfriends and the trouble they had gotten into throughout the years. Then he would wake up, thinking Stefan would walk through the door any minute with something witty to say. Then reality sat in, and he realized he would have to live out the rest of his life without Stefan, and the tears started to come again.

Paris wondered had Kenneth and Jamal caught up with Stefan and, if so, would he be next. He wanted to ask Simone if she had told Jana where they lived. He needed to tell Simone what had happened in New Orleans. He couldn't leave her in the dark. If Stefan's murder had resulted from what they had done while they were in New Orleans, both he and Simone were in danger of undergoing the same fate.

⬥

Simone sat on the sofa where she had fallen to sleep the night before. Her eyes were swollen and blood red. It was three o'clock in the afternoon and the phone had been ringing off and on since six o'clock that morning. Some of the numbers on the caller ID she did not recognize; the ones she did were Jewel, Crystal, and Eugene. Jewel was not even Stefan's friend; Stefan and Crystal had not talked to each other in months. She hoped Eugene did not miss Stefan now; he should have seen him more than once a week. She didn't have one nice thing to say to any of them. She picked up the phone and slammed it down when they called. Unless they could conjure up some spell and bring Stefan back to life, to hell with them.

Simone thought back to her mother's words earlier that summer, about how Stefan was going to die behind what he had done to spite her. She snatched the phone off of the base and called her mother.

"Hello," Tessa said, answering the phone on the first ring.

"I know you had something to do with the shit that happened to Stefan," Simone snapped.

"Who the fuck is this?"

Simone knew her mother realized who she was and why she had called. She'd answered the phone too quickly not to know. Simone screamed into the phone. "Oh, bitch, you know who the fuck this is!"

"Look, Simone, you don't have to talk to me like that," Tessa said. "I've been trying to get my life together—"

"Well, it's about to come to an end," Simone spat.

"What did you say?"

"You heard me."

"How the hell you gonna call me out the blue and threaten me?"

"Don't play stupid with me," Simone said. "I know what you did to Stefan."

"What are you talking about?" Tessa asked. "I ain't seen Stefan since who knows when and haven't talked to either of you for months now."

"Remember that bullshit you said about how Stefan spited you and how he was gonna die behind it?"

"Look, I know what happened to Stefan," Tessa said. "And I meant to call you this morning to say I was sorry to hear about it, but I didn't do anything to that boy."

"It seems funny to me that you said that shit and now he's dead."

"What seems funny to me is, as many people as he's fucked over, he's just now being put to sleep," Tessa said. "Seems like somebody would've done that shit way before now."

"Bitch, fuck you," Simone spat. "That's why I hate your ass."

"Don't be mad at me," Tessa said. "You know what he was and how he was; grow up."

"I'll tell you what I do know."

"What's that?" Tessa asked.

"That you're about to be keeping him company."

Simone slammed down the phone. Snot and tears ran down her face. *If it's the last thing I do, I'm gonna make sure that bitch leaves this world in an untimely fashion.* She could use some of the money she was getting from Wayne to hire someone to rid the world of her mother. *Damn, the money.* With all that had happened, she'd forgotten to call Wayne and set up another time to pick up her money. She hoped that he had not changed his mind. If he had, oh well, she would sell it to the highest bidder. Hell, she might sell it even if he gave her the money. She'd never gotten a break so she damn sure wasn't about to give somebody else one.

❖

Wayne sat back in his lounge chair in front of the pool at his Florida home where his wife and children resided. He watched his children splash water and take turns dunking each other back and forth in the pool. He looked over at the house, thinking of his wife in the kitchen preparing dinner. He had not felt that kind of happiness in years and he knew the happiness he felt being there was mutual. He wanted to be a family again.

He was tired of using loose women to entertain himself. He had been with more women than most men will during their lifetimes, all different creeds and nationalities, all beautiful in their own way. But they all had one thing in common; they would do unimaginable things to get his money and that was only a good thing when it came to sex.

Simone made him realize that it was time to stop playing around. Although he was able to shut her up permanently, it had been a close call; one that took years off of his life. It was time for him to settle down. Nicole had stood by him through everything; if not as a wife, as a friend. She was the type of woman that he wanted in his life. Simone had made him realize that. He had grown tired of playing games with scandalous women. He planned to make love to his wife that night and afterward, he would tell her that he wanted to reconcile.

Wayne's cell phone rang and he looked down at the caller ID. *What the fuck?* Why was he getting a call from Simone's house? She was supposed to be dead. His guy had assured him that she was. There was no way she could be calling him. *My conscience must be fucking with me*, he thought. Wayne let the call go to voice mail. A few minutes later his phone beeped, alerting him of a new voice message. He closed his eyes and took a deep breath to brace himself as he lifted the phone to his ear to listen to the message.

"Yeah, it's me," Simone's voice echoed. "Just because I

wasn't able to make it last night, don't get to thinking I don't want my money. You need to have it to me by tomorrow morning. If not, this DVD is as good as the media's and everyone will know how much fun you had getting it on with my cousin."

Wayne became dizzy and every hair on his body was erect. He couldn't believe it; it was her. His guy had never lied to him before. Wayne needed further confirmation. He dialed Simone's number and waited to see who picked up.

"Hello," Simone answered.

Wayne hung up the phone and called his guy.

He answered after a few rings. "Damn, Wayne, more work already? What you been into these days?"

"I thought you said you handled that for me."

"And I did."

"That's odd 'cause she just finished calling me."

"Are you saying I'm a liar?"

"Naw, I'm saying the bitch still has air in her lungs."

"Man, look, I went to the house. She was driving the car you described. It had the same license plate and everything. And she fit the description."

"Are you sure it was a woman?"

"What do you mean, am I sure it was a woman? It had on a dress." The guy paused for a moment to think; if it was a man, that would explain why he had given him so much trouble. "Man, what type of shit you into?"

"Just answer the question."

"All I can tell you is my work is done."

"Naw, man, you need to fix this or give me my money back."

"All I'm going to say is this, I don't shit in the same place twice, and I damn sure don't hand out refunds."

"This is bullshit."

"It's no longer up for discussion, but call me if you have some work for me in the future."

Wayne threw his phone on the ground and lay back in his lounge chair. He covered his face with his hands and screamed. His kids jumped out of the pool and approached him.

"What's the matter, Daddy?" they asked.

Wayne didn't answer; he continued to lie there with his hands over his face, trembling. There was no need to answer them. They would soon find out what had caused his anxiety and then they would be deaf to his words, forget his face, and deny he was their father. He could restore his reputation from the accusations of assault and rape. It was Simone's word against his. People would side with him, not because they knew his character, but because they liked what they saw of him on TV. But from this, there was no redemption. His fans would not forgive him for portraying himself to be an alpha male and then participating in a homosexual act. They would deny him his manhood. He was ruined.

Simone gritted her teeth. *Damn, I wish she'd stop calling.* Tessa was calling back for the tenth time. Simone did not want to miss Wayne's call due to her mother's compulsive behavior.

Simone picked up the phone. "What!" she shouted.

"Don't do nothing stupid, hear."

"Whatever," Simone said. "Stop ringing my damn phone."

Paris made his way downstairs as Simone hung up the phone. "Simone, I need to talk to you."

Simone shook her head. "I don't feel like it right now; maybe later."

"It can't wait 'til later."

"What is it then?"

Paris took a deep breath. "Did you tell Jana where—" Paris was interrupted by a knock on the door.

Simone rolled her eyes. "I swear, this better not be either one of those dumb asses that kept calling this morning."

Simone walked over to the window and looked through the blinds. Detective Warner stood on the front porch with a black female officer by his side.

"Oh, it's the detective from last night," Simone said. "Maybe he came to tell me that I can get my car back."

Simone opened the door. "Yes," she said, looking at the female officer's badge that read "Evans."

"You're Simone Simmons, right?" Detective Warner asked.

Simone nodded. "Yeah, that's me."

"Good," Officer Evans said, grabbing Simone by her arm. "You're under arrest."

Simone snatched away and ran toward the kitchen.

Officer Evans pinned Simone down and handcuffed her. "Evading the police is a felony."

"You would think being charged with murder would be enough for her," Detective Warner said.

"Murder," Simone bellowed. "But I didn't kill anybody."

Officer Evans grabbed Simone's arm to escort her to the police car. Simone bent her knees and collapsed onto the floor.

"Get up!" Officer Evans shouted.

Simone pressed herself against the floor.

Detective Warner laughed. "Well then, Evans, I guess we'll have to drag her."

"Hold on!" Paris exclaimed, as he rushed to help Simone. "You can't do that!"

Detective Warner placed his hand on the gun strapped to his left side. "I can do anything I want to, boy." Detective Warner looked at Paris and smirked. "Or should I say girl?"

Paris's skin became hot. His blood boiled. He wanted to beat Detective Warner. He wanted to smack him and watch the blubber on his big pink face tremble. He wanted to tell him that he hated his type; scared-ass criminals who hid behind the badge of the law and did their dirty work. But Detective Warner's eyes warned that he was a miserable, insecure, trigger-happy bastard and Paris valued his life.

Detective Warner and Officer Evans dragged Simone out of the house.

"Come get me, Paris!" Simone yelled. "Look under my mattress and get some money so you can bond me out!"

Paris ran upstairs and lifted up Simone's mattress. A stack of money lay in the center of the box spring, held together by a rubber band. Beside the money lay Paris's earrings and bracelet. Paris picked up the bracelet to make sure that it was his. He looked for his name engraved on the clasp and, sure enough, it was there.

That bitch, he thought. How could she steal his jewelry? He had asked her if she'd seen his jewelry in Michael's room and she'd looked him in his face and said "no." Maybe he was foolish to think better of her. Maybe he was stupid to take their friendship so seriously. Both of them were thieves but never once had he stolen from her. But she'd seized the opportunity when she saw something she wanted. Something she could've bought herself; the stack of money under her mattress was proof that she was not hard up for cash. Maybe she didn't think of him in the same way that he thought of her; as a friend.

Paris picked up the DVD underneath the stack of money that had "Jackpot" written on it in big bold letters. Paris wondered why she had given the DVD such a name. He put the DVD in Simone's DVD player and pressed

PLAY. Paris grinned as he watched Stefan get it on with Wayne.

Well, he sure got the chance to live out one of my fantasies before he left this world, Paris thought. Simone had given the DVD the proper name. Paris was sure he could get a lot of money for it. If Simone thought it was okay to steal from him, he had no problem returning the favor.

30

Simone sat in the interrogation room at the mercy of Detective Warner and Officer Evans.

"How long have you been using your dead granny's identity to obtain credit?" Detective Warner asked. "Weeks, months, ever since her death?"

Simone's pulse quickened. *Who the fuck does this fat, sloppy, old white pig think he's talking to?*

"Did you hear the question?" Officer Evans asked.

Simone glared at her with rage-filled eyes.

"I suggest you answer the question," Officer Evans said.

"Never," Simone said.

"Excuse me," Detective Warner said.

"Never, I never used her identity to obtain credit," Simone reiterated.

"How do you explain your car?" Officer Evans asked.

"I paid cash for my car. It's just in her name," Simone said.

"Where did you get the money from?" Detective Warner asked. "Hooking?"

Simone looked away and didn't offer a response.

"We found a camcorder in the home of two murder

victims," Detective Warner said. "It was hidden on the dresser in that dump they called a room."

"They were being entertained by two prostitutes when they had a dispute over payment and were killed," said Officer Evans.

"Guess who we have on tape committing those murders?" Detective Warner said.

Simone got a knot in her stomach. They were bluffing. There was no way they had a tape of the incident.

"Would you like to see the tape?" Officer Evans asked.

Simone lowered her head. After all that had happened to her during the last few months, she couldn't be spared from this.

Officer Evans smirked. "Warner, I think she's embarrassed."

"Are you, Simone?" Detective Warner asked. "Are you embarrassed about being a hooker?"

"Aw, don't be too hard on her, Warner," Officer Evans said. "It's understandable. If I did any of the things she did on that tape, I wouldn't show my face in public."

Detective Warner nodded his head in agreement. "I sure am glad your grandmother didn't live to see this."

Simone could not hold in her rage any longer. She hated how they stood in front of her with their holier-than-thou attitudes, knowing damn well they had committed their own offenses. The only difference between her and them were they wore badges. It was apparent that Detective Warner was lonely and so desperate that he was a turn-off to even the most undesirable women. He gorged himself, trying to cure his loneliness. His distorted figure was proof of that. He would be more than happy to pay for a woman's services, even if it was only to keep him company.

Officer Evans was the plain Jane-type. There was nothing special about her. The way she stood, the placement of her arms near her sides, her not being able to veil how fascinated she was with having control over the situation showed that she was goofy. Simone was sure she had clients who had treated her better than any man Officer Evans had ever been with had treated her. She would bet her bail money that Officer Evans' job was the primary way that she met her men. She pretended to look out for the criminals that she and her coworkers arrested, hoping that in return, she would be sexed by them later.

"Don't worry about my grandma. She sure wouldn't have given a shit about a fat piece of trash like you," Simone said.

Detective Warner's face grew redder and redder with each passing second until it resembled a tomato. He tried to mask his anger with a smile but Simone realized that she had hit a nerve.

"I bet your fat, lonely ass be cruising the streets looking for a woman like me, but you don't have enough money to talk a junkie into sleeping with you," Simone said.

Detective Warner became furious. "Listen, you little bitch…"

"Hey…hey…hey…" Officer Evans shouted, cutting

her partner off. It was time for her to take over. She was disgusted with how her partner had allowed Simone to get under his skin so easily. She was certain that he had heard a similar spiel several times before. If he couldn't deal with it, he needed to hand over his badge and let someone else have his job.

Officer Evans looked Simone over. Simone had her flaws. She sat in front of them with her clothes wrinkled up, sweaty, and with her hair tangled. She wondered had Simone slept in her clothes the night before and if she'd had a chance to bathe before they arrested her.

"Seems like Warner hit a nerve," Officer Evans said. "If your grandmother meant that much to you, you should've honored her by living a better life."

"Nothing's wrong with my life," Simone said. "I make more money in one night than you do in a month and I have clients that treat me better than any man will ever treat you."

Officer Evans laughed.

"I don't know what you're laughing for," Simone said. "You know it's true. I could have your man if I wanted him, although I doubt you have one."

Officer Evans held up her hand and pointed to the one-carat ring on her left hand. "This is an engagement ring, something you will never have, being that men don't marry women like you."

"Whatever, he's probably a junkie or some criminal you locked up and made your boo." Simone giggled. "I wouldn't be surprised if you had to pay for the ring yourself."

"Even if I did buy my own ring, I still have something you will never have; a man who's committed to me. And by the way, my man wouldn't have you." Officer Evans looked Simone up and down, sizing her up. "My man might be a criminal, but he does require his women to take baths."

Simone jumped out of her seat and charged Officer Evans. Officer Evans grabbed the can of mace off of her side and sprayed it into Simone's face.

"Arrgh!" Simone screamed and fell to the floor.

Detective Warner cheered Officer Evans on. "Good job, Evans; mace her like the dog she is."

Two officers lifted Simone off of the floor. One grabbed her feet and the other grabbed her arms. They took her to solitary confinement and threw a dingy white pillow-case and a mattress into her cell.

Simone sat on her bunk and cried. There was no one to help her. No one to tell her what to expect or how to get out of the mess that she was in. There was no one to tell her everything would be all right and she couldn't assure herself of that; she knew better. Was this what her life was about: tragedy? God always found a way to bring her down, to weave misfortune into her life. She'd witnessed others perform cruel acts without facing consequences. But for everything she did, Judgment Day came and arrived quickly. She recalled the story that she was once told as a child. The story of Maat, whose feather the hearts of the dead were weighed against, and if their hearts outweighed her feather, their souls would be devoured. She thought about how refreshing that would be, her soul being devoured; it would be the end of her existence. She would not have to worry about her fate. She would no longer wonder if Officer Evans was right about a man never committing to her, or if Detective Warner was right about her being equivalent to a dog. She wouldn't grit her teeth with anger when she thought about how much pleasure her enemies would feel when they learned of her misfortune, or how the girls she had gone to school with would laugh and talk about how they knew that she would never amount to anything. She envied the dead. Stefan was lucky that he was allowed to take the easy way out.

Stefan's father lay back on his couch and cried. Memories raced through his head. He remembered the day that Stefan was born. He had his mother's complexion and her hazel eyes. He'd held Stefan in his arms while they cleaned up his wife, Sarah. Stefan looked at him and smiled.

"He just smiled at me," he told his wife.

His wife laughed. "He's too young to do that. He probably has gas, Dennis. They say it tickles their bellies."

He didn't care what his wife had said. Their baby had smiled at him. After all of the hard work that he had done to free himself from his mother's womb, he still had the strength to smile. His son was a winner, a survivor. He was a proud father. He was grateful to his wife for bearing him a son.

He remembered taking his three-year-old son to the park to socialize with other kids. Stefan had picked flowers with the girls and fought the boys. He was a flower picker and one hell of a little fighter.

His wife told him not to worry about their son's behavior. Their son was fine. He was still so young and wasn't aware of the dos and don'ts for boys and girls, let alone his sexual orientation. He was a free spirit. He would eventually grow to know the ways of the world but, meanwhile, let him be.

When Stefan was four years old, Dennis noticed that he was still urinating sitting down after he had showed him the proper way for men to urinate for what seemed like a hundred times. Then there was the time he had overheard Stefan asking his mother when he would develop breasts.

Dennis looked back on the day he had walked out on his wife and his son. How his wife had begged him to stay.

"Please don't leave," she'd pleaded. "It's too soon to tell whether he's gay or not and even if he is, we'll find a way to deal with it. That's what families do."

He'd ignored his wife's pleas, grabbed his suitcase, and made his way to the door. Stefan stood by the door, crying as he made his way out.

"Daddy, please don't leave," he'd said.

He'd pretended not to hear his son and left.

What would people say when they found out that his son was gay? What would his mother and father say, whose roots were deeply embedded in the church? He had brought shame to his family.

No matter what good deed he had done, when people heard of the deed, they wouldn't praise it. They would be too busy saying, "You know his son is gay." Stefan was his dark shadow; his curse.

He blamed his wife. He thought she had some genetic defect and that's why his son's body didn't match his spirit.

He tried to forget them. When his wife committed suicide, he told himself that it wasn't his fault. He hardened his heart and spent whatever free time he had volunteering at the church, so he could stay busy.

But now the floodgates were open and there was nothing he could do to keep his mind off of the family he had started and then ran out on. There wasn't anything he could do to keep his mind off the loss of his son. Oh, how he was foolish. What man would turn his back on his family so he wouldn't be defamed by others?

Stefan wasn't his curse. His pride was. It had caused him to lose his wife and now his son. He kept replaying the day he had left them over in his head. He imagined that he had made up with his wife and they had worked things out, and now they were all sitting around the table having dinner and that he wasn't lying in the house by himself grieving the loss of his Sarah and Stefan. Instead, he was enjoying their company. But no matter how much he daydreamed about what would have happened if he hadn't walked out on them, that chance had come and gone and there was nothing he could do to change the past. All he had were memories, a few pictures of Stefan as a child, and the pictures they had taken of Stefan in his coffin before he was buried. He would have rather seen his son prancing around in one of his dresses, with his heels and makeup on, than lying in a coffin.

When the medical examiner informed him that Stefan had HIV, his heart almost stopped. Everything was his fault. He was the one who had left his son to fend for himself. He was the reason Stefan had allowed men to violate him for money.

Dennis couldn't conceive that no matter how tough things had gotten for Stefan, he had lived his life to the fullest. Regardless of whatever happened in life, he'd made it his business to be happy.

Dennis looked through his photo album and found a picture of Stefan and Simone together as children. They both looked so happy. Stefan's death had to hit her as hard as it had hit him. They were born cousins but were more like siblings. Both of them had been abandoned by their parents. With a father like him and a mother like Tessa, they never stood a chance.

He was thankful that Simone was still alive; in a sad predicament but alive. After Mrs. Sandra told him Simone was incarcerated he vowed to do everything within his power to help Simone. He would be to her what he had never been to Stefan; a father. He would do everything in his power to get her off. He would call in favors and give up church members that were laundering money and involved in other shady activities. And when she came home, he would make sure that she lived out the remainder of her life as comfortably as possible.

31

All Simone did was sleep and cry during the week that she spent in solitary confinement. She left her cell once to go to medical. While she waited to be called in the back to have her blood work done, she overheard the other women bragging about the different jails they had been in and how they wished they could be transferred to a particular jail instead of serving their time in the one that they were in. She thought jail was jail. She couldn't imagine how anyone could have a preference or could possibly wish to go anywhere but home. She could not wait until her preliminary hearing. She hoped Paris had called to find out what day she was to appear in court so he could come, find out how much her bond was, and then bail her out.

The first day of the second week of her stay, Simone lay in her bed staring at the wall. She wondered what time of day it was; the filth that covered the window in her cell prevented the sunlight from giving her a clue as to whether it was morning or night. She wouldn't know if it was morning until the lights came on or the deputy came around to announce chow. *This shit is torture*, she thought. To be confined so long she had no concept of time, to be fed things domestic animals would turn their noses up at, to consume fluid that smelled like juice but looked and tasted like water; it was inhumane. Was this the place she had heard so many people brag about going to? The same place they had said you could grow accustomed to after a while. They had to be crazy or had not yet found anything to live for. Even if that were the case, how could anyone get used to such a place? It was a place that shattered hope and stunted spiritual and physical growth. It was one of those places that you would die just to leave.

"Simmons! Medical! Bring your things!" the deputy shouted, bringing Simone back into the moment.

Simone shoved her sheets and hygiene products down into her pillowcase, grabbed her mattress, and then waited by the door for the deputy to escort her.

Simone walked past the pregnant women lined up at the door, waiting to be escorted back to their tiers. She walked to the back and took a seat. She wondered would she ever have the opportunity for a life to be planted within her womb.

The doctor stood in front of Simone, looking down at the sheet of paper that he held in his hand. "Simmons, your blood tested positive for HIV."

"HIV? How is that possible?" Simone asked as tears rolled down her cheeks. "I didn't have that shit before I got here."

The doctor looked at Simone and sighed. "I'm going to start you on Combivir and Ziagen."

A nurse walked in with two small cups; one with water and the other with several tablets. One of the tablets was familiar to Simone; it was yellow and had the same imprint as the prescription medication that she'd discovered in Stefan's gym bag. Her tears grew heavy as she struggled to swallow the tablets. Ever since Stefan had died, her life had seemed to get worse each day.

How could he do this to me, she thought. *How could he be so careless?* They'd shared the same clients and often had unprotected sex with them. How could he do her like that? He was the only one who gave a damn about her and if that wasn't true, then no one did. He was always there for her. He protected her. But why didn't he protect her from himself?

The nurses in the back observed Simone crying. Simone could hear them talking amongst themselves.

"I feel so sorry for her," one of the nurses said.

The other nurse rolled her eyes. "I don't. That's what happens when you run around selling your ass."

Simone held her head down as she was escorted to the medical tier. She felt so low; there was no need for the deputy to unlock the door so she could get in. She could've crawled under the door and gotten in all by herself. Simone didn't bother to look around to see the faces of those that sat in the dayroom as she made her way to her cell. Hopefully, she wouldn't get to know anyone. She would go to sleep and never wake up. Simone threw her mattress on the bottom bunk and then lay down and cried until she fell asleep. She slept through lunch, dinner, and breakfast the next morning.

Simone was awakened by her cellmate who brought a letter in the room that was addressed from Stefan's father. She could feel photos in the envelope as she opened it.

Simone,

I'm sorry that you and Stefan had to live the way you did. I only wish that I had been there for the both of you when your grandmother died so you and Stefan wouldn't have had to raise yourselves. I wish that I would've stayed in Stefan's life in the first place. Maybe I would still have a wife and a son. I can't change what happened and I will never have the opportunity to make things right with Stefan, but I can make things right with you.

I'll be at your hearing next week and if they give you a bond, I'll post your bail. Your mother has moved back into your grandmother's house. You know your grandmother left that house to her? You can stay with me until this whole thing is over with and you get back on your feet.

Paul gave your money to Sandra. I'll use that to post your bond. If it's not enough, we can use some of the other money he left you. He gave Sandra ten thousand dollars today. He said you won the jackpot and said you'd split the money with him. He said the ten thousand is your cut. He told Sandra he was moving to New Orleans and to tell you good luck and that he found his jewelry under your mattress.

Well, I'll see you soon. Keep your head up, baby girl.
Love,
Uncle Dennis

Simone sat up on her bunk. *Muthafucka*, Simone thought. *I can't believe he stole my DVD. Mister "money ain't everything."* Simone wanted to cry but thought she didn't have enough fluid in her body to shed another tear. She looked at the pictures that Stefan's father had sent her. She and Stefan were toddlers, dressed up and holding hands with their bushy hair all over their heads. They were smiling and staring wide-eyed into the camera. She looked at the next picture. It was Stefan lying in his coffin, wearing a suit and tie. Simone covered her mouth. *He's dead; I can't believe he's really dead.*

"Ladies, chow!" the duty yelled as she walked past the tier.

Simone rushed to the window and screamed for the deputy.

"Deputy, I can't stay here; I want to die! I want to kill myself!"

32

T wo different days, one day at dawn and the next at dusk, Kenneth, Jamal, and Jana waited outside of Simone and Stefan's house in the 2003 Buick they'd paid ten thousand dollars for from some old fellow they'd run across in front of his house taking groceries out the trunk of his car. They had been in Richmond for five days now, staying at a rinky-dink hotel. They could barely sleep while they were there. There was something about the bed, the sheets, the detergent used to wash the sheets, or maybe mites. Whatever it was, it made them itch.

This was the third day they had staked out the house, waiting to see Stefan, Simone, or Paris; preferably all three of them. Nightfall slowly approached. Kenneth sat in the car, slurping the last of his soda out of his cup. He was becoming agitated. This was the *last* day he was coming back to stake out the house and something had to give.

Jamal sat in the passenger side seat with his eyes closed. He was starting to doubt that anyone lived in the house. *This has been a fucking waste*, Jamal thought. *All the time we spent trying to hunt their asses down, we could've made up for what they stole and then some.*

Jamal looked at Kenneth out the corner of his eye and huffed. He closed his eyes again. The image he got of Kenneth stuck with him; red eyes, flared nostrils, sweat running down his face. Kenneth was intent on killing. He was psyched up for it, just itching to tear flesh apart like a rabid animal. Jamal shook his head. *This nigga needs to lay off the coke. That shit's fucking with his brain.*

Jana sat in the back seat with a book in her lap, pretending to read when she had really spent the few hours they had been there praying that they had the wrong house, that Simone didn't live there and if she did, that that day she would have a revelation and decide she was too young to stay cooped up in such a small city and decide she wanted to travel and see the world. Then she would leave town, not worrying about packing her belongings, and she would never return. Jana didn't care what happened to Stefan or Paris, but there was something so naïve, so innocent about Simone that made Jana want to protect her and that made Jana love her. But she wasn't about to put her life on the line for Simone. Kenneth had that look in his eyes and whenever he had that look, there was no reasoning with him. He would kill anyone who stood in his way. That's why there used to be six of them and now there were only three. Jana wasn't about to try her hand. Then there would just be two of them; Kenneth and Jamal. And she guessed after Kenneth eventually killed Jamal, he would go out on a limb and live out the rest of his life as a serial killer.

Damn, I like the bitch but she ain't worth all that, Jana thought. *And she ain't give me no ass. If she shows up, she's shit out of luck.*

Kenneth crushed his Styrofoam cup in his hand. "This shit is really starting to piss me off. I'm ready to kill the next person that walks past this bitch."

Jamal looked at Kenneth and shook his head.

Kenneth turned up his nose as he looked over at Jamal. "What the fuck's wrong with you?"

Here we go, Jamal thought. "Shit!"

"Something's up with yo' bitch ass, shaking yo' head at me like you think I'm some mutherfuckin' punk," Kenneth said, spit flying from his mouth. "Keep doing that shit and I won't have to wait for the next person that walks by; I'll smoke yo' ass."

Jamal turned toward Kenneth. "Yeah, and after you finish smoking it, you can suck out it for me."

Kenneth grabbed for his gun.

"Hey!" Jana shouted. "Stop that. We came here to get even. How we gonna do that if we kill each other?"

Jamal turned around and looked at Jana. "Who the fuck asked you?

"I'm just saying... Look, forget it. This shit's stupid. I don't even think anyone lives here."

"You're the same bitch that thought a chick was in the bathroom taking a shit when her ass was long gone, so don't tell me what the fuck you think," Kenneth said, swinging his arms wildly as if he was fighting the air. "Just keep yo' fucking mouth shut."

"I say we go in the house and look around," Jamal said. "I mean, if they live there, there's got to be something like pictures; mail; some shit to let us know we're on the right track."

"Oh, that's a good idea," Jana said.

"It's a dumb-ass idea; especially since I told y'all shit-heads that this is where the fuck they live," Kenneth said.

"I'm just saying, it won't hurt to go in and look around," Jamal said.

"You know what I'm going to say?" Kenneth asked.

Jana shrugged and Jamal took a deep breath and looked out of the window.

"The next one of y'all that's got an idea about how I should do shit is getting their brains spilled," Kenneth said, gritting his teeth. "That should put an end to that shit."

The car became silent. Kenneth sat there, trembling with rage like a teakettle about to boil over.

Jamal sat there thinking about how to cut ties with Kenneth. Dealing with him was getting to be too much. He didn't know what to expect from him. One minute they were friends and Kenneth would do anything for him and the next minute he was threatening his life. Kenneth wouldn't let him walk away that easily. If he tried to keep his distance, Kenneth would stalk him, pop up wherever he was, and try to buy him back into his circle. When that didn't work, the threats would come next, and then he would follow through with them. Kenneth was like an abusive parent. When you were around, they talked about how they wanted to get rid of you, but when you ran away, they would hunt you down to get their punching bag back. Maybe one day soon someone would put Kenneth out of his misery. If not, he would have to make a move. He couldn't spend the rest of his life enslaved by a psycho.

Jana was relieved that she'd managed to put an end to Kenneth and Jamal's spat, even though they'd both dumped on her. If Kenneth shot Jamal, he would have to shoot her. She didn't know where Jamal stood on the matter but she couldn't sit there while Kenneth killed him. If Jamal was gone, she'd be left to deal with Kenneth by herself, and he'd eventually kill her, too. She couldn't let shit go down like that. Why should she and Jamal be slain when ridding the world of Kenneth would make it a better place; especially considering it would bring the murder rate in the USA down by at least ten percent?

After thirty minutes of silence, Kenneth decided to do what Jamal had suggested. They got out of the car, shadows in the darkness as they made their way to the house. They checked the side windows but were unable to force them open.

"Why can't we break a window to get in?" Jamal asked.

Kenneth slapped Jamal on the back of his head. "Why

the fuck would I do that? You think I want someone to hear us?"

Jamal took a deep breath. *Ain't no helping this nigga.*

They made one last attempt to get into the house, checking the windows on the front porch to see if one had been left open. Jana walked over to the front door, turned the knob, and it flew open. Jana gave Kenneth and Jamal a smug look and then smiled.

Kenneth grinned. "Girl, you must be my good luck charm."

They walked into the house. It was a clean and cozy-looking place. Nothing like the places they resided in, where you had to be careful not to slip on whatever clothes were left on the floor, and there were no dishes sitting around waiting to be placed into the sink. It didn't look like a place inhabited by two restless young adults like Stefan and Simone.

Jamal looked around the living room and shook his head. "I swear, this don't seem like the place."

"Did I ask yo' dumb ass what it seems like?" Kenneth asked. "You should know by now, things are hardly ever what they seem."

Jana went into the kitchen and walked back out with a dingy white shoestring and a used syringe. "Look what I found."

"Oh naw," Jamal said in disbelief. "I know they don't get down like that."

Kenneth sneered at Jamal and then made his way upstairs.

Jamal and Jana followed Kenneth upstairs. They went into Stefan's room and searched for any indication that Stefan and Simone resided there, to no avail. Next, they searched Simone's room and found nothing. As Kenneth was about to make his way to the grandmother's room, Jamal pulled the headdress Jana bought for Simone out of the closet.

Jamal held up the headdress. "Look at this."

"So what?" Kenneth said. "Don't waste my time."

"Naw, this is the headdress Jana bought for Simone during Southern Decadence," Jamal said. "Isn't it, Jana?"

Jana shrugged.

Kenneth took the headdress from Jamal and looked it over. "It damn sure is. It even smells like her." Kenneth handed the headdress to Jana. "Doesn't it, Jana?" Kenneth asked with a grimacing smile on his face.

Jana ran her fingers over the headdress. *Fuck, there ain't shit I can do if she shows up. She's just late.*

"Is something wrong, Jana?" Kenneth asked.

Jana shook her head.

Jamal grinned. "Why would it be? She ain't even give you no play."

The front door opened and the three looked at each other. Kenneth motioned for Jana and Jamal to get into the closet while he hid behind the bedroom door.

Tony shut the front door and then pulled the pack of chicken breasts he had stolen from the supermarket from under his shirt. He slapped Tessa on her ass. "Now get in there and cook this shit," he said, pointing to the kitchen.

Tessa grinned as she took the pack of chicken out of his hand and made her way to the kitchen. "We got food and smack. We gonna have us some fun tonight."

Tessa noticed her syringe and shoestring missing from the table and slammed the pack of chicken down. "Tony, where the fuck is my shit?"

"What?"

"You heard me, muthafucka," Tessa spat. "Where the fuck is my syringe and my shoestring?"

"How the fuck am I supposed to know?" Tony asked.

"Ain't nobody been here but me and you."

"How you know that?" Tony asked. "You left the fucking door unlocked all day."

"You better not have had some bitch up in here, using my shit."

"Why the fuck you always jumping to conclusions?" Tony asked. "I don't like it when you do that shit."

"Who gives a fuck what you like?"

"You better watch how you talk to me, you ugly bitch."

"Oh, I'm an ugly bitch? Is that why you was fucking some tramp and letting her use my shit up in my own damn mama's house?"

"Man, shut the fuck up."

"And I'm an ugly bitch. Well, this ugly bitch gonna cut yo' ass if I don't find my shit."

"I swear, you've got to fuck up everything," Tony said.

"I should've left your trifling ass alone when I found out you was fucking my nephew." Tessa made her way upstairs. "Maybe you had some bitch upstairs fucking her in her ass, playing make-believe like she was Stefan. Let me check his old room. Maybe you were in there reminiscing."

"You can check wherever you want," Tony snapped. "If it's up there, it ain't 'cause I put it up there."

Tessa looked around Stefan's room and became frustrated when she didn't find her drug paraphernalia. She became sweaty and her eyes watered. Tony placed his hand on Tessa's shoulder, about to tell her that it was okay, that he could go out and find them a needle before they killed each other, but before he could, Tessa jerked away.

"Get the fuck off me!" Tessa yelled. She stomped into Simone's room. "I'm gonna find my shit. You better hope it's still in this house and you ain't give it to one of your bitches."

Tony followed Tessa into Simone's room and they stood in the middle of the floor, arguing.

Tony got in Tessa's face. "And if I did?"

Tessa drilled her finger into Tony's forehead. "Muthafucka, don't play—"

Kenneth slammed the bedroom door shut. "Is this what you're looking for?" Kenneth held up the needle and the dingy shoestring.

Tessa turned up her nose at Kenneth and then looked at Tony. "Who the fuck is that?"

Tony shrugged. "I thought you brought him up in here."

Tessa pointed to the door. "Nigga, you better get the fuck outta here."

"Tell me where Stefan and Simone are and I'll leave."

Tessa placed her hands on her hips. "Nigga, who the fuck are you?"

"Just answer the question," Kenneth said.

"Tony, get this nigga out my gotdamn house," Tessa demanded.

Tony motioned forward, ready to tie up with Kenneth. He figured if it came down to it, Tessa would help him out by hitting the nigga over the head with something.

Kenneth grabbed his gun off of his side and cocked it. Upon hearing the gun cock, Jana and Jamal came out of the closet.

Tony froze. He didn't want to do or say anything to put his life any further in jeopardy. On the other hand, Tessa sucked her teeth and continued to mouth off. Tony didn't know whether she was feigning so hard that she didn't realize her life was in danger, or whether she simply didn't give a fuck.

"Oh, you had to bring your posse, that toy-ass nigga and a boy-girl," Tessa spat.

Kenneth fixated his gaze on Tessa. "Whoo, Jana, give me a cigarette; I need something to keep me from killing this bitch before I find out what I want to know."

Tessa placed her hands on her hips. "You ain't gonna do shit."

Kenneth bashed Tessa on her forehead with his gun.

"You one of them bitches that don't know when to shut the fuck up."

Tessa fell to her knees and grabbed her forehead while blood poured down her face. "Muthafucka," she uttered.

Jana handed Kenneth the cigarette she had gotten out of her pocket and lit it for him. Kenneth held it between his lips and took a few pulls.

Kenneth pointed his gun at Tony. "Where in the fuck are Stefan and Simone?"

"Stefan and Simone?" Tessa screeched. "You done gashed me in my head over a fucking punk and a hoe?"

Kenneth looked over at Jamal. "Handle that for me."

Jamal slapped Tessa and she fell down on her side.

Tony tried to make a move for Kenneth's gun while his eyes were on Jamal and Tessa. Kenneth saw Tony out the corner of his eye and backhanded him. Tony grabbed his cheek and Kenneth kicked him in his groin. Tony quickly removed his hand from his cheek and grabbed his groin as he fell to his knees and joined Tessa on the floor.

Kenneth pointed his gun at Tony's head.

Tony quivered. "Please don't kill me."

"If you want your life, you better talk fast," Kenneth said.

Tony began to stutter. "Stefan's dead; somebody killed him a couple of weeks ago and Simone, she down in the city jail."

"For what?" Jana asked.

Kenneth gave Jana a nasty look. *Who the fuck do she think she is?* he thought.

"She's being held on murder charges," Tony answered.

Kenneth shook his head while he looked down at Tony.

After seeing the disapproval in Kenneth's eyes, Tony began to offer up additional information. "That's her mother right there," Tony said, looking over at Tessa.

"You sonofabitch!" Tessa yelled.

"I ain't no kin to none of them," Tony said. "I'm just in the wrong place at the wrong time. Please don't kill me."

Kenneth directed his attention back to Tessa, who was lying on the floor with her face covered with blood. "So that would make you Stefan's aunt."

"Fuck you!" Tessa snapped. "I ain't kin to that faggot."

Kenneth drew his leg back like he was about to kick a field goal and kicked Tessa in her back. Tessa screamed.

"Yeah, she's Stefan's aunt," Tony announced.

Kenneth looked at Jamal and Jana. "Well, somebody has to pay for what they did. Jana, shoot her."

Jana hesitated to pull out her gun and shoot Tessa.

"Did you hear what the fuck I told you to do?" Kenneth asked.

Jana nervously reached for her gun. Disgusted by Jana's reaction, Kenneth pointed his gun down at Tessa and shot her in the head. Kenneth then drew back his hand to slap Jana and Jana drew up.

Kenneth laughed at Jana. "I'll deal with you later."

Kenneth directed his attention back to Tony, who was on his knees with his hands in a praying position.

"So you aren't going to kill me?" Tony asked.

"Oh yeah, you a dead man," Kenneth said. "I don't like the way you gave her up."

Kenneth shot Tony in his stomach and the three stood there and watched as Tony groaned and pleaded with God for his life until he died.

Kenneth, Jamal, and Jana crept out of the house and made their way back home to Florida, leaving Tessa and Tony in the house to rot.

Tessa had burned so many bridges that no one would come to check on her. On Halloween, kids would knock on the door but no one would answer. They would swear they heard knocking and bumping inside of the house and that the house was haunted. No one would be worried when Tessa didn't show up for Thanksgiving or Christmas dinner. She had never graced her family with her presence, so there was no need to be alarmed.

Tony had no family and the so-called friends that he used to shoot up with had abandoned him years ago when they had found out that he had HIV. They couldn't shoot up with him anymore and they were too scared to be in the same room with him while he breathed, thinking somehow sharing the same air with him would contaminate them.

It wouldn't be until the Fourth of July, when the summer heat forced the stench of their rotting flesh out into the neighbor's yard during their cookout, the foulest scent they had ever smelled, that the authorities would be called and their bodies would be found.

❧[Epilogue]❧

Winter came early that year; especially in Richmond, Virginia, with temperatures below forty
in October. Children crowded around the oven,
trying to keep warm while they waited for their parents
to come home with dinner. Old folks sat around the table
eating Sunday dinner, gossiping about Wayne Jasper
being found guilty of sexual assault on a Richmond
native, Simone Simmons. They shook their heads whenever someone mentioned his punishment; seven years
probation.

"The things they let celebrities get away with," they
would say.

Then there was the video of Wayne having sex with
Stefan. The explicit video was discussed on every television and radio station in the U.S. Stories about the nature
of Wayne's relationship with Stefan were featured in
every tabloid on grocery store shelves. When all of the
talk about the video started to dwindle, it was posted on
the Internet and gossip about Wayne reached an all-time
high. It gave people one more thing to gossip about, in
order to keep their minds off of their miserable lives
and cold homes.

Rats made their way into the house where Tessa and Tony had lain dead, in order to keep themselves warm. Mother Nature showed her anger at the events of the summer by thrusting freezing winds in the faces of all the mothers that thought they had better things to do than take care of their children; who thought running around town using their looks to persuade men out of their money and having a good time was more important than nurturing their children. Mother Nature did the same to the fathers who chose to be absent from their children's lives; who were more concerned with finding a woman that would show them a good time, no strings attached, than taking care of their children. Her cold air made them age before their time. Mother Nature gave frostbite to those who sat in the alley getting drunk and high all night and having sex on the side of sheds, instead of being at home nourishing the bodies and minds of their children. A lot of them became amputees by the summer and were still determined to maintain their reckless lifestyles.

Dennis visited his son's grave every day. He would sit down in front of his grave and weep, begging for his forgiveness. His teardrops froze as soon as they hit his cheeks. Maybe he should have prayed and asked God to give his message to Stefan. Although Stefan's body lay in its cozy coffin, warm under six feet of dirt, Stefan was long gone. When Dennis wasn't at Stefan's grave, he was searching for mediums, hoping they could help him to communicate with his son. The mediums sold him stories about his son. One told him that his son had been reborn and was living happily as a peacock. Another one told him that his son was his guardian angel; to repay the kindness he showed him when he was alive. The weirdest thing he was told by a medium was the child that he was trying to contact was a white woman who had died in a car accident. Dennis spent a couple thousand dollars consulting with mediums over the telephone and on the Internet, trying to contact his son. He only wanted to say that he was sorry.

Sandra tried to comfort Dennis. She told him that she didn't give a damn what any person or book said, Stefan was in Heaven, he was with God, and he was fine. She spent many hours of her days and nights trying to drill into Dennis's head that Stefan had already forgiven him; now he needed to forgive himself. She convinced Dennis to write a letter to Stefan, telling him how he felt. They went to Stefan's grave and burned the letter, visualizing the smoke spreading throughout the universe and Dennis's message reaching Stefan. That was the day Sandra realized that she was in love with Dennis. After burning the letter he had written to his son, Dennis started to forgive himself and the love he had for his son made his skin glow. He was starting to heal.

A few months later, Sandra and her husband filed for divorce and Sandra and Dennis moved in together. They focused their energy on getting Anthony and Charlie into rehab and getting Simone out of jail. They didn't want her spending an entire year in jail, awaiting her trial. Although Simone had only left the state of Virginia once in her life, to go to Louisiana, the Judge didn't grant her bond. The Judge agreed with the commonwealth attorney who argued that Simone was a flight risk.

Wayne decided to go into hiding. He stayed in the house with his wife, Nicole, and they hired help to run their errands and a teacher to home school their children until the situation blew over. Nicole stood by Wayne and they decided to salvage their relationship. Two years later, Wayne found out he had HIV and Nicole tested positive for HIV also. The news made Nicole's soul ache and made Wayne despondent. Again, Nicole stood by him and gave him hope. What was done was done; there was no way they could change it. All they could do was take their medication, eat right, and live out the remainder of their lives, which they did together until their midseventies.

Paris used Valium to get high during the day; they calmed the tremors he experienced when the thought of Stefan decaying in a coffin popped into his mind. At night, Paris got drunk and walked the streets of the French Quarter going from club to club. He often watched the female impersonators sing, dance, perform monologues, and mimic famous entertainers. He wondered did he have what it took to perform in a show. After a few months, Paris decided to audition for shows.

During his stay in New Orleans, Paris performed ten shows using the name Madame Mojo. The show he was most proud of was the one he performed at Starlight by the Park, where he danced around in a skirt and a midriff top both made with bananas and yellow fishing rope. Just when New Orleans was starting to feel like home to Paris, that bitch of a hurricane hit. She tried to drown New Orleans. It seemed like she was sent to suck the carefree city deep into the earth and deliver it to the devil himself. After the looting, killing, and all the mayhem, Paris fled to Rhode Island and started his own brothel.

Simone was shipped to Pamunkey Regional Jail. She was in Hanover County's custody awaiting her trial. The first five months she was there, she spent more time in the infirmary on suicide watch than she did in medical quarantine. While Simone was on suicide watch, the corrections officer monitoring Simone recognized her. She remembered seeing Simone in a compromising picture; her husband, Mason, had hidden it in between some papers underneath the driver's seat of his car. Mason's wife made Simone's stay a living hell. When Mason's wife took Simone out of medical quarantine and put her into general population, she bribed another inmate to bully her in exchange for putting money on her account each month. Her supervisor confronted her about taking

Simone out of medical quarantine and Mason's wife explained her error by telling her that Simone was HIV positive. Mason's wife decided to get tested for HIV. When she got her test results back and found out that she had HIV, she went home and killed Mason and then headed to work, planning to kill Simone and make it look like self-defense. When Simone was bullied by another inmate, did the only friend she had stand up for her? Were Simone's grievances taken seriously? When Simone told the foreign psychiatrist, who couldn't discern what she spoke, how she was being treated, did he pretend to understand her and increase her dosage of Paxil and Klonopin, or did he put forth more effort to find out why she was distressed? Did Simone stand up for herself and become her own hero, or did she surrender her life to Mason's wife?

What happened to Simone? Well, that's another story.

ABOUT THE AUTHOR

Abnormal Lives is Rae's introduction into the literary world. Rae resides in Richmond, Virginia with her family and is currently working on her next novel.

Discussion Questions

1. Which character was your favorite and why?

2. Do you think Stefan would have lived a different lifestyle if his father would have remained in his life?

3. Do you think a parent who disowns their child because they disapprove of their lifestyle could have ever genuinely loved their child?

4. Should Simone have shown her mother more respect in spite of her transgressions against her?

5. Have one of your parents ever done something that made you want to hit them? If so, did you hit them or did you restrain yourself? Explain the reason for the action you took.

6. Which character did you empathize with the most? Explain why.

7. Do you think Stefan's father would have felt less guilty about the way he treated Stefan after receiving the news of his death if he would have acknowledged him when he saw him at church?

8. Did you have a sexual relationship with an adult while you were a teenager and swore you both loved each other? If yes, do you still think your relationship with that adult was based on love?

9. Do you think Paris made the right decision by ending his efforts to have a relationship with his father?

10. Do you think Simone should be convicted of murder?

11. Should prostitution be legalized in all fifty U.S. states? Why or why not?

12. If you were Wayne's wife, Nicole, would you have salvaged your relationship with Wayne after finding out he had sex with a man while the both of you were separated? Would you have stuck by Wayne during his rape trial? When you found out Wayne had HIV and infected you with it, would you have still been willing to remain married and work past your issues?

If you enjoyed "Abnormal Lives," be sure to check out

by S.K. Collins
Available from Strebor Books

CHAPTER ONE

Early Spring 2004

"**D**amn! I can't be late for work again!" Zeek cried
as he slammed the door behind him and sped
off down the street. He had only two minutes
to catch the 8:35 a.m. bus, so he ran desperately to the
bus stop. His heart raced as he broke out into a heavy
sweat, praying he would reach his destination in time.
His red Staples shirt blew in the wind as he forced himself to run faster knowing his job was on the line. He
made a sharp left and took a shortcut through a vacant
park. He knew taking the detour would give him the

best chance at making the bus. He tucked the back of his shirt in so he wouldn't get it snagged on the fence he had to get over. He jumped the fence, but he somehow managed to bang his knee on one of the raised rusted posts. He ignored the pain and rushed and made it to the corner.

Zeek's pupils enlarged as his eyes zoomed in on the last passenger stepping onto the bus. He knew he only had seconds to make it there before the bus pulled off. "Hold the bus, please! Miss, can you please hold the bus?" he yelled as he ran desperately.

The woman rolled her eyes and let the doors close behind her. "Yo, driver! Hold the bus!" He immediately started to wave his hands in the air, hoping to obtain the driver's attention.

Unfortunately, the driver never checked his rearview mirror, so the bus proceeded to pull off, leaving Zeek utterly down and out. While holding his knees in an attempt to catch his breath, Zeek hopelessly yelled, "Aww, come on, man! Come on! Damn…I know you seen me… How the hell could he not see me?"

Now with the bus gone, he had to think fast. He knew he could either wait for another bus or run another twenty blocks to Brookline Metro Station and catch a train. Right then a bus that ran a different route pulled up in front of him. He knew it wouldn't take him to his job, but he would be close, at least in running distance. Without a second thought, he ran up the steps and sat as close to the front as possible. He wiped his clammy hands off on his shirt as he thought about being late.

"I hope there ain't no traffic," he said nervously to himself as the bus pulled off.

The twenty-minute ride into town felt more like hours as Zeek sighed heavily. Before the doors of the bus were fully open, he squeezed out of the tight space and took off running. He dodged and weaved through crowds of people who were on their way to work as well.

"Sorry!" he yelled as he ran out in front of a taxi as the driver smashed down on his horn in anger.

He checked the time on his phone and became even more nervous as Staples was now only a short distance away. *What the hell am I going to say this time?* he thought hopelessly. He'd pretty much run out of excuses for being late.

Zeek quickly entered the store and tensely peered around for his manager. "He must be in the back." He sighed in relief as he headed for his register.

His co-worker, Tara, was finishing up with a customer when she looked up and saw Zeek trying to creep in. She shook her head and waited for the customer to be out of earshot before she spoke. "Boy, why you late again? You know Dan gonna go off on you, right?"

"Dan can kiss my ass," he said in a hushed tone as he tried to clock into the register.

"If he can kiss ya ass, then why you whisperin'?" she said after sucking her teeth.

"I ain't whisperin' shit. Dan's tight shirt-wearin' ass know what it is. Fuck...why can't I clock in?"

"Boy, you always be fakin'. You are such a bama." Tara

quickly cut her eyes to the back of the store and happened to see Dan making his way to the front. She smiled and looked back over at Zeek. "Here come Dan. Let's see you talk that shit now."

Zeek's eyes widened as Dan made his way over to his register. Dan's yellow, overly round frame walked tall in his snug-fitting shirt as he had Zeek in his focus. Zeek's lips started to quiver as he thought about what excuse to use. All he could do was tap his shaky fingers on the cash register keys as Dan moved closer.

Zeek swallowed hard and said the first thing that came to his mind. "Hey, what's up, Dan? I've been trying to clock in for the longest time, but it's not working. Is there a problem with the system?"

"Nope. Ain't no problem with the system. The problem is you," Dan said as he stared at Zeek with his hands placed firmly on his hips.

Zeek swallowed hard as the realization of what was happening started to set in.

"I decided to let you go."

"Come on, Dan. I need this job. Just give me another chance." Zeek begged.

"I'm sorry, Zeek, but you brought this on yourself. I can't give you any more chances," Dan said, standing his ground.

Zeek knew Dan was overly tired of his call-offs and late-to-work routine. It was clear to him after being late this morning that it was his fault that he was fired. He looked over at Tara and became even more embarrassed after he saw that she had been laughing at him. With nothing else to be said, Zeek lowered his head and slowly walked toward the door. He looked back at Dan one last time to see if there was any slight chance he could salvage his job, but Dan had already walked off. He shook his head in disappointment that he had to move on.

Zeek forcefully pushed through the doors and started to walk fast down the busy street. He tightened his lips and balled up his fists as he thought about what had happened. "Damn, I shouldn't have been late! I can't do shit right!" He cursed himself after failing to try to be more responsible.

He'd intended to stretch his twenty-first birthday weekend until the crack of dawn and still get up for work on time. He had hoped this morning would have been the start of a more mature Ezeekiel Harris, but yet again, he was dead wrong. "What the fuck am I going to do now?" Zeek said as he wiped his eyes.

His mind was racing a mile a minute and he couldn't help but feel worthless. He headed back to the bus stop and looked enviously at everyone who drove past him. The summer hadn't even begun and with the money he would've made working, his mind was set on buying a car in September. Now losing his job had ruined his plan. Zeek needed to come up with another way to get a car, but for now, he wanted to go home and sulk in his sorrow.

Once the bus arrived, Zeek stepped up on the bus and

took the first available window seat. He still couldn't believe he'd been fired. He shook off the thought as his eyes started to water again.

"Damn, I'm such an asshole," he said as he thumped his head against the glass.

He peered dejectedly out of the window as the bus left downtown and headed back to his neighborhood. His surroundings altered drastically as the business buildings turned into rundown row houses, and the professional working class shifted to corner boys and drug addicts. Zeek shook his head as the U.S. Capitol came into view. The immaculate structure represented a country that attracted millions of tourists from around the world. It also symbolized the power and security that every country respected.

Damn, there's such a thin line between wealth and poverty. I gotta find a way to get in between, Zeek thought as the bus moved deeper into the hood.

Zeek arrived back at his house but didn't bother to go in. He sat down on the porch steps and tried to clear his head. He was so distressed from losing his job that he didn't want to make it worse by sitting in an empty house. All Zeek's friends were at work so it made him feel even worse about being unemployed again.